Terror 404

Book 4 in The Amy Lane Mysteries series

by

Rosie Claverton

D0532378

Terror 404 © Rosie Claverton
ISBN 978-0-9933815-3-9
eISBN 978-0-9933815-4-6

Published in 2017 by Crime Scene Books

The right of Rosie Claverton to be identified as the author
of this work has been asserted by her in accordance with the
Copyright, Designs and Patents Act 1988.

A CIP record of this book is available from the British Library.

Book design by Clockwork Graphic Design
Cover design George Foster Covers
Printed in the UK by Marston Book Services Ltd

Acknowledgements

Thank you to my editor Deb Nemeth for providing the ever-climbing scaffold for my writing tree – you have made me the writer I am today. Many thanks to Sarah Williams and the team at Crime Scene Books for giving me and The Amy Lane Mysteries a home.

The main research contribution to this novel is from the Royal College of Psychiatrists, without whom I would not have a medical career.

Thank you for my education, even if this isn't quite what you thought I would do with it.

And thank you to my family: my husband Huw and my daughter Faith, who encourage me every day – mostly by blowing raspberries.

Chapter 1: *The Sea's Sway*

When everything was too fast, too intense, too crowded with worry, her only respite was the sea. Its calming blue or its stormy grey or the white horses riding over it - she could watch and find a tiny space inside her that was still tranquil.

Emma Mason sat cross-legged on the damp grass, looking out through the clear plastic fence. She had been disappointed it wasn't cool glass, to calm the hot turbulence inside her head, but it couldn't be glass, could it? Not here. Too *risky*.

Three months. She had been imprisoned here for three months. No, not imprisoned - what was that word they used? *Detained*. She had been detained, because she had a mental disorder and she posed a high risk to herself. There was that word again: risk. It permeated the very atmosphere of the rooms, the breath of the staff, the wary glances between patients.

It was the kind of prison that lied. It showed you bright, open spaces, good food, the garden overlooking the sea - and it tried to convince you that you were free. Merely resting here a while.

But she felt trapped and itchy. They wouldn't give her paper to write down all the things she needed to remember. They wouldn't let her spend two hours in the shower, making sure every inch of her skin was given equal attention. They wouldn't let her fold her clothes and order them how she chose on the shelves. They wouldn't let her abate the storm, even if only for a few moments.

As the days had eked out into weeks and expanded into months, Emma's concerns had grown. The nurses knew nothing about her and the doctor only pushed his cocktail of pills on her. The therapist wanted to talk about her mother and her father and her brother, even though Emma never said a word. She was overwhelmed, consumed by the idea that this was a hospital that didn't actually want her to get better.

Was she finally losing her mind, turning into one of those conspiracy people from the internet, the kind her brother Max made mocking documentaries about? Or was she merely being realistic? Her mother was paying a small fortune for her stay at this "elite establishment", which made it sound like a yoga retreat or wellness spa rather than an asylum with fake white smiles. Why would the staff here want her to get well? She was making them a ton of money by staying ill.

She had only two saving graces in this place. Max, returned from his exotic travels and somehow turned human by them, wanted to give her gifts of sweet treats. Perhaps to make up for years of little brother bullying, doing anything and everything to get their father's attention. Now it was too late for either of them to gain his approval.

The gifts made the hours more bearable, though between them and the drugs, she was increasing in size like a balloon waiting to burst. She tried to give them away, but most people here were suspicious. Emma could understand their fears. This place was supposedly designed to soothe them, but it made Emma feel watched, scrutinised.

She had one other saviour. Little Amy, as she called her inside her head, had only been with her six weeks but Emma knew her immediately as a kindred spirit. Her struggles were all on the inside, not on display like some of the others, but she didn't deserve this place either. She had arrived with an escort of police officers, but someone so slight, so pale, couldn't possibly be a criminal.

Amy didn't like to leave her room. Amy didn't leave her room at all, in fact, so Emma couldn't show her the distant sea and explain how much it helped her. More than the drugs, more than the therapists, more even than the conversations they shared - such as they were.

"Time for bed, Emma."

The nurse touched her arm before she could react. Emma cried out and jumped to her feet, her arm stinging with the brush through her cardigan. She fought it for a moment, trying to remember all those things the therapist said, but the urge was too great.

She touched her other arm in the same place, evening out the sensation, but then her left leg flared, demanding its own attention. *Your father is dead. What will happen to your mother? Pay attention to the details. Make it right and God will spare her.*

She touched her legs, one after the other, and then her cheeks, one-two. The nurse - Miriam, that was her name - tried to distract her, and Emma's hand slipped, brushing her chin instead.

Start again. Arm, arm, leg -

"Stop, Emma. Come inside."

- leg, cheek -

"What's the worst that could happen?"

My mother will die. Everyone will die. I can prevent it. I can make it right.

She'd lost the pattern again. She hadn't even managed it once, let alone completed the holy three sets. She felt the anxiety rise in her, the flutter in her chest that meant she was losing control. She had to get back to her room, finish the job. Ward off Death for another day.

She sped past the nurse, dodging left and right to avoid the other patients and staff, allowing no one to touch her. She had to get back to her room. Her skin was burning all over, screaming out the pattern, begging her for symmetry and alignment.

Emma didn't see her. She collided straight into her, almost knocking her over in the bedroom corridor. The ghost of a woman, already starting her night of pacing, with her grey hair in disarray and her rictus smile without teeth.

"Let go of me, demon!"

But it was Ffion gripping Emma's arms, over the points of their burning, shaking her in desperation, in fear. Emma tried to protest her innocence, but she couldn't find the words, the *right* words. What could she say to make it better, apologise, undo her mistake?

"Demon! DEMON!"

Ffion's bellowing drew the nurses, who carefully pulled them apart without much force at all. Emma watched her eyes, how they rolled in her head, how she was getting worse every day, her shouting louder, her words about demons more frantic and terrified. Ffion had been here for months - was this what happened to people who stayed here?

Ffion continued her pacing as if nothing had happened and Emma retreated to her room, shrugging off their hands, their comfort. So many touches that she couldn't possibly keep track. How could she make it right? How could she undo?

She couldn't. It was hopeless. She couldn't do this alone. She couldn't do this with other people. She felt like she had only one friend in the entire world, but how could she say all these things and make herself understood? She never seemed to have the words.

But if she gave up, she would stay here forever. She had to try - for her family, for herself. To appease the God who had taken her father and would surely come for her mother. To avoid the demons that haunted Ffion, and might yet come for her.

For that, she needed an ally.

She carefully wrote a note on a paper towel with a stolen pen. The words smudged and the letters were uneven, but the twenty-third attempt was passable. She folded and refolded it a number of times, aligning the edges perfectly, before she crept out into the corridor and pushed her note under Amy's door.

Returning to her bed, she pushed open her window, wrapped herself in her blanket, and waited. Only a few minutes later she heard the answering sound of a window opening.

"Are you there?"

"I'm here."

Amy's voice was soft, rasping, as if her mouth was too dry and her words barely formed by it. Emma took a few moments, a few minutes, to find the right words. To tell Amy exactly what had happened in the corridor, how she felt. However, the spectre of the ward round tomorrow filled her head and she could talk of nothing else.

"Max thinks I'm getting worse." She paused, took a breath. "He thinks I stutter more. It's only with him, though, and the nurses. I don't stutter with you."

It was true - Amy's silence, through the window, allowed her space to think and form her words. At first, Amy had tried to ask her things, but Emma was derailed by questions and prone to panic when confronted with them. Now Amy just listened.

"I've lived with my little rituals for a long time. I don't know why they've shut me away now. I felt a bit strange that day, that's all - but I can't describe it, not to them."

From what Emma could remember, she'd broken down in her brother's car and panicked in the street, calling out a torrent of things that made no sense. The psychiatrist called it psychosis. Emma feared it was a worn-out brain finally reaching its breaking point.

She could hear crying through the wall. Ffion's bitter tears, the ones that begged for a mercy that never came. Emma knew that all too well. So she listened - to Amy's silence, Ffion's tears, and the gentle move-

ment of the sea against the shore.
    And willed her mind not to break.

Chapter 2: The Escaped Crusader

Bradley Thompson got in from work at seven o'clock, reheated leftover spaghetti bolognese, and watched an hour of mindless television. He took a brief shower, sluicing away a day's worth of grime and grease from the garage, before dressing all in black and stuffing his balaclava in his pocket. He left behind the knife, because it was a distraction - when a man had a weapon, he forgot how to use his body to fight. Using the back door, he stepped out into the night and started walking.

The secret to living a lie was to live it completely. As soon as his sister had dropped him off on the outskirts of Bristol, he no longer had a sister. Jason Carr was dead - and Bradley Thompson was born.

With fake ID and a wad of cash, he floated around Bristol's hostels until he found a garage willing to take on a mechanic with no questions asked - and none answered. The boss found him a place to rent, owned by a mate who didn't mind the lack of references, and the boys at the garage welcomed "Taffy Lee" into their small business of dodgy car fixing.

From experience he could no longer name, Bradley knew his way around a stolen motor and cash in hand suited him just fine. For a couple of weeks, he kept his head down and fixed up the cars, silent and avoidant until the others left him alone with his work. When a big guy with a shaved head and tats didn't want to talk, you didn't push him.

Yet it wasn't enough any more, a nine-to-five and a place of his own. One time, he would've given anything for a fresh start, like the one gifted to him. The man he had once been had dreamed of that, between prison and Amy -

He couldn't think of her. That one piece of his past was not so easily forgotten. If he started down that road, he would up and leave, run back to Cardiff and his former life as assistant to an elite hacker. Find her, protect her - and end up in prison for helping her. She had arranged all this to keep him safe. He would not let her down.

Except he was already putting that safety in jeopardy. Walking towards Clifton Down, he was looking for trouble. If he were caught, the police would soon rip through his false identity and he would be back in jail.

But he couldn't leave it alone. Night after night, he had entered the dark parts of the city, stopping muggings, protecting the homeless. This latest crime seemed made for him: a spate of rapes over The Downs, the perp unknown and making the police look like idiots. Bradley Thompson wouldn't know anything about how to hunt down a rapist, but Jason had not forgotten, could not forget. Was he supposed to just sit at home and do nothing?

That's what *she* would want him to do. But Jason's strengths were in his ability to sniff out the streets and break heads. He wanted to be something more than that, but that was the truth of him. Denying it was futile - even under a different name and in a different city, he couldn't unmake himself.

After an hour's walk across the city, Jason reached the edge of Clifton Down. The green space was part of one of the most affluent areas in Bristol, which was probably why the sexual assaults had caused such panic and raised so much media attention. Jason relied on the press for most of his information these days, no direct link to the police to guide his investigating.

He missed them, his friends with the police - and he never thought he'd say that. Ex-cons didn't have friends who were coppers, men who'd watch his back, cared about his fate. He had no idea what that friendship had cost them, as they'd turned a blind eye to his flight. He wanted to know, but then again he didn't. He had enough guilt to carry.

As he'd done every night this week, he started jogging along the most obvious paths, keeping an eye out for a likely suspect. He wasn't used to running, out of the habit since the prison treadmill, but this week of jogging had given him some stamina for the hours ahead. Despite the assaults, he wasn't alone, though the huddles of women gave him the eye when he passed them.

The crowds thinned as the night drew in, until it was only Jason jogging the paths and only rarely spotting another loner. This was the prime time for the attacker to strike, his hunting ground ripe when his prey were scattered. Where was he hiding? Could Jason find him before another girl met with him?

Jason ran for another thirty, forty, sixty minutes before deciding he'd better call it a night. He was the only one on the paths now and that made him look guilty, skulking around the park at night.

Then he saw her. A lone woman with her head down, jogging ahead of him with bulky headphones covering her ears. And behind her, about fifty feet away, an anonymous man running in black.

Jason increased his speed, putting on a sprint to cover the hundred yards between them. The man reached for the woman's shoulder - and Jason collided with him, knocking him off the path and rolling him down into a ditch.

The woman ran on, oblivious, as Jason straddled the man's back. He tugged on his balaclava, before rolling the man and peering into his face through the murk. He looked like any other guy, shocked but guilty as fuck, struggling to get away.

"Thought you'd try your luck with another one?"

His confession was written all over his face. Though that wasn't Jason's job here. He hauled the guy up and pulled out a pair of handcuffs. It was amazing what you could buy on the internet, and old-fashioned police handcuffs were in high demand. Jason doubted anyone else was using them for cuffing a rapist to a tree.

"You can't just leave me here!"

The man's voice was whining, nasal, but Jason ignored him. He checked the bloke's pockets, removed his phone and dialled 999.

"Hello - which service do you require?"

"Police. I've got your Clifton rapist. Come and get him."

Jason dumped the phone at the man's feet and walked away, ignoring the man's crying and swearing and shouting, as he slowly smiled to himself.

Maybe, somewhere, Amy was proud of him.

One day, he would tell her how proud he was of her.

Chapter 3: Fear the Reaper

They were coming. She could hear them in the walls.

The little box on the ceiling flashed its red light, the eye of the devil, watching her. It was only a matter of time now. She'd thought they had gone away but they never would. They had merely been sleeping, waiting.

Now they were coming - she knew it with absolute certainty. She had no hope now.

Ffion curled up beneath her blanket and tried not to meet the eye's gaze, bony fingers clutching at her hair. Her body was weak, so very weak, and she could not summon the energy to even turn in her bed, so she could see the eye no longer. She was wasting away in this stifling box, moving slowly towards death by inches.

Some nights, it was better - when the drugs were so strong she was unconscious within moments, falling into dreamless sleep, or when her therapist's words stayed in her head: "What are the alternative explanations, Ffion? What else could be going on? Why don't you colour in this mandala?"

But what was the point in fighting it? The fear would always return, that unstoppable feeling of being watched, of her punishment being prepared just out of sight. She could hear their laughter, the anticipation.

She had done terrible things, unspeakable things. If only she could remember what they were, she might be able to plead for forgiveness. Yet she could not remember, her thoughts thick, sucking mud that would barely let words pass her lips. She knew she had wronged many, and could not be saved, yet the details of her damnation escaped her.

The doctors and nurses tried to tell her it would be okay, but they couldn't see that she was hollow inside, nothing but bones and skin to cover the rot. Something was eating away inside her, wrapped around her stomach so she couldn't eat. It had loosened its grip this week, and she'd had a piece of toast and a few chocolates that could slip past the constriction. Even tea no longer soothed her, the burning reminding her of the impending hellfire that awaited her.

It was hot now, for October. Or was it November? She had been here for weeks, months, and time had grown meaningless to her. Her brain scrambled to remember the date before she checked the little phone her daughter had brought her - October 31st. Hallowe'en.

It was twenty minutes to midnight, the witching hour. She had never believed in such things - or, at least, that any such thing could harm her, as long as she attended chapel and said her prayers. She had never been one for churching in her youth, but she had learned to appease God if she wanted to live.

Now the dark things were getting louder, closer. Whatever she had done, perhaps now was the hour of her reckoning. Would God have mercy on her? Or would the demons drag her down without trial, her sins too weighty for contemplation, redemption?

Her skin was blistering already - the fires must be close now. Her heart pounded in her chest, her temples pulsing, like a war tattoo on a single, sonorous drum. She saw them creeping into the corners of her vision, little blurry shadows scuttling up the walls. *They're here, they're here…*

They were a chorus unseen, a hundred voices surrounding her, but only one or two calling clear, and their message was death. Her death and eternal torment. She had been living with its weight for months now, unable to escape the impending doom.

Briefly, she had surfaced - over the past few days, the grip of Death had loosened and she had begun to hope. Smiled, even, and told the nurses she thought she might be a little better. A little closer to life. What a fool she had been.

She tried to be brave and remember to breathe, to concentrate on the breath moving within her body, the sensations that were real. That's what her therapist told her - concentrate on reality, on what you can feel within you. But her body felt too tight, too hot, her arms and legs throbbing with the beat of her racehorse heart. She tried to contain herself, but her body was flooded by fear.

She wanted to cry out, to scream for help, but the sound wouldn't leave her mouth, her throat closing under the pressure of the weight around her neck. A warm, sticky trickle ran down from her left nostril and onto her lip, the salty iron taste telling her she was bleeding. She had been right all along - she was dying, and they were coming for her. She had no recourse, no escape.

Lights started flashing above her head, the red fires of hell rising, and she could smell burning flesh, the thick smoke invading her nose and throat, choking her. One eye was enveloped in fire and she could see no more. Her limbs left her control and shook violently, ceaselessly.

This was the end and she had predicted it.

Hell on Earth.

Chapter 4: Girl Offline

Amy woke to the sound of sirens outside her window.

As her stiff, tired body jolted upright, she saw the blue lights pulsing through her permanently-shut curtains. They were here - were they here for her? Had the National Crime Agency suddenly changed their mind and decided to bring her in?

Then she heard the commotion in the corridor, the barely-contained panic in the voices, and the sound of a woman crying. One voice counted aloud, "…twenty-three, twenty-four, twenty-five…"

Amy swung her legs over the bed and then stopped. Did she really want to know what was happening outside? Did she want to see, to become part of it? Meddling in dangerous situations was exactly what had brought her here. These were the parts of the world that she wanted to keep away from her.

"Oh no…oh no…"

The sobbing woman's voice made her feet hit the floor, snatching up her sister's old hoodie and tugging it over her hospital nightdress. Emma was crying. Something bad had happened and Emma was crying.

The voice had stopped counting and had been replaced by a digital monotone.

"Analysing heart rhythm. Do not touch the patient."

Amy crossed to the door, the silence of the corridor enshrouded by a communally-held breath.

"Shock advised. Press the flashing button now."

For the first time since she'd been admitted to this place, Amy opened her own door and peered out into the corridor. The lights were bright, blinding, and a cluster of people were spilling out of a room two doors down. Emma stood in the corridor, hugging herself, shaking with her sobs.

"Stand clear!" someone called, and the cluster edged back, afraid.

"Shock delivered," the mechanical voice said, as if this was nothing more interesting than the weather.

A stampede of boots came down the corridor and two paramedics rushed past, moving Emma aside and trying to dislodge the crowd by the door.

Emma saw Amy in the doorway and ran to her, throwing herself on Amy's slight frame and crying into her shoulder. Amy barely caught her, startled and out of her depth. She was usually the one to be comforted, wrapped in Jason's arms and plied with tea. Her own attempts had always fallen short.

"She's dead," Emma cried. "Ffion's dead."

Ffion… The ghostly woman sailing past Amy's door, night after night, muttering about the monsters coming for her. Amy felt something lurch in her chest - someone she knew was dead.

The only other loss she had known was her grandmother, who went to the hospital one day and never came back, leaving Amy and Lizzie alone. Yet they had lost the old woman long before that, their souls slowly fading in her eyes day by day until she didn't know them at all.

"They can still save her," Amy mumbled.

However, while the paramedics were still working, they did not look optimistic. Ffion was transferred to the stretcher they had brought, out in the corridor, someone still jumping up and down on her chest, but their movements were listless, hopeless.

As the trolley flew past her, Amy caught sight of Ffion's face - her staring eyes, her mouth slack around the tube inside it, the trail of blood from her nose, the pinkish froth around her lips. But it was her hands that startled Amy - the claws they had formed, the nails broken and bloodied. Desperate hands.

Ffion had not died quietly. Yet no one had heard her.

Amy had lived with death for many years, had made it her business when the opportunity presented itself. But confined by her anxiety, she had always been one step removed. Seeing the details in photographs, hearing their horror in the slight tremor of Jason's voice as he recounted the crime scene to her.

Now she had seen the face of death, and it brought back that familiar lurch of panic, the fear of her own mortality. I am not safe here.

Abruptly, Emma's warmth moved away from her and Amy saw the bulk of Sandy fill her vision, the strict nurse's face twisted into an unhappy line.

"You both need to come with me," she said, Scottish brogue thicker with sleep deprivation. "Terrible, terrible business."

Amy froze, her feet rooted to the spot. "C-come with you?"

Sandy sighed. "Yes, with me. Now. You cannae stay here."

Amy backed towards her door, fingers finding the frame. "This is my room."

"You'll have to be moved. Come and have a cup of tea now."

No…no…no…

Amy heard shouting, and realised it was her own voice. The surge of panic was immediate, vicious, like an unstoppable tsunami of emotion. A woman had died here and they wanted to take Amy away from the one sure place she had?

She'd been a fool to think her anxiety had gone away. It had only been contained by the four familiar walls of her hospital bedroom, but now it was back, and raging, and there was no comfort to be found. Amy Lane was a brilliant hacker, ally to the police and champion of justice. But Amy Loach was a sad little girl who was flying apart in the face of her fears.

Emma had started crying again, and Sandy was calling for help, for someone to do something - to stop these hysterical women from getting out of hand.

"She needs some PRN - quickly, now."

Pro re nata - "when necessary". That's what the ward manager Lois had told her, when she'd asked. She was young, with shiny black bobbed hair, but her smile was an iron fist within a velvet glove. The nursing staff here thought her favourite little blue pills were a lot less necessary than Amy did, but what the hell did they know about it?

Amy's chest felt tight, the world spinning away, the air thinning. She fell into it wearily, too tired to fight the rising panic. She should be used to this by now, her body's revolt against sanity. Was this how Ffion had felt, just before she died? Terrified of the monsters in her head?

Could a person die from fear? Could she?

That thought threw petrol on the fire of her panic, and Amy was consumed in it. The tiny plastic pot with its blue saviours barely registered, as she swallowed them dry. Sandy and a man, a healthcare assistant, led her unresisting body down the corridor, away from her sanctuary. Her heart slowed, her breathing eased, but the maelstrom continued in her head. She needed a whole bottle of red wine for this, or a vat of pills.

Or Jason.

The communal area of the hospital ward opened out before her, but the edges were dark as she struggled to breathe, Amy collapsed onto a sofa with broken springs, a puppet with her strings cut, as Emma was ushered in beside her. Two lost little girls.

"Don't cry, hen. Here now."

Sandy pressed a tissue into her hand and Amy wanted to protest - she wasn't crying, she barely knew Ffion, why would she cry? But when she pushed her lank brown hair out of her eyes and touched her cheeks, they were wet, and she knew then that she was crying for herself.

This was a hell of her own making. She had chosen to turn herself in to the police, allow Jason to escape. Her assistant's past crimes would've ensured he served prison time for helping her and she couldn't allow that, not again. She would always choose that path, no matter the circumstances. Anything to save him.

Could she repent her life of crime, of entering forbidden doors, seeking the truth no matter what digital defences barred her way? She had helped people, from the wrongfully-dismissed employee to the families of murder victims. She had helped her friends in the police - and brought shame and suffering down on their heads with her own.

Yet the reason she was here, the one thing she had done that had condemned her, she could not regret. Stealing money from the parents who had abandoned them, her and her sister Lizzie - no, she cared nothing for those selfish gluttons. But in her move to punish them and to break free, she had closed the circle and put herself where they had always wanted her - locked away, out of sight, the mad daughter in the attic.

Amy sat on the couch, her fingers dancing on her lap, seeking comfort. They itched to touch a keyboard again, a tablet, a phone, but she was not even allowed near a landline and her wristwatch had been confiscated. What on earth would she do with a digital watch? Maybe they thought her a true evil genius, or they had watched too many movies.

She would give anything to see Jason again. He was the rock upon which she had rebuilt her life and, without him, she couldn't see a way out. If she got better in here, she would go to prison. If she didn't, she would be condemned to stay here forever. And always without Jason.

Alone. Like Ffion.

Yet there was still a spark within her that rebelled at being so constrained. She had been tormented before, and survived. She could not allow herself to sink beneath the rising tide, give over her brilliant mind to this half-existence.

As long as she had her mind, she had hope.

Chapter 5: By the Book

First day back at work and Death came calling.

Bryn had treated his suspension like a trial run for retirement and loathed every minute of it. He had more grey than black in his hair now, every day of stress adding a year or more to his face. After he'd weeded the garden and put up a few shelves, he was ready to return to Cardiff's robberies, swindles and violence. The work that was in his marrow.

When he'd got the call from the chief that his suspension was over and all charges dropped, he could've kissed the man. However, a small part of him had wondered why. When last they'd met, National Crime Agent Frieda Haas had made it very clear she was gunning for him. Frieda had been determined to bring down Amy Lane and all those associated with her - so what had changed?

The most likely explanation was lack of evidence. With Amy's computer wiped clean, the NCA had only speculation to link Cardiff Police with Amy's useful yet highly illegal hacking investigations. With nothing to tie Bryn to her supposed crimes, he could walk back to his work as if nothing had changed. Except everything had.

Fortunately, he'd only had to tolerate the stares and whispers for half an hour before the call came in - a death at a private mental health unit in Penarth, the exclusive institution that stood on top of a cliff and gazed out over the sea.

The unit where Amy Lane was currently an inpatient.

Bryn's heartbeat echoed loudly in his ears, only quietening when the death was confirmed as a woman in her sixties - Ffion Ellis. The nurses didn't think it was suspicious, but Ms Ellis had been detained under the Mental Health Act and so it was like a death in custody or prison. Every one needed a thorough investigation, and it was exactly the kind of work Bryn needed. At least, that's what he told himself.

He volunteered for the job, and no one protested. Taking a pair of Scene of Crime Officers with him, he arranged for the body to be brought from the hospital morgue to Indira Bharani's autopsy room.

If anyone could persuade a body to give up its secrets, it was Indira.

Penarth wasn't really part of Cardiff, not yet absorbed into the city's sprawling havens - an idyllic seaside town housing the wealthier residents of Glamorgan, enjoying the sea air and the dilapidated pier. Cliff House was a name that evoked either a Georgian mansion or a cheerful fisherman's cottage. The glass and metal construction that owned it couldn't be further from either.

Bryn parked up his car and stepped out into the largely-deserted car park. The unit was right on the cliff top, with a sculpted wooden fence blocking the car park from the sea. Next to it, glass walls separated a beautifully manicured garden from the cars, the cliff edge and the adjoining wild grass - but it was empty, despite the late autumn sun.

The front entrance was at the opposite end of the car park to the designer fence. They were greeted by a middle-aged man, with his origins in the Middle East and his suit from Savile Row. He held out his hand as Bryn approached.

"Dr Al-Dosari - I am the psychiatrist here. The hospital manager is in London on business, but I can help you with anything you need."

"Detective Inspector Bryn Hesketh." He shook his hand briefly. "Are you usually here on a Saturday, Doctor?"

"It is my busiest clinic time. We must all fit in our health around our jobs now, yes? Please, come in."

Bryn followed the man's extended arm through a set of automatic double doors and into a large atrium. It resembled an airport lounge or a shopping centre court more than a hospital, with a sleek reception desk on the right and a deserted café in the far left corner. The chairs opposite the reception desk were utilitarian but comfortable, and the unobtrusive doors that lined the back right corner told nothing of what went on behind them. Bryn felt uneasy, as if the whole thing was faked for him, too new and just out of the box to be real.

Dr Al-Dosari nodded to the receptionist before heading to an unmarked double door in the centre of the left wall, one that Bryn had entirely failed to notice. However, this one did not open on their approach. The psychiatrist waved his photo ID at the door and then it yielded, admitting them into a smaller corridor with another door beyond.

The left side had a window, with a small gap beneath, like at the bank or post office. Behind it, a young woman blinked up at the doctor, seemingly in awe of him, and wearing a neat grey trouser suit with a colourful scarf.

"These gentlemen are with the police," Dr Al-Dosari said.

The receptionist nodded and opened the second door for them, which the doctor pushed out into the room beyond.

Whatever Bryn had been expecting, this wasn't it. It resembled the photographs of the youth hostels his oldest daughter had sent back from her travels abroad, a jumble of sofas and a large television set dominating the room. A square table was covered in craft materials and puzzle books, with pots of pens dotted about, and a table in the corner was piled high with jigsaws and board games. What was this place?

To his right, a room resembling a goldfish bowl stood in front of a vast glass cylinder, a central greenhouse-like room full of broken garden furniture ("Closed for Maintenance") surrounded by an arc of rooms with closed doors. To his left, a glass-walled dining room looked out onto the garden he'd seen before, and the sea beyond. Half a dozen faces gazed out at him, some curious, others frightened.

And one he recognised.

"I'll need to interview your patients afterwards," he said.

"I doubt our *clients* heard anything," Dr Al-Dosari said. "The nurses found her during the hourly checks - it was unusual for her to be in her room, actually."

"How many…clients do you have here?"

"We have nine beds in total. This is a small, exclusive facility. Please, this way."

Dr Al-Dosari led him away from the dining room and towards the goldfish bowl, which Bryn could now see was an office with three people inside. They all wore smart-casual clothes with name badges around their necks, the same distinctive purple lanyard.

"The night staff are waiting in the Conference Room, when you're ready for them."

Dr Al-Dosari indicated a door on the left wall, but Bryn shook his head.

"I'll see the room first," he said. "This isn't your first death here, is

31

it?"

The doctor's mouth settled into an unhappy line.

"We most tragically had a suicide in our first year - but that was 2011, Detective. I assure you we run a very safe hospital."

Bryn didn't respond to that comment, the SOCOs following him down the left corridor towards two uniform officers standing guard. He counted three doors in total, before a locked door cut off the corridor.

"They open them depending on the mix, sir," the nearest constable said.

"The male/female mix, he means," the other said, rolling her eyes. "Six men and three women - full house. Well...not anymore."

Bryn stepped into the little room and took it all in. The floor was dotted with packaging and emergency equipment, contamination from the resuscitation attempt - the SOCOs would hate every minute of cataloguing that lot. The single bed was unmade, with a smear of dried blood on the pillow, and the window pushed open to its limit. The walls and wardrobe doors were decorated with sheets of elaborate patterns, each painstakingly coloured in with a variety of rainbow markers.

One SOCO took the small *en suite* shower room, as Bryn craned his neck to peer in. It was neat, with minimal toiletries, and an automated rubbish bin. The SOCO started work on the bin and Bryn decided he was better off leaving him to it and starting the interviews.

Part of him wanted to talk to Amy, and the rest of him really didn't. The nurses had never let him speak to her during her stay there, saying she was unable to use the phone. Unless she'd suddenly lost the use of her hands, Bryn assumed that meant she was banned - and that Frieda was behind it.

But, with the charges against him dropped, what was the harm in taking her witness statement in this investigation? He had no conflict of interest here. Emerging from the corridor, he made his way towards the dining room, striding purposefully across the lounge.

"Excuse me, Detective - the Conference Room is that way."

Dr Al-Dosari was not to be shaken off, it seemed.

"I need to interview the patients - clients who were on the corridor last night."

Dr Al-Dosari raised an eyebrow.

"Then, as you surely know, Detective, you must see them with an appropriate adult. My clients are far too ill to suffer an interrogation."

"Interrogation? No one is a suspect here, Doctor."

Dr Al-Dosari smiled, but it was a professional veneer, well-oiled and not to be trusted. "Of course not, Detective."

Bryn would not give up so easily. "You suspect foul play? Or did Ffion Ellis…?"

"She was not suicidal, no," the doctor said, matter-of-fact. "She was also a very healthy woman for sixty-eight. We will obviously release her medical records as the coroner demands, but I cannot think of a reason why she would die like this."

So much for Bryn's straightforward work.

"Start from the beginning," he said.

Chapter 6: The Art of Death

Indira loved nothing better than a fresh corpse.

The state of a body when it arrived with her determined the entire course of the autopsy. A waterlogged body that had been missing at sea for several days, for example, was very different to one buried beneath a sand dune for ten years.

This body, however, was contaminated. The heroic efforts of the staff at Cliff House, the paramedics, and the A&E department meant that it would be difficult to imagine the body in its pre-resuscitation state.

Indira called up the context details for the autopsy. Ffion Ellis, sixty-eight years old, female. Detained at Cliff House under Section 3 of the Mental Health Act for three-hundred-and-twenty-seven days with a diagnosis of recurrent depressive disorder with psychotic symptoms. Her university psychiatry lecturer would've called the woman "sad and mad" – how Indira had hated that man and his 1950s values.

Indira looked through the list of medications Ffion had been taking - an impressive cocktail of unusual drugs, the treatment of choice when all other choices had been exhausted. She filed it away for later comparison to the toxicology results, to see what was meant to be there and what wasn't. Her past medical history was unremarkable for a woman of her age - high blood pressure, high cholesterol, underactive thyroid. That made Indira's job easier.

Before she started the full post-mortem, she would need to wait for the medical photographer and one of Bryn's SOCOs to make sense of the evidence. However, she could make a few preliminary observations - the coroner would want the report as soon as possible, to know if they were dealing with a suspicious death.

Indira turned to the body. She was not a sentimental woman, but she always paused to consider the person, if only for a moment.

"You're all right," she murmured. "You're safe with me."

She cleared her throat, her eyes already scanning for clues, but she first needed to ensure her actions were recorded. "Dictation on."

The computer beeped and the software appeared on screen, the red "recording" button flashing to acknowledge its readiness. Indira read the case number and identified herself for the record, before turning her attention to the task.

"Sixty-eight-year-old Caucasian female. Apparently of average height and underweight - measurements to follow."

Indira moved closer to the head, scrutinising every inch with a professional eye.

"Medium-length grey hair - appears wet, possibly due to perspiration. Eyelids open, with a large subconjunctival haemorrhage of the right eye."

In fact, the white of the eye was almost entirely obscured by blood. Indira would need to look at the backs of the eyes for more evidence of bleeding.

"Evidence of multiple small haemorrhages - I note petichiae over both cheeks, possible purpura over the chin and forehead, and evidence of bleeding from the right nostril. Note the intubation tube *in situ* currently limits observation."

Indira's mind was already skipping ahead, trying to come up with reasons for so much bleeding and bruising - a clotting problem? An infection run rampant? Uncontrolled blood pressure? She would need the full records from Cliff House to see if any signs had been noted in the days leading up to her death.

"Pink staining around the lips may indicate pulmonary oedema - lung dissection will clarify."

She dimly heard the back door to the laboratory swing open. The courier was probably dropping off samples, as they weren't expecting another body today. He was a jolly man, always cracking jokes and whistling off-key, never perturbed by the things he saw in their laboratory.

"Dictation off." She raised her voice to call out. "Just put them on the side and I'll sign for them in a minute."

Refocusing her thoughts, she returned to the body. "Dictation on. Again, I note purpura over the neck, but in no fixed pattern. This is unlikely to be traumatic but skin reflection will provide more clarity."

Indira paused. Something was nagging at her, but she couldn't quite work out what. Had she seen this pattern of bruising before? Or was it something else that didn't feel right?

She took a step back from the table, considering the whole. The nightgown had been cut to apply the defibrillator pads, which were still stuck to the chest - though they appeared to have slid. A closer look confirmed that the torso was also drenched in sweat.

Sweating and haemorrhages… Sepsis was looking more likely, but had the mental health unit really ignored such severe symptoms? Or had this woman harboured a suppressed immune system, perhaps from one of her medications? Indira's drug knowledge was rusty but she was sure some of them could do that.

But that wasn't what was bothering her. What the hell was it?

The computer beeped, reminding her that she had left the recording running without speaking for a minute, the noise echoing in the soundless lab.

Soundless. If the courier was here, why wasn't he whistling?

Something heavy connected with the side of her head, knocking her into her instrument tray with a clatter. Another blow and she was down, the room spinning away from her and blood filling her mouth from her bitten tongue.

She clung to consciousness, trying to lever herself off the floor to confront her assailant. But there were no more blows, no coup de grâce, and after what could've been moments or hours, she heard the laboratory door close once more.

Sticky wetness flowed into her eye, stinging, and she tried to move, to shout, to do anything at all. Instead, she slumped back to the floor, looking up with one bleary eye at the fading lab.

Only one thought registered, as all others vanished:

The body was gone.

Chapter 7: Run for Mother

He had never watched the news, not before. However, Jason had grown vain, drunk on his crime-fighting success - he wanted to see what they had to say about him, "The Bristol Bat". The local news loved him, wanted more of him. He'd even started collecting newspaper articles detailing his exploits.

It was much better than following the news after his flight from Cardiff. The local press was full of the museum story, which had overshadowed all else for several days. Then stories began to emerge about possible corruption in Cardiff Police and that a police consultant had been arrested, but later committed to a mental institution. That had almost been enough to send Jason running back to Cardiff, but he'd stayed put. Was an asylum worse than a prison cell?

This news was much more to his taste. He'd usually catch the headlines before work, but Sunday was his day off. For a man with no life, no family, that meant idly flicking through channels after a fry-up round the corner. Full of sausage and bacon, he turned on the TV, landing straight on the news.

He recognised Cardiff Central Police Station immediately, having seen it more times than he wanted to remember. The banner across the bottom of the screen said:

BODY STOLEN FROM MORGUE. PATHOLOGIST INJURED.

The details were sparse, scanty. They didn't have much information on the body, or the name of the pathologist. Which was why the vultures were circling, staking out the police station until someone threw them a morsel or two.

Bradley Thompson had no interest in this story. But Jason couldn't let go - was it Indira who was injured? Who was working the case? Was his best friend watching this somewhere, wishing she were part of the action, missing the thrill of it? Or was she too folded up within herself to know anything but misery?

He couldn't think about that. Not if he wanted to stay away, stay safe, like she wanted. If he thought of Amy in pain, he would go home in an instant. She would never forgive him for that.

He couldn't look away from the television, glued to the non-existent updates. The perpetrator had used a white van, no one had seen him come or go, and they were reviewing the CCTV footage. The pathologist was in a critical but stable condition.

Then came the afternoon press conference from the Chief Constable, the time for putting rumours to rest. Jason's stomach lurched as he recognised Bryn standing beside him, grey-faced and worn. He looked years older - that's what corruption charges did for you.

"We can now identify the victim as Indira Bharani, one of our most senior pathologists."

Shit. Jason liked Indira - she knew what she was about, and she tolerated Jason in a way her predecessor had never managed. He would've liked to know her better, but they had always been working, too busy for social calls. Really, he knew next to nothing about her - and that made him feel a hundred times worse. Maybe he would never get that chance.

"The body cannot be identified for legal reasons. However, the death had not been considered suspicious prior to this incident."

Why did a person steal a body? The most obvious answer was that they didn't want Indira to find something, maybe the cause of death? This non-suspicious death was looking more and more like a murder investigation.

A journalist stuck her hand up. "If the death wasn't suspicious, why was the body in a police mortuary for a coroner's post-mortem?"

The Chief Constable looked undecided about whether he should answer such a question, before coming down on the side of brief disclosure. "This person had been detained under the Mental Health Act. All deaths under those circumstances require investigation."

Mental Health Act. That meant the death had occurred in a psychiatric hospital, didn't it? A hospital like the one where Amy was kept. There must be a few of those in Cardiff, right? It could be nowhere near Amy. Or it could be right next door to her.

Suddenly, Jason was aware that Bryn was looking at him. Right through the television, straight into Jason's soul. He knew that look, had seen it a hundred times or more on the detective's face: *leave it alone.*

It was meant for Jason. Bryn was looking at the camera like that, because Jason might be watching. That meant he thought he was going to do something stupid - like run to Cardiff and see if Amy was really in trouble.

If Bryn felt the need to warn him off, then Amy must be involved. There was no chance Jason would leave that alone.

He packed in minutes, the barest essentials, before liberating a bike from the garage. Within an hour, he was leaving Bristol behind and crossing the Severn Bridge into Wales. He couldn't march up to the police station and demand answers - he was still a wanted man, after all. But he had one place where he could find both rest and information.

He left the bike on a side street, dusk falling around him, as he made his way to the small, familiar house in Butetown, a small area of Cardiff that was struggling out of its poor origins. He picked up the key from under the mat and let himself in, not wanting to take his helmet off before he was safely indoors and away from prying eyes.

Something hard hit his helmet, momentarily knocking him back. Through the visor, he saw his furious mother brandishing a broom and preparing to strike again.

"Mam! It's me!"

Gwen took a step back, squinting up at him in the dark corridor. Jason fumbled for the light switch and yanked off his helmet, shooting his mam a wounded look of betrayal.

Instead of sympathy and regret, Gwen's anger seemed to swell until it consumed her entirely. "What are you doing, you stupid boy? Do you want to get arrested again?"

Jason scowled. "I saw the thing on the news. About Indira."

"Indira's fine. Go away."

Jason looked up the staircase, where his sister Cerys was descending, hair wet from the shower.

"Nice to see you too," he quipped.

"You're an idiot. Amy is stuck with those bloody headshrinkers to protect you, and you decide to fuck it all up."

"Language, bach," Gwen said, absently.

Jason wouldn't back down so easily. "Is the body from the same hospital that Amy's in?"

Cerys didn't have to say a word - it was written clearly all over her face.

"It's a murder investigation now, isn't it? They must think that man was murdered, for someone to steal the body?"

"Woman," Cerys said, then scowled at herself. "And that's all you're getting from me."

Jason jutted out his bottom lip in a childish act of defiance. "Fine then. I'll go ask Bryn, shall I?"

"You're fucking mental! If you see Bryn, he'll have to arrest you. Do you know how much shit we're in because of you? I have weekly meetings with my supervisor to see whether you've 'been in touch.'"

Jason felt bad about that. He was putting Cerys' career as a police office in jeopardy just by existing, but if Amy was in trouble, then all other things faded away. He was her friend, her assistant - she needed him to take care of her, and he hadn't been there.

"If you won't help me, I'll do it myself."

Cerys smacked his arm. "You're bloody impossible, you are."

Jason smiled tentatively. "Does that mean you'll help?"

"I'll keep you out of jail and that's all."

Gwen sighed softly, a bare whisper of sound that nevertheless commanded the attention of her two children.

"Don't spoil this for her, love," she said, and retreated into the kitchen.

Jason swallowed. He was asking Cerys to put her future on the line for him - she was still a probationary constable, but that would all be over if she was found to be helping him. Could he ask that of her?

"She's all right, you know," Cerys said. "Bryn's seen her."

And that was all it took. Amy came first - Amy would always come first, and Jason would walk into fire for her, ask his sister to sacrifice her career over her.

If that's what it took to keep her safe.

Chapter 8: Personal Question

For a fleeting moment, Amy had thought she might see Bryn, enjoy some familiar human contact - and then he was gone. She was to be denied even that.

But the next day, the hospital was swarming with police, suddenly demanding full access to the hospital and to the patients. Something had changed. Perhaps something about Ffion's death had made them suspicious?

A couple of patients decided to seek better healthcare, and Emma and Amy were moved to other rooms, with a nurse posted in the corridor at all times in case a male patient wandered too close. Once evicted from the sanctuary of her room, Amy found the hospital tolerable - she spent little time in the main rooms, trying to seek out the quiet spaces, but she didn't die from it. All it had taken was Ffion's death for her to make progress, give her strength to push past that low-level buzzing in her veins that told her to be on high alert.

Dr Al-Dosari, however, was not interested in Amy's improved mental health. Instead, he was doing his level best to prevent the police talking with his patients. He seemed to want to protect them, demanding advocates, but did he really have something to hide? Had one of his treatments killed Ffion?

The updates filtered round the hospital over the weekend, after the nurses had banned the news channel due to "distressing content". Their gossiping, however, provided plenty of intelligence:

"Did you hear - Ffion's missing?"

"Someone stole her!"

"I can't believe it. Who would do that?"

By sneaking a look at a discarded newspaper, Amy had learned of Indira's injuries, but no more than that. Amy had never met Indira, but she had heard her voice and received her emails, knew that she was valuable to the little police team that Amy was a part of. Or had been, before all this, before her secrets and crimes had destroyed everything she had built.

With the body missing and without access to the patients, how were the police to learn the truth about Ffion's death? Amy was living at the crime scene, in the perfect position to obtain answers from all the witnesses locked in with her - a captive audience.

But they were all strangers to her, all except Emma. Could she really walk up to someone and start interrogating them? Wouldn't she die from embarrassment, their laughter killing her as effectively as any knife?

She knew a few nurses, enough to nod to and mumble "I'm fine", but they wouldn't disclose information about their patients. Of course, if she had her usual technological capabilities, she could plant bugs, tap into cameras, and spy on their casual conversations. Except she was stranded here with nothing but her trembling hands.

Could she break into the nursing office and their computer system, accessing patient records and cameras, undetected? Her hands longed to touch a computer again, and she kept an eagle eye on every visitor that entered the unit, coveting their smartphones and their tablets. The patients often kept their toys locked in the office but Amy was always aware of exactly where they were at all times. Longing for that vital connection to be restored to her.

It was too risky. Even if she could pick the lock on the office door, the unit was too small to hide effectively, even at night. She would be discovered immediately, and then further questions asked, more jail time looming in her future. They had to think her docile and innocent if she was to make progress here.

She missed Jason and Bryn. They got answers by asking direct questions. It was the reason she sent Jason out into the world and into danger - to find the answers she couldn't gain through technology. But Jason wasn't here, and Bryn couldn't talk to her or any other patient.

Of course, she could just leave it alone. She wasn't a police consultant any more, nor a private investigator. She was little Amy Loach, fragile in mind and weak in body, struggling to get up and dress every day.

Could she leave it, though? A woman was dead, a woman she had known - if only vaguely - and she was the one with access to the crime scene and the witnesses. She could hide away, or she could put her mind to use before it rotted away. *What would Jason do?*

It was late Sunday night before she'd made her decision. She would start small, try it out. Test the danger, like her therapist always told her. See if the feared outcome matched up to reality.

When she returned to her room after dinner, she nudged a small folded piece of paper under Emma's door, like Emma had done to her countless times. She curled up on her bed, pushing open the window despite the chill, and waited.

She hadn't really spoken to Emma since the night of Ffion's death. Emma had been a ghost, inconsolable, stuck in a pattern of rituals that barely allowed her to leave her room. If Emma could talk to her, it would take time and patience. Thankfully, Amy was blessed with an abundance of one if not quite the other.

It was over an hour later that Amy heard the click of the window opening. She took a deep breath and closed her eyes.

"Are you there?"

The silence was long, stretching into the cold of the night. Emma hadn't expected her to ask, wasn't prepared.

Eventually, her answer came: "I'm here."

Amy knew it was her turn to speak, but all her words were inadequate. Was this how Emma felt every time they spoke, fumbling around for words that would not come, that couldn't possibly add up to what was contained inside?

"How are you?" she said, chickening out of the tough questions.

"Sad."

The immediacy of the response surprised Amy, who was used to waiting on Emma's deliberations. The first time, Amy had thought she'd fallen asleep, but she'd soon learned that Emma always took time to choose her words. She wanted to be understood, but she could never find what to say.

"Do you miss her?"

The pause stretched out like warm toffee turning to goo, making up for that first quick response. Amy thought she heard a stifled sob.

"No. Is that bad? I feel bad about it. But she was always loud, shouting in the night, stopping me sleeping." Her voice dropped to little more than a murmur. "Is she dead because of me?"

Amy blinked, taken aback. Was this a confession? Had Emma done something to bring about Ffion's death? That made no sense. What

45

did make sense was Emma blaming herself for something that wasn't real.

"You had nothing to do with it."

"What if I did? I've been lax with my little rituals. The therapist keeps making me change them, saying nothing will happen. Now Ffion is dead! Did I do that? Maybe I need to pray more, keep things neater, better."

Amy knew enough about Emma's "little rituals" to know they were all-consuming, paralysing. They made Amy's total avoidance of the outside world look like a slight inconvenience. "I don't think it works like that."

"Then why is she dead? Why are the police here? They're looking for me, aren't they? How can I undo it? How can I stop anyone else dying?"

Emma was breathing too quickly, talking too fast. Amy was out of her depth, flailing in the darkness. When she panicked, Jason held her and made her tea. She couldn't do those things for Emma.

Her breathing wasn't slowing down and she had started to make little muffled sounds, as if she wanted to scream but something held her back. Amy hit the nurse call button in her room, hearing all the alarms go off around the ward.

The healthcare assistant outside threw open the door. "What is it?"

"It's Emma," Amy said. "I can hear her panicking."

The cavalry arrived, anxious and out of breath, and they did what Amy couldn't: calmed, reassured, settled. She had stirred up Emma's fears by talking about the case and yet she couldn't deal with the consequences. She should've listened when Dr Al-Dosari had forbidden the police to question anyone without supervision.

Amy had thought the rules didn't apply to her, had always believed it. Which had ended her up in this hospital, ruined her friends' lives, and now caused Emma pain. She'd thought she was doing the right thing. What was that phrase - the road to hell, good intentions? This was hell.

Enough. She had to say enough, and stop this before she hurt anyone else.

Chapter 9: Evidence of Absence

The secret to digging a grave was patience.

Sure, a man could spend all night digging and have something usable by dawn. But who wanted to spend all night digging? If you went camping for a few days out in the wilderness, you had plenty of time to dig between drinking, smoking and fresh mushroom omelettes.

He was a patient man. He could play the long game.

He could also act fast when needed. Like stealing that body before any discovery could make things…problematic. Adaptable - that was what he was, a fine quality in a man. If only *some people* could understand that.

Shame about that girl. Though she was just staring into space like a dozy cow and, really, what could you expect? You had to pay attention to the details, to life around you, or you would never get on. You wouldn't see the body snatcher coming at you with a weapon.

Body snatcher. He liked that. No doubt his antics were the talk of the town. Would the media give him a nickname, like they had the Cardiff Ripper? What would it be? But no, what was he thinking? He didn't want too much noise around this. He didn't want anyone to look too deeply, even scratch the surface. Who knows what they might find? It was just too bad he couldn't capitalise on the publicity.

After the old woman was in the ground - somewhere nice and out of the way, where no dog walker could accidentally stumble across her - he would return to town to see what was what. What the pigs and the hounds thought about him. How much they wanted him. How much they knew.

He returned to his temporary home just before dawn, too wired to sleep, a thousand ideas bubbling up through his mind. This turn of events was unexpected and he needed to rethink his plans. He hadn't been prepared for the involvement of the law, the hospital. Who knows what bits and pieces they might've taken from her. The little things that might tell of what he had done. At least he had the body now. There would be no tell-tale heart to betray him.

He drew the curtains and lit some incense, allowing the scent to carry him far away - half a world away and more, his mind struggling to break free of his worldly cares. He needed to chill out, calm down, focus. He didn't want to fall over the edge. That way lay madness.

Quite literal madness. How he fucking hated it. He couldn't bear to look at the old woman, the derangement in her face, even in death. Fucking mental cases, all locked up in that hilltop house, with a sea view. It would be quicker to set fire to the place and have done with it.

It was patience he needed and patience that would see him home. He had waited this long. What was a few more days, a week? He was investing in his future - no need to be hasty. He had all the time in the world.

Watching other glasses fast run out of sand.

Bryn stood outside the doors to the morgue, his knuckles white as he gripped his Monday morning coffee, double strength and black.

Yet no amount of caffeine could prepare him for what he would find within. He did not want to cross the threshold, to enter into the scene that he knew lay beyond the door. To become part of the cold, objective investigation into his friend's assault.

His phone buzzed in his pocket. Bryn considered ignoring it, but the uniformed sentry was already looking at him as he was losing it.

"Hesketh."

"Report back on the number plate, sir." Detective Constable Catriona Aitken did not waste words. The Cyber Crime Unit was analysing the CCTV footage, their remit encompassing everything from online fraud to digital evidence. "It's registered to a tradesman in Hull. He just got back from Ibiza last night and his van's safely locked in the garage, where he left it."

Another dead end. After spending all of Saturday and Sunday hunting down the body, they were still no closer to finding it. The daughter of the victim lived a distance away and had no notion who might want to steal her.

He'd managed to contact the two former patients who had discharged themselves at the first sign of trouble. Paul Yates was a depressed lawyer who had retreated to Italy to find his recovery in an idyllic vineyard, and Roshan Vara was a disgraced surgeon using his new-found freedom to rediscover his cocaine addiction. Neither man had seen or heard anything, though both agreed to contact local police to submit formal statements. Dead end after dead end.

"And the CCTV footage? Have we cross-referenced it with the car park surveillance from Cliff House?"

"Owain's on it," she said.

Which meant that Owain Jenkins was also back at work, returned from the same disgrace that had banished Bryn. He should call the boy, make amends, but something held him back. They had gone a long way towards mending their relationship on the night that Amy had surrendered herself to the National Crime Agency, but it was still far from where they had been. Bryn had trusted Owain, and the copper had collaborated with their enemy, unknowingly bringing the whole house down around them.

Indira had been invaluable on that night. They owed her for Amy and Jason's lives, but Bryn wasn't sure he had ever thanked her. Now she was unconscious in the hospital, her brain swollen inside her skull. They were talking about operating, but it was risky. They couldn't tell if she would ever be the same - would she work, or even walk and talk? Would she breathe by herself? Too many unknowns.

"Keep me informed," he told Catriona, and hung up.

He couldn't ignore it any longer. Taking a deep, steadying breath, Bryn nodded to the uniform and entered the scene of the crime.

Bryn had been inside the Cardiff Police morgue many times before. To witness autopsies or harangue his colleagues for evidence. Seeing it in this state felt like his entire world had been knocked off-kilter, that something that had been sturdy and dependable had been shattered beyond repair.

Like the room at the hospital, this one had also been trampled by paramedics. Their interference was focussed around a series of blood stains at the end of the examination table, with a blood pool interrupted by the sole of a size nine foot. Contamination, distraction.

He knew he had to focus on the evidence, on catching this bastard, but he could not stop staring at the blood. It had altered with exposure to the air, dark and congealed, deprived of its host. Spilled from Indira, who should be at his side, pointing out its properties and marvelling at the science behind the horror of the scene.

Tearing his gaze away from the blood, Bryn took in the rest of the corrupted room. The SOCOs had already catalogued, labelled and photographed all the relevant evidence, leaving gaps in the picture. The samples had been sent to Bristol, as their police station was no longer secure and the techs didn't want to process these pieces next door to the crime scene.

Even with bits missing, the actual theft appeared to be fast and efficient. The thief had taken a direct route to the table and retreated the same way. His soft-soled shoes had left only scuff marks on the linoleum floor. He had worn thick, woollen gloves, which had shed a few generic fibres and nothing more.

All this Bryn had gleaned from the preliminary SOCO report, from the photographs they had taken. He had come into the room to experience the scene first-hand, to look for some missing piece, but now he regretted entering this still, unnatural place. It felt haunted - not by the many bodies who had passed under the medical examiner's hands, but by the absence of the woman herself.

Bryn forced himself to concentrate. What was there to be learned here? The examination table was clean, so Indira hadn't yet started her autopsy. Yet she'd been found wearing gloves and gown, so she was ready to begin.

Bryn looked around the autopsy table, knocking the computer terminal with his hip. The monitor blinked on, opening up a piece of software with a recording panel on the screen. The last entry was dated November 1st, around the time of Indira's assault.

With a gloved hand, Bryn pressed play. Indira's voice filled the room, describing the woman she was examining and the signs she'd witnessed upon her body. They may not have the body, but they still had expert testimony.

Abruptly, the recording went silent. Bryn could still hear Indira breathing, as a long, slow minute passed.

Thwack! Bryn flinched, the sickening sound of weapon connecting with skull making him sick. *Crash!* The clatter of instruments flying, and then another crack. Small, pained whimpers coming from further away, as harsh breathing filled the microphone. The thief's breathing, interrupted by a grunt as he lifted the body, and then silently made his retreat.

The recording stopped. Bryn's hand shook as he hovered the mouse over the "Play" button, before deciding against it. He couldn't listen to that again. He would have to send it up to Owain and Catriona, though he wished he could spare them. No one should have to hear the sounds of their friend's violent assault.

For the first time in a long time, Bryn wanted to call on Amy. But he couldn't ask her to help him, couldn't ask that ever again. He could've used Jason's skills on the street, sniffing out the best places to hide a body or who could be hired to steal one. The less he knew about Jason's whereabouts, the better. He wouldn't have to arrest the boy if he couldn't find him.

He'd have to rely on those people who were still on his team. The pathologist Rob Pritchard had moved on to bigger and better things in London, but he would help Bryn - if only for his protégée Indira. With her audio description and the scans from the hospital, they may be able to put together a picture of what had happened to the body.

Because if they solved the riddle of this first death, it would lead them right to the man who had attacked Indira. Bryn couldn't wait to find him, arrest him, spend a few intimidating moments alone in a dark cell. Accidents happen.

While Rob worked on this *post-mortem in absentia* and Dr Al-Dosari dithered over how his patients could best be interviewed, Bryn needed to look deeper into the life of Ffion Ellis. While he couldn't confirm this was a murder, it was looking suspicious. Had someone wanted her dead? Was she killed by accident? Who would benefit from covering it up?

Bryn needed to put aside his feelings as a friend and colleague, and look through the eyes of a detective. Ffion Ellis was the key - he just had to get to know her.

Chapter 10: Bar Room Brawler

Jason sat in a dark corner of The Black Sheep, Cardiff's dodgiest of dodgy pubs in Canton's grubby back streets. But his pint was barely touched and he wasn't looking to score drugs or find a special friend for the night.

He was watching his sister suck up to her ex-boyfriend, Detective Sergeant Owain Jenkins.

Jason wasn't sure exactly how they'd come to separate, but he expected it had a lot to do with him and Amy. After Owain had helped the National Crime Agency come for Amy, Jason had seen his sister struggle to take sides. He was just a little bit smug that she had ultimately chosen him.

Except they needed Owain now, needed his expertise with computers and his police access. Jason wanted some assurances that Amy was going to be all right and, if there was the slightest chance she wasn't, he needed to get her out of there.

Unfortunately, Jason wasn't sure there was a legal way to get her out. He'd borrowed Cerys' laptop to look up a few things, and all the advice said that only a person's "nearest relative" could get them out of hospital. In Amy's case, her nearest relatives - her parents and her sister - all lived abroad and therefore didn't count. If Jason could contact Lizzie, he could probably persuade her to help out, but to what end? If Amy wasn't in the hospital, would Frieda Haas send her to prison instead?

Therefore, if he couldn't get Amy out, Jason had to make sure the police were keeping her safe. The best way to do that was to find out how the woman had died and make sure it didn't happen again - end of. But if Indira had been hurt just for investigating this crime, what might happen to Amy if the killer thought she had witnessed it?

Jason was convinced they were looking at a murder, and Cerys was inclined to agree with him. However, from his position, Jason didn't think Owain was quite on board with it. He couldn't seem to meet Cerys' eye, nursing a glass of orange juice and giving its murky depths his entire attention.

He looked drained, thin, a different man to the one Jason had seen six weeks ago. His floppy hair had grown out, so it looked shaggy and unkempt, his suit crumpled with a stain on the left lapel. He looked defeated. Betrayal would do that to a man.

Suddenly, Owain looked up and straight at Jason. He tried to pull away from Cerys' restraining hand on his arm, tried to leave the pub behind. Jason stood up, as Owain yanked his arm free and made for the door.

Jason was tenacious as a pit bull, following hard on his heels despite Cerys' warning call. He grabbed hold of Owain's shoulder and dragged him into an alley.

Owain yelped, but said nothing, trembling under Jason's grip.

"What the fuck is wrong with you? You think you've got it bad? Try being me or Amy for a week." He released him, looking at the pathetic man with disgust.

Owain slumped back against the wall, trying to shove his hair out of his eyes. "I just want to move on," he mumbled. "I don't want any more trouble."

"You're a police officer - you go where trouble is! And trouble has found Indira, or don't you give a shit?"

Owain looked up then, a hint of challenge in his eyes. "Of course I do."

"Then why won't you help me?"

"Because helping you is what got me suspended. Helping you almost got me killed, remember?"

Jason remembered well enough, the way Owain hadn't been quite himself since he'd been seriously injured on an arrest. But he wouldn't take the flak for Owain's suspension, not when he'd brought that hell down on himself.

"You chose to work with Frieda fucking Haas. You need to own that."

"Amy broke the law!"

"Amy put away murderers!"

"She stole money. Millions of pounds, from innocent people."

Jason laughed, which seemed to startle Owain more.

"Innocent? She took that money from her parents - her shitty, absentee parents. That's not theft. That's compensation."

Owain deflated, folding his arms protectively across his chest.

Cerys skidded into the alley, looking seriously pissed off. "Killed each other yet?"

"Just getting started."

"I am not helping you," Owain said, vibrating with stress. "I like my job and I want to keep it. Amy is fine - we don't even know if it's murder!"

"Why else would someone steal a body? They almost killed Indira. That's a person with nothing to lose, right there."

"Why are you even here?" Owain's face was red, his arms raised in agitated incomprehension. "You're on the run. There's nothing you can do here."

Jason felt the words hit him like missiles, battering him until he could barely stand up. What was he doing here? What could he possibly hope to achieve, with no resources and no access, hiding in the shadows?

"That's what I thought." Owain pushed past Jason, out of the alley and into the fading afternoon light.

Cerys tentatively put her hand on his arm. "Let's go home, yeah? Pick up your things, so you can be on your way."

Jason shook her off. "So, you agree with him, do you? I'm a waste of space who should just hide his arse until it all goes away?"

"Do you have a plan? Any plan at all? Because running in head-first hasn't worked out any time before."

Jason didn't want to admit it, to himself or his sister, but she was right. Amy was the one for grand plans, and he was the organ grinder's monkey. He didn't have the first idea where to start.

"I'll think of something," he said.

"Think fast - if Owain decides to shop you, I can't stop him. You need to be working on something, or you need to be gone."

"The victim," he blurted. "We need to know about the victim."

For a moment, he thought he'd lost her, that she'd had her fill of his idiocy. Then her anger faded, her eyes alive with that desire to pursue a mystery to the ends of the earth. That same desire that fuelled Jason, the one he'd learned from Amy, the one thing that could draw her into the light.

"Go on," she said.

"We just need a name and Google, right? We don't need Owain's fancy tech or Bryn's badge. We can find her."

"And that's how we find who killed her."

Chapter 11: Collective Memory

Amy didn't get out of bed on Monday. What was the point? Nothing awaited her except institutional green walls and judgemental looks and healthy food that tasted of green.

Nurse Will brought her a sandwich at lunchtime, which she ignored. His tanned, handsome face was the picture of concern, but Amy knew anyone could fake that if you paid them enough. Even if he was worried, it wasn't her job to ease his conscience.

At one o'clock, Will returned, telling her there was a mandatory therapy session in the lounge. Amy had no intention of attending, but the covers were stripped away and she was bundled into her dressing gown before she could protest. She was beginning to think prison might be kinder.

In the lounge, the other patients were gathering, in various states of dishevelment. Lois, the only nurse she trusted, pressed a cup into her hand and thankfully it was tea. Amy had realised with her first cup that the coffee here was decaffeinated, and what was the point of that?

Amy vaguely recognised her fellow inmates by sight, even if they were now reduced in number. Emma was there, curled up at one end of a sofa, double her usual size in fluffy pink pyjamas and a winter coat. She didn't meet Amy's eye, didn't even seem to realise she was there. Amy perched on the opposite arm of the sofa and sipped her tea, observing.

Next to Emma, in the only armchair, Ron stared straight ahead, his lips moving soundlessly. In her brief periods out of her room, Amy had noticed him talking to himself a lot and had stayed out of his way. He was well over six foot, his toned muscles barely contained by his tight T-shirts and sports trousers, his dark bluish-black skin barely reflecting any light at all, not even from his shaved head. She had stared the first time, and averted her eyes ever since.

Carwyn was wheeled into the awkward circle that had formed, shirt stained with old cereal. He was easily seventy or eighty years old, grey curly hair spilling over his ears like a judge's wig. He had never

57

said anything in Amy's presence and she had no idea why he was here, or how long he'd been in residence.

Mordecai staggered into the lounge and threw himself over the other sofa, jewellery jangling as he landed. Amy was certain that Mordecai was not his real name, but she had never spoken to him to question it. However, she had overheard him talking to Paul, one of the patients who had left. She hadn't found out anything about Paul, as Mordecai talked exclusively about himself. He was the lead singer in a band, which was apparently quite famous, though Amy had never heard of them. He had a problem with pills and booze, but he was getting clean, for his fiancée. But it was so hard, so terrible, oh how he ached, he wished he was dead, *et cetera et cetera ad nauseam*.

The last person to arrive was Tony, sitting next to Amy on an upright chair that one of the nurses had brought from the dining room. He was wearing a pressed shirt and trousers, with a neat crease running precisely down the front of each leg. His salt and pepper hair was cropped, tidy, and he held a folded newspaper under one arm. Amy had no idea why he was here, because he seemed perfectly sane. He kept himself to himself, much like Amy, and only read quietly in the corner.

One chair remained empty. From the door to the unit, a sparrow of a woman emerged, her skeletal frame draped in a loose blouse and skirt, with a long trailing scarf. She perched on the edge of the chair and surveyed them all from behind frameless spectacles.

"I am Dr Lourdes," she said, with a faint French accent. "Dr Al-Dosari has employed me to help you…recollect the late Ffion Ellis."

Amy's stomach dropped. Beside her, Emma started crying into her coat sleeve. Lois brought her a box of tissues. She was the only nurse present, hovering behind the sofa while the others hid in the goldfish bowl.

Dr Lourdes glanced over at Emma, before pressing on. "Would anyone like to start?"

The silence fell like a stone, broken only by Emma's hitching sobs. After a long minute or two, Tony cleared his throat.

"I didn't know her at all. We never spoke. I saw her in the dining room and that was all."

Dr Lourdes seized on the point regardless. "What was your impression of her?"

Tony looked awkward, fishing for the right words. "She had obviously been ill a long time," he said, eventually.

By which he clearly meant that she looked completely mad and that was unlikely to change. They could not have been more opposite, Tony and Ffion. He was contained, together, immaculate, and she was crying in the corridor late at night, tormented.

Abruptly, Ron stood up and walked towards the dining room, pushing straight through both sets of doors before lighting up in the garden. Lois didn't try to bring him back.

"She was whacked out," Mordecai said, with a shrug. "Whatever good stuff they were giving her, they definitely weren't sharing with me."

Dr Lourdes looked towards Emma and Amy. "Ladies? Do you remember Ffion?"

She said her name like it was vanishing - *fee-yoh* - and that grated on Amy for a reason she couldn't name. Singled out, Emma only cried more, sometimes trying to start a sentence but always being sucked back into her tears.

Amy avoided Dr Lourdes' eyes, refusing to be drawn out. She wished she'd stayed in bed. What good would this do, dredging up people's memories of the dead woman? Would it stop Emma crying? Would it help find Ffion's murderer?

Suddenly, Amy looked up at Dr Lourdes, at once suspicious and filled with a new respect. Perhaps she wasn't Dr Al-Dosari's minion at all - maybe she belonged to Bryn and the police.

Dr Lourdes caught her gaze. "Did you have something to say?"

"She paced all night," Amy said, her voice mumbled and thin, even to her own ears. "Except the night she died. She was in her room. She was never in her room."

Dr Lourdes made an "mm" noise, beloved of therapists everywhere, supposedly to encourage confidence. When Amy didn't elaborate, she was forced to question further: "And does that mean something to you?"

"I want to know why she died." Her voice was suddenly bold, stronger. "I want to know who killed her."

The words rippled through the room, like a pebble thrown into a placid lake. Tony looked curious, while Mordecai threw himself upright. Emma stopped crying, staring at Amy as if seeing her for the first time. Lois came forward, trying to place a hand on Amy's shoulder, but she shrugged her off.

Carwyn started laughing.

It was quiet at first, like the creaking of a rusty gate, before erupting into a full belly laugh that seemed completely unstoppable. But it did stop, after a minute or so, and a toothless grin filled his face. "It's because she was a murderer. She got just what she deserved."

He started to laugh again, cackling like a dozen witches around a cauldron. Lois seized the handles of his wheelchair and swiftly directed him towards his room, her low voice firmly chastising him as they went.

Dr Lourdes was all at sea, clearly unprepared for what had happened. "We'll…we'll leave it there, for today."

She floated away in a waft of gauzy fabrics, swiftly exiting through the front door. Tony left the room, returning to the bedroom corridor. Emma remained, still staring, and Amy belatedly realised Mordecai was staring too.

"How do you know it was murder then?" he asked.

Amy shrugged one shoulder. "Sudden death. Stolen body. Not rocket science."

Mordecai considered her for a moment longer, before mirroring her shrug and heading into the garden for a cigarette.

Amy felt a tug on her sleeve.

"Do you really think she was murdered?" Emma asked.

"I don't know," Amy said.

But she knew now that she couldn't leave it alone, that despite everything the passion still burned within her. She had to know. She had no other choice.

"I intend to find out."

Chapter 12: The Past is Her Story

Bryn arrived at an unassuming house in the centre of Roath, the area that marked the passage from posh, moneyed denizens to scruffy, downmarket dwellers. The end-terrace house had a faded ceramic plate bearing the name "Ty Coch".

The house lived up to its moniker, the red brick gleaming from recent rainfall, and the door a respectable black. Bryn pressed the door bell and waited, trying to ignore the cat curling around his ankles.

A discreet intercom burst to life, reminding Bryn of the paranoid access rituals for Amy's house. "Hello, can I help you?"

Bryn held up his badge to the camera. "Detective Inspector Bryn Hesketh - I have some questions about Ffion Ellis."

The door opened and he stepped inside. The cat followed, disappearing down the corridor before he had even closed the door.

"Don't worry about her. She's always in here - I suspect my residents are feeding her scraps."

Bryn smiled at the sensible, middle-aged woman who had appeared in the corridor, almost as swiftly as the cat had vacated it. She wore a white shirt and black trousers, not quite a uniform but suggesting that she hadn't much choice in it.

The woman held out her hand. "Mared. I fear you've had a wasted journey."

"As I said - "

"I do understand you're in a terrible rush, Detective, but you can't expect me to find out the information just like that. I've given your assistant all I could lay my hands on for now and you'll just have to call back tomorrow, at the very earliest."

Bryn felt his heart sink. Someone had been here before him, using his name to gain access to the house and gather information. Probably some journalist chancing his luck - and succeeding. Of course, he could think of a worse scenario...

"I just wanted to see Ms Ellis's room for myself," he said, unwilling to confront the situation head-on in case his suspicions were correct.

Mared gave a disapproving *tsk*. "Very well then. The girl said you'd send over some forensics people to do it properly, but I suppose looking's the next best thing."

Bryn frowned. "Girl...?"

Mared laughed. "Oh, she was certainly a young woman, but she looked like a slip of a thing. And such hair! I'm surprised they allow that kind of thing in the police."

Bryn tried not to let his disappointment show. It seemed that even without her brother on the scene, Cerys Carr was unable to stay out of trouble. Her peroxide-blonde tufts were as distinctive as a fingerprint.

He followed Mared upstairs. The first floor was long and thin, but they didn't linger long on the landing. Bryn noticed that the nearest door had a white sign with the name "George" printed on it, surrounded by musical notes, before Mared led him up the next flight of stairs.

The second floor was smaller, with a small bathroom at the front and two long bedrooms at the back. On the left door, the name "Enid" was enclosed in a wreath of flowers. On the right, the sign had peeled away, the flopped-over paper concealing the name beneath.

Mared unlocked the door with a key from a large clanking ring, before pushing open the door and stepping aside. The overwhelming smell was stale air, overlaid with something sweet and rotting.

"I can't find the apples," Mared said. "I know she had a stash somewhere, but I have no idea where she put them."

The little room was sparse, the single bed pushed against the only window and a chest of drawers along one wall with no personal touches at all. A generic print hung on one wall. The only distinguishing feature was a small bookcase that was crammed full, a mixture of romance and science fiction and textbooks about everything from gardening to crochet.

"I'm not sure she even read half of them. She just couldn't bear the library throwing them out. She would tell you the most bizarre things over supper."

"How long had she been in hospital?"

Mared counted on her fingers. "It was coming up eleven months."

"Is it usual to keep the room that long?"

"Her daughter paid for it, and Cliff House and all. She thought giving up this room would make her lose the last bit of hope she had. I visited her most weeks, and the other staff too. She wasn't getting any better, though - seeing and hearing things again. They thought the dementia might be setting in."

"Can you think of anyone who might want to harm her?"

"Your friends asked the same thing. Right fixed on that terrible accident. I can't imagine anyone would come after her for that, not after all these years. The only one who still fretted over it was Ffion herself."

Bryn itched to ask for details, but he wanted to maintain his ruse a little longer. *Friends.* Owain wouldn't come along with Cerys, not anymore. Which meant someone else had been here with her, and it wasn't a long list of suspects.

"Had she mentioned it to you recently?" he said, subtly fishing.

"Only that hell was coming for her. She felt she still had to be punished, even after she did her time in that…what did they call it? 'Forensic unit'. Worse than prison, if you ask me. Her daughter reckons she was never the same after that - though I don't know what she would know about it. She's so busy up in London, you see."

Bryn retreated from the sad, little room, and Mared locked the door behind him.

"I'll have that information about her probation officer and all those bits for you tomorrow, Detective. You can just give me a call if there's anything else you think of."

"Thank you," he said, but he wasn't truly listening.

It wasn't Mared or this house that would yield the information now. He had to hunt down Cerys Carr and her idiot brother - they needed to stop interfering in his case, but first they had to give up what they knew.

If they ruined this murder investigation, Bryn would arrest both of them, Amy be damned.

Chapter 13: Friends in Unlikely Places

For the first time, Amy really wanted to talk to Carwyn.

She could put his outburst down to the ramblings of a madman, but he had never called out before. In fact, he was always quiet, watching the world go by, keen interest behind his eyes.

However, the nurses had tucked him away in his room, claiming he was "overexcited", and Amy suspected they would be watching him closely from now on. She had also noticed them watching her, when they had never bothered before. In the closed world of the unit, an accusation of murder meant they were all suspects.

So far, the only person Amy could definitely rule out was herself. She didn't want to suspect Emma, couldn't quite believe in the possibility, but she'd had opportunity. Calling for help could be a ruse.

All of the nurses on the night shift had touched the body. If she hadn't been dead when Emma called, one of them certainly could've killed her. All sorts of drugs in that emergency bag - who knows what the wrong dose might do?

Before she let her imagination run away with her, she had to take a step back. Why would anyone want to kill Ffion Ellis? Was she a murderer, as Carwyn said? Had everyone known that except Amy?

At dinner, nobody said anything at all, a taut silence over the tables - the word "murder" hanging invisibly in the air, yet making its presence felt. Certainly Emma, sat across from Amy, couldn't muster a word. Carwyn did not make an appearance, his dinner delivered to his room, and Amy chewed over what to do next.

Having decided to leap into an investigation with both feet, she now had nowhere to go. Was she really up to this? Yet she felt alive again, sluggish but functional, the dark thoughts and the anxious flutters simmering away under the surface but not threatening to emerge. She could do this.

But could she do it without Jason? They had fallen out before she'd ended up in hospital, because he didn't feel she appreciated his talents, thought of him as just her attack dog and snoop. He was so much more than that. She ached with how much she missed him, just to talk to, to share a silent cup of tea.

Where was he? Was he safe? Staying out of trouble, lying low? How long could she expect him to live in exile from his hometown and everyone he knew? If he returned, would he be arrested and locked away? Perhaps he was already in prison - Amy had no knowledge of what was happening beyond her room. But she suspected that Frieda Haas would've come to gloat if that were the case. She would never pass up the chance to tell Amy how utterly she had failed.

So, Jason wasn't here. Jason would never be here, not if he had followed her instructions. It was up to her to do this alone. She had to find a way to get to Carwyn without the nurses' interference, and without letting on what she was doing.

Her best chance was now, while they were all busy with dinner. The nurse in the corridor appeared only at night, so Amy could pretend to go to her room but just keep wandering down the hallway to Carwyn's room. Whichever room it was.

Amy mumbled apologies to Emma before abandoning her peers and hearing for the bedroom corridor. She passed the empty nurses' office and walked towards her room, the one right on the end. Emma was next door to her and then, somewhere further down the corridor, was Carwyn.

As she neared her room, she saw a healthcare assistant emerge from the room two doors down, with a cleared tray. *Target acquired.* She opened her own door, ducking inside to avoid the staff member. She closed it and crouched below the slatted glass, waiting for the woman to pass by.

After a few minutes, Amy stood up and opened the door, looking both ways before heading for Carwyn's door. The corridor light was flickering, an irregular pulsation that made Amy's temples throb in time to its beat. She turned her face away from it and caught sight of something silvery echoing its light, on the floor beneath the boxy radiator.

She crouched down and fished it out with careful fingers. It was a film strip of tablets, half-full. She didn't recognise the printed name and there was nothing else to identify it. How had medication ended up in the corridor? The nurses were always careful to dole out the meds in their clinic room and, if they did bring tablets out to patients, they were popped out in little plastic pots.

Had a member of staff taken this away from the clinic room and then accidentally dropped it? Or had a patient smuggled it in to feed their addiction? Amy's mind leapt to Mordecai, the drug-fuelled rock star. Yet from the information he couldn't keep himself from spilling to all who would listen, his problem was with diazepam, the same little blue pills that had soothed Amy's soul on difficult nights trapped in her flat. Amy didn't know what these tablets were, but she was fairly certain she would recognise any and all brands of benzodiazepine at a glance.

In the wrong hands, could these tablets be used in a murder? In an unstable old woman, would half a strip of this mysterious medication rob her of her life?

Amy slipped the tablets into her pocket and stood up. Yet another question that needed answering, but for now, she would focus on Carwyn and his information. She passed Emma's closed door on the right, a glitter-covered sign declaring it to be hers. Carwyn's door had no such adornment, plain wood, window slats closed.

And door locked. *Damn.*

"What are you doing?"

Amy started at Tony's voice, panic trilling through her as she whirled to face him. How much had he seen?

"Hoping the old boy has a confession, mm?"

With a composure she didn't feel, Amy folded her arms across her chest. "I want to know the truth."

Tony smiled, but it didn't quite reach his eyes. "Don't we all, Miss Lane? But some clearly know more than others."

His eyes were on Carwyn's door, but Amy wasn't sure it was him they were talking about.

"You know something," she said.

Tony continued to smile. "My room is at the end of the corridor. I heard the woman screaming. I have just as much interest in finding out who killed her."

Amy felt a warm thrill fill her. "You believe she was murdered."

"Now that makes two of us. Perhaps we can be of assistance to each other."

Amy gestured to the bulging top pocket of his shirt. "You can look up Carwyn's accusations. Find out - "

"Oh, I've already done that. Nine years ago, Ms Ellis drove her car in front of a bus, hoping to die. The driver swerved to avoid her, crashing into a wall. Five people were injured - and one little boy died."

It was true then. Ffion Ellis was a murderer, or at least a killer. But how could the family of that little boy get to her in here? Why now?

Tony, clearly pleased with his research, was keen to show off. He removed his phone from his trouser pocket and started tapping at it. Amy watched it covetously. If she could have only a few minutes alone with it, she could reach out to her computer's backup servers, harness the power of technology to assist her. Or simply Google the medication that was burning a hole in her pocket. She could be free again.

"Spent two years in some special facility. After that, she couldn't go home - small town, all hating her - so they set her up somewhere. No idea where. This murder is the first time anyone's heard of her since the trial."

Amy's focus returned at that. "Has she been identified?"

Tony smirked. "You really are out of the loop, aren't you? Her name's everywhere now, and everyone's talking about the bus again. 'Diminished responsibility' - that's what they called it. But we're all responsible for our crimes, aren't we, Miss Lane?"

Amy felt the hairs rise on the back of her neck. "I think she was just...very sad."

Suddenly, she felt the need to bolt and hide. She started back towards her room, but realised Tony was blocking her path.

"What? Did I say something to offend you?"

"No, nothing. I need to sleep."

Tony looked at his phone. "At six o'clock?"

"Let me pass."

She felt the darkness falling, the heat and the closeness and constriction at her throat. But he stepped aside and she fled, fumbling desperately with the door handle until it opened, feeling him watching her all the time.

She closed the door, locked it, and crawled along the floor into the bathroom. Hidden away. Concealed.

"But we're all responsible for our crimes, aren't we, Miss Lane?"

Miss Lane.

Her heart stopped. He'd called her Miss Lane - not once, but twice. Yet here she was Amy Loach, her pseudonym stripped away, returned to the frightened teenager she'd once been.

Tony knew her name - her true name. How? How could he possibly know? Had her name and picture been on the news? Was her arrest public knowledge? Did they know she was here, in this building?

Amy had helped put men in prison, destroyed gangs, cost some people a lot of money and pride and freedom. What if they knew exactly where she was - and she was vulnerable?

Is that why they had come for Ffion Ellis?

Chapter 14: A Family Affair

"You have to stay out of sight."

"Fuck off, Cerys."

The jibe was casual, good-natured, but Jason could tell his sister was serious as a seizure. She stopped them in the middle of the path, two doors down from their suspect's house, and gripped his sleeve so hard her knuckles turned white.

"Wait round the corner. I'll be fine."

Her voice was intent, firm, but he could see the edge of fear in the lines of her face. She didn't want to do this alone, and he wasn't going to let her.

"What if he is the killer? What then?"

"I'm in uniform! You think he's going to off me in the street?"

"He killed an old woman and stole her body!"

"We don't know that! He might have nothing to do with it."

"Then we're all just wasting our time here."

"That you are."

The deep, stern voice cut through their squabbling and Jason's muscles tensed, deciding whether or not to run. He slowly turned his head and took a good look at Detective Inspector Bryn Hesketh. He looked unhappy and unimpressed, but he wasn't waving handcuffs in Jason's direction. Yet.

He stared for a long moment, before turning to Cerys. "What do you think you're doing?"

"Taking a walk. You?"

Bryn stifled a sigh. "You just happen to be walking through the dodgy end of Gabalfa, right on the street where I'm about to make inquiries into a murder investigation?"

Cerys gave him a shit-eating grin. "That's about right, yeah."

"Probationary Constable Carr, are you lying to me?"

Jason watched Cerys squirm under the pressure, though only her eyes and a twitch of her cheek gave her away. He'd watched a similar reaction occur under their mam's interrogation techniques. The threat of no pudding could work wonders in their house.

"We're here to see Cezary Kowalski."

The name was mangled in his mouth, probably nowhere close to its Polish origins, but it didn't seem to matter to Bryn. Jason had thought to save his sister admitting her fibs, but the detective continued to blank him.

"Cerys, I'm waiting."

She scowled, acting her nineteen years, before gathering her churlishness into a response. "We're looking for the father of Oskar Kowalski. The child that Ffion Ellis killed."

Bryn's mouth was a hard line, disapproving father and judging copper all in one. "I guess you found him after you went to Ffion Ellis' house and asked her carer."

Jason winced. Bryn knew everything, including how much Cerys had abused her position - before they even got into how she'd carted her wanted brother around with her.

Cerys' reply was a shrug, before she rallied herself to fight back. "I was trying to help."

"It wasn't the police you were helping though, was it?"

It was the closest Bryn had come to acknowledging Jason's presence since that initial spotlight glare, but Jason resisted the urge to leap in and defend her again.

"I had to keep him out of trouble," Cerys said, pleading for understanding. "Or he would've blundered into this by himself."

Jason was being characterised as an idiot by his own family now. From the look on Bryn's face, his friends agreed. If they were even still friends.

"He needs to go back where he came from. Now. Before someone arrests him for being a right pain in the arse."

"I'm not leaving until I know Amy's safe." The words were out before he could think them through, tripping off his tongue like a melody he was born to sing.

Bryn finally turned to him. "She's fine. I've seen her."

"Have you spoken to her? Does she know who did it?"

"She's in hospital for treatment, not to run a murder investigation."

"You really think she could stay out of this? I know her! She's already in it up to her eyes."

"What are you going to do then?"

At the blunt question, Jason faltered. He couldn't wander up to the hospital and demand to see her. They couldn't run this investigation together, not without serious help from the police or someone on their side.

"The best way to protect her is to stay out of this - and stay out of prison."

"What the hell are they going to arrest me for anyway? I didn't know about her parents' money."

"Anything they can. You've met Frieda Haas."

Jason really didn't want to be reminded of that woman. He had trusted her, and probably more, but she had been spying on him the entire time - using him to get to Amy. If he'd only thought with his head instead of his junk, they wouldn't be in this stupid mess.

Unable to argue against that woman's name, Jason changed tack. "Where's your partner? You just going in there alone?"

"They haven't got round to..."

Replacing Owain. The unsaid words were deafening, and Jason saw that Cerys felt them most of all. Bryn's expression was hard as flint, silently blaming Jason for dividing them.

"You need backup," Jason said.

"From you?"

"From me." Cerys had shrugged off any sign of teenage petulance and stood tall, her uniform hanging neatly off her slim frame.

Bryn assessed her, then nodded - before rounding on Jason. "You," the glare was back, "stay out of sight."

Jason restrained his irritation. He'd united them, only for them both to turn on him. How was that fair? At least he wasn't getting arrested.

Unable to stay entirely apart from the action, Jason followed about fifty feet behind them before crossing the street and settling on a garden wall. He took out a cigarette and lit up, all pretence of quitting long since forgotten. A man on the run needed his little comforts.

Bryn knocked on the door, and then they waited. After a minute or two, it opened only a crack, a chain across the gap.

"What you want?"

The voice carried easily, slurred and heavily accented. Through the narrow opening, Jason noted a tall, thin man in worn clothes, unshaven and swaying on his feet. Probably not up to killing a woman, smacking a pathologist, and hauling a body out of the morgue. But appearances could be deceiving. If petite, scrawny Amy could fight off a killer...

"Detective Inspector Bryn Hesketh, Cardiff Police. Can we come in?"

"What you want?"

Bryn squared his shoulders, but Kowalski didn't have the wits about him to back down.

"Does the name Ffion Ellis mean anything to you?"

Jason couldn't see the man's expression, but he imagined it to be sour.

"Why?"

"She's dead."

"That is sad. She kill herself?"

He didn't sound angry. Jason had expected anger, but maybe Kowalski was too burned out by life to feel it. To Jason's ear, he almost sounded regretful, as if it was genuinely sad to hear the news.

"No," Bryn said. "She was murdered."

Kowalski laughed, though it was more of a wheezing cough than a sound of mirth. "So you come for me. You think I kill the mad old lady."

"Did you?" Cerys was a blunt instrument. Like Jason, she never had time for finesse.

"No. She writes me letters. Many letters. Every month, the same. Who even writes letters anymore?"

He reached behind him and shoved something through the gap, Cerys fumbling to catch the letter bundle before it fell.

"They're unopened," she said.

"That's because they are mad, and all the same. The devil is coming, always the devil. Now you will leave me alone?"

"Where were you on the night of the 31st October?"

"I was home, for *Zaduszki*. I returned last night."

An iron-cast alibi. Unless this man had two passports like a high-rolling Bond villain, that excluded him from Ffion's death.

"Thank you - "

Kowalski slammed the door, shutting them and the world out. Jason got off the wall and met Bryn and Cerys on the opposite pavement.

"What now?"

Bryn looked resigned. "I can't persuade you back into whatever hole you crawled out of?"

"Not a chance."

"Then lie low for now. I'm driving up to the hospital tomorrow. If you happen to climb into my boot, I'm not responsible for what happens after. We clear?"

Jason grinned. "When should I break in?"

Chapter 15: Supermassive Black Hole

Amy didn't sleep, couldn't sleep, Tony's words ringing round and round in her head. She was known here. She was vulnerable.

She sat on the edge of the bed, until the nurses' pleas for her to sleep became too much and she curled up under the blanket, staring at the wall. The investigation had given her new life, but one man's words had stripped it all away. She had started to feel safe here, leaving her bedroom, speaking to strangers - and it had exposed her.

As dawn came, like a slow, orange syrup oozing through the curtains, she faced a dilemma. In her room, she had the security of four walls surrounding her, guarding her - but if someone breached that flimsy defence, she was lost. If she ventured out into the communal areas, she would be protected by visibility - but Tony could see her too, anyone could.

How had he known her, and what did he mean to do with that knowledge? Had he also known everything about Ffion? Who was this man? Was he even a patient at all? Surely, Dr Al-Dosari and the nurses must think him a patient - or did they? Was this some elaborate plan of Frieda's to spy on her?

She was growing deluded, lack of sleep and lack of coffee and lack of Jason turning her sharp mind into a jangle of nerves and nothing more. When Jemima the healthcare assistant came to call her for breakfast, Amy ignored her. When Emma appeared at her door like a shadow, Amy couldn't muster a reply to her stutters, even when she offered to share her tea and organic, artisan peanut butter on thick, white toast.

At ten o'clock, Lois knocked on the door, her dark hair framing her artificial smile. Amy had to give her points for persistence.

"Amy? Dr Al-Dosari wants to see you."

Amy had never yet attended a ward round. On a few occasions, Dr Al-Dosari or his minion (Dr Lock? Stock? Barrel?) had hovered in the doorway and asked some vague questions about her mood and how she spent her time and did she want to kill herself today? They prescribed mind-altering tablets and therapy, and Amy did her best to avoid both. She wasn't going to try anything new without detailed information, and no one was going to hand over access to a computer and a high-speed connection.

"It's really important, Amy. And afterwards, the police need to have a word."

The police. They had let Bryn come back to take statements. This was her chance to tell him what she'd learned - and what Tony knew about her. He would be able to investigate the man, find out his connections and his motives. Bryn was her path to safety.

Amy stumbled out of bed, feeling groggy and washed out, and tugged her dressing gown over her Wonder Woman nightdress. She toed on her hospital-issue slippers and headed out of the corridor and into the lounge.

Emma, Tony and Mordecai were sitting round the table with one of the staff, painting eggcups. Amy wasn't sure if she actually owned an eggcup - she would have to ask Jason when she got home. If she got home, and Jason was able to join her. That possibility was looking very far away right now.

Opposite the dining room, the door to the grandly-titled "Conference Room" was standing ajar. Amy approached slowly, with trepidation, wondering what the room might hold in store for her. Lois opened the door wide and ushered her inside, before closing it behind her.

"Amy? I am Dr Al-Dosari - we have met before."

But she wasn't listening, because Lizzie was sitting opposite her. She looked nervous, pale beneath her Australian tan, wearing clothes more appropriate for the beach than a Welsh November. Why was Lizzie here? How could her sister be here?

"Please sit down, Amy. I know this is unexpected, but we must all work together."

Lizzie looked nervously to her left and Amy's eyes followed her glance. And her stomach fell through the floor and the bottom fell out of her world.

She hadn't changed. Of course, she had altered - a few more lines on her face, despite the surgeons' best efforts, and a deep tan that made her dyed blonde hair ridiculous. But the look on her face, that look of pity - it was as if the past twelve years had never happened.

"Oh, Amy," her mother said, voice laden with disappointment, "look at you."

"I expected better than this, Amy. We both did, didn't we, Margot?"

Amy didn't look at him, because she couldn't see any more. The room had been swallowed up by the black, all at once, and her heart had seized in her chest. Someone's hand was on her shoulder, but it was too small and cool to be Jason's, too steady to be Lizzie's.

"Is she going to faint?" Her mother's voice was high, trilling, panicked.

"Not in front of all these people." The next words were left unsaid: *because I would never allow that.*

The panic didn't creep or crawl today - it surged up over her in a wave, engulfing her and sweeping her away. The room was gone, the people were gone, and she was left alone with the crushing certainty that she was about to die.

She was pushed down into a chair and someone, somewhere told her to breathe, remember her therapy, keep breathing. Somehow, she breathed and she lived and the black went away. But the panic didn't leave her, an ugly black mass in her chest.

She slowly realised it was Lois who was rubbing circles into her back and muttering calming words. Around her, behind the wall of anxiety surrounding her, the other people in the room were talking. Talking about her.

"The doctor we saw told us it was bipolar. He gave her lithium, but she never took it. She was always a difficult child." Her father had always been to the point, brusque. Business-like.

"We didn't raise her like this, Doctor. Our Elizabeth has turned out very well. She's a nurse, you know."

"We're not here to talk about me, Mum."

When Lizzie spoke, Amy felt for the first time that she wasn't alone here. Her sister may be with her parents, but she was on her side. The ghost of panic receded a little further into the darkness.

"They went to the finest primary school in the area, and Elizabeth attended an exclusive boarding school. But Amy has always had problems." He spat the last word. She heard what he meant: *weakness, inadequacy.*

"Tell me what she was like in her childhood. Before."

Amy didn't remember a "before", not really. She remembered being younger, remembered primary school and collecting Pokémon cards. Pretending to be princesses and knights and dragons. Getting into Star Wars, because her best friend in the whole world was a huge fan and she wanted to be just like her.

Her parents wanted to send her to boarding school, like Lizzie. Somewhere far away, remote, away from all her friends. She said no. She begged and pleaded and cried, but they were adamant. She remembered that day, though the churning of her stomach had begun days earlier, the nagging sense of doom hanging over her.

She had made it to the school gates. And vomited all over Lizzie's shoes.

Her sister's friends had laughed. Lizzie had shouted at her, screamed. Her parents had to drive her all the way home again, a constant litany of comments that implied she had done it on purpose, to ruin Lizzie's return, out of spite.

They applied for a local school, but it was too late. Amy never wanted to repeat that experience, the terrifying clawing anxiety of that first day. She wouldn't leave. Her parents found her the best psychiatrist that money could buy, who filled her full of tablets. She got wise to that, eventually, spat them out - and then refused to eat or drink anything they'd prepared. They were willing to stoop to any depths to make her "normal".

Then they gave up on her, on Lizzie, decided they'd had enough of parenting. Vanished off into the sunset, leaving them with a grandmother who couldn't remember where she put her glasses. And then couldn't remember her shopping list. Her friends. Her granddaughters. Her name.

Amy survived. That is what she told herself, every day. She was a survivor. She would live with the dark days and the anxious days, because she wouldn't accept that drugged haze again. The cocktail of medication rammed down her throat.

Yet here she was, the same fate hanging over her. Had the intervening years meant nothing at all? Her friends and allies and work were all gone, and she was back in the stifling embrace of her family.

"At least Lizzie's made something of herself." He sounded like a man congratulating himself on a sound investment.

"Thank you, Mr and Mrs Loach. Your comments have been very enlightening."

The psychiatrist's voice was neutral, careful. It was a comment that could serve anyone in the room, and that was clearly its intention.

"We're not here for long." Her father's voice was clipped, laying out his terms. "We're flying out in a week, after we've disposed of my mother's estate. If the police will ever let us get on with it."

Amy wanted to laugh and cry at the same time. She'd thought that the police wanted to see her - Bryn, or even Owain, someone familiar and holding some degree of affection towards her. It was Frieda Haas who wanted to talk to her, to manipulate her, to own her. Could she refuse to speak to her without a lawyer? How did it work in this hospital? She was as much in prison here as a jail cell.

"I won't keep you longer today. Thank you for your time. Thank you, Amy."

Amy didn't move. She wasn't sure if she could stand unaided. Lois lent her an arm and she stood on shaky, coltish legs, the post-adrenaline crash hitting her hard. She didn't fall, and that was the most important thing. She couldn't be any more humiliated, not without crying - and she wouldn't give them the satisfaction.

"Amy? Wait, please."

She turned at her sister's voice, and Lizzie hit her like a train, almost bowling her over as she hugged her. "I'm sorry. I didn't call them - I swear I didn't."

"I know." And she did. She knew it was Frieda's doing and no one else's. Despite the evil she'd brought with her, she was glad that Lizzie was here, even if only for a brief time.

"I'll come back and see you - every day, any time you want."

Amy shook her head violently. "You can't - it's not safe."

Lizzie looked incredulous. "It's locked up like the Bank of England."

"There was a murder here last week."

Lizzie's mouth dropped open. "A murder?"

"Come on, Elizabeth. We need to meet the estate agent." Her mother was hovering a few feet away, looking everywhere but at Amy.

Amy's stomach lurched again. "Gran's house?"

"The police have already gutted it. Our parents are determined to get every penny they can, as always." Lizzie hugged her again. "Stay out of trouble. I'll see you tomorrow."

Amy watched her leave, her eyes focussed only on her sister - the other two figures fading into insignificance, if only in her sight.

Chapter 16: The Drop

The boot of Bryn's car was hot and stuffy and smelled of wet dog. Jason was pretty sure Bryn didn't own a dog, so maybe all car boots came with that stench as standard.

Bryn had pulled up outside Gwen's house in Bute, seemingly to talk to Cerys. While he was inside sipping a cup of tea, Jason had climbed into the unlocked boot and waited. It was fake and it was absurd, but whatever Bryn needed to sleep at night.

Jason was filled with both excitement and trepidation at the thought of seeing Amy again. They had parted under bizarre circumstances, Amy begging him to run and save himself from prison, handing herself over to the authorities. He hadn't wanted to leave her, but she had prepared for it, forming her new identity, determined to fall on her sword for him.

Would she be pleased to see him? Or would she be furious that he had disobeyed her request and put her careful plans in jeopardy? Worse still, what kind of state would he find her in, away from home and the care of her assistant? What could this place have done to her?

Jason had no experience of psychiatric hospitals or headshrinkers. He'd known a prison counsellor when he was in Usk who had been nice enough, and a few of the inmates at the Vulnerable Prisoners Unit had been mental. Jason had steered clear of them - nobody wanted a friend who could go off the rails at any moment.

Except Jason's best friend was Amy, who was unpredictable on a good day. He might've started out as her assistant, but he had grown attached to her - too attached, if he was honest, far more than any carer or friend. He had missed her, hidden away in Bristol, unable to look after her, unable to talk about nothing at all or listen to her unique silence.

Jason was a doomed man. If he caught sight of her now, would he be able to walk away?

The car started half an hour after he'd climbed inside, and immediately set off. Jason wasn't entirely sure where this hospital was or how long it might take to get there, so he huddled inside his favourite leather jacket and resigned himself to bruises.

He hadn't quite figured out his plan of attack - how was he going to contact Amy? He had bought a pair of cheap mobile phones off the market and his main objective was to get one of them to her, some-how. Cerys had told him that Amy wasn't allowed visitors or phone calls, and he reckoned it was something to do with Frieda and the investigation. Giving Amy access to any technology would give her an opportunity to exploit it.

Supplying her with a mobile phone could get them both in a lot of trouble. But she could be in danger and none of them could reach her to find out. Jason had thought about contacting her lawyer, a princi-pled man who had helped him out in the past, but he didn't want to compromise the man by asking him to lie about the whereabouts of a wanted criminal. Instead, after much soul-searching, he had asked Cerys to look into it. Jason hated how much he didn't know - he wasn't even sure what Amy had been accused of.

After about twenty minutes, the car came to a stop and the en-gine died. Jason heard a door open and slam, louder than necessary: Bryn was signalling his departure. Waiting five long minutes, Jason felt around for the internal boot release and tugged it, before lifting the boot lid and peering out.

His eyes met an arty wooden fence and, beyond, the sea. The wa-ters were choppy, tossed by the strong wind off the Bristol Channel, a dark, moody blue beneath the white foam. At least the place had a view.

Jason slid his body out of the car and dropped to the ground. Crouched behind the vehicle, he cautiously leaned out half an inch. The car park was half full, with mostly pricey motors and a few hurry-ing people. Bryn had parked flush against the fence, far from the main entrance. The hospital garden was close by, but he couldn't see Amy. No surprises there.

A small group of people were headed towards his corner of the car park, and Jason pulled himself under the sleek 4x4 parked next to Bryn. He kept an eye on them, hoping they would bugger off prompt-ly, when he recognised one of them.

Lizzie, Amy's sister.

The couple with her were older, the man's face like thunder and the woman looking like she didn't think too deeply about anything at all. The more he stared, the more he could see a familiar nose, the shape of the lip, that particular shade of green-hazel eyes.

They were Amy's parents, and Jason had to resist the almighty urge to leap out and throttle them.

If they were coming from the hospital, that must mean they had been in to visit Amy. Pushing aside for a brief, angry moment the pain that would've caused her, Jason realised this was an opportunity. If he could get a message to Lizzie, she might be able to help him reach Amy.

True, he wasn't Lizzie's favourite person, his shady past leading her to doubt his intentions towards Amy. But they had parted on good terms and he felt he could persuade her to his cause. If he could draw her attention without alerting her parents.

Awkwardly checking his jacket pockets for a coin or a pen, anything, he pulled out a few dog-eared business cards that Amy had ordered for him: *Jason Carr. Assistant to Amy Lane, Independent Police Consultant.* Of course, the phone was now disconnected and Amy couldn't check the email address, but that wasn't the point. Jason only needed Lizzie's attention.

A car immobiliser beeped a couple of cars down. He was going to lose them! He scrambled out from under the 4x4, ducked down between the cars, and lobbed a handful of cards into the air.

The wind gusted them away immediately, tossing them here and there, like a snowstorm of cardboard knives. Instead of swirling around Lizzie, they were carried out to sea, tumbling over the cliff edge to oblivion. Shit.

"Mummy, I've dropped my ring somewhere. I need to go back."

"Oh, Elizabeth - how careless!"

"Hurry up then. We haven't got all day."

Jason seized his chance. Standing up slowly, he mimed locking the nearest car and set off across the car park. He didn't look to see if she was following him, or if she'd even seen him, hunched over like a man on a mission. Only when he reached the automatic doors of the hospital did he pause for a moment, allowing her to pass him on her way into the hospital.

Thankfully, there was a short queue at the reception desk and they were finally able to hover together.

"Are you mad?" she muttered, each word sharp as flint.

"I'm leaving a message in the garden. Tell her."

"You'll get her in trouble."

"I'm protecting her."

Lizzie laughed under her breath but said nothing more.

Jason stepped out of the queue and looked quickly over the leaflets arranged by the desk, before selecting one on cosmetic dentistry.

"Can I help you, sir?"

Jason smiled quickly, tightly at the receptionist. "Just browsing for my mam."

The woman handed over a thick pack of forms and told him to call with any questions, any at all, and he mumbled his thanks before tearing himself away. Out of the corner of his eye, he saw Lizzie being let in to a door at the side and wished he could run and follow, see Amy, hold her, tell her how badly he had fucked up and how sorry he was that they were in this mess.

Instead, he walked back towards the main door and headed down the side of the car park nearest the glass wall of the garden. Looking at the ground, he saw that the smooth plates rested in metal supports embedded in the ground. Up close, he saw that the "glass" was actually hardened plastic, scratched up in several places, including with graffiti scrawls and doodles. The panels were flush against each other and Jason couldn't see a single gap. How the hell was he going to get the phone to Amy, short of lobbing it over the fence in full view of God and everybody?

In the middle of the garden, a seed table drew a few wild birds, drawn to scraps - until a large seagull chased them all away. Jason wished he could drum up an unladen swallow to deliver his message, but his luck wasn't that good.

If he kept hanging about by the fence, he would draw attention to himself. Reluctantly, he changed course and headed back towards Bryn's car. Jason almost missed the maintenance man coming the other way, crossing from the other side of the car park to approach the glass. Jason hovered by a nearby car and watched.

The bloke bent down to a particular point on the fence, drew something out of his toolbox, and pressed it to the bottom edge. He then removed the tool with a perfect circle of plastic attached. He drew out a small package from his box and pushed it through the hole, under a shrub. Calm and cool, he then replaced the circle and hurriedly stood, turning on his heel and striding across the car park.

Jason leapt into action and intercepted him. "Excuse me, mate - you got the time?"

The man hesitated, his tanned, clean face not the one Jason expected to see beneath the blue cap. He also didn't expect the cut-glass English accent. "You don't have a phone?"

"Battery's dead," Jason blagged.

Drawing up his sleeve, the man consulted a large analogue watch with a leather strap. Jason had cased a gold exchange shop - he knew an expensive watch when he saw one. "It's just after eleven o'clock."

"Thanks mate." Jason wanted to stall him, find out more, wishing he could bump the man's phone with his own and set up a traceable connection. Without Amy, he couldn't do anything but talk.

"Does it pay well, this gig? I'm between jobs myself."

"Great. Just great. But busy. Excuse me."

He was off before Jason could think to stop him, but he had enough to be suspicious. If that man was in maintenance, Jason would eat his mam's fascinator, feathers and all. Jason quickly approached the fence and examined the damaged fence. Without skill or delicacy, he pushed the plastic circle in, letting it tumble to the grass beyond. Reaching through, he retrieved the package and slid it into his pocket, before walking away.

Leaning against the fence at the back of Bryn's car, Jason kept an eye on the car park. He saw Lizzie hurrying back first, not looking in his direction, and getting into a sleek silver BMW. It drove off too fast, but Jason caught half the licence plate, typing it into the twin of the phone he would leave for Amy.

Five minutes went past, then ten, with no sign of Bryn's return. The garden was no longer empty, a few people milling about with cigarettes, the sight making Jason itch to light up. He couldn't see any sign of Amy, but it had always been unlikely. Even if she had received Lizzie's message, it would take some time to work up the courage to step outside.

One man wandered down the side of the fence until he reached the position of the cut circle and planted package. Jason started towards him, removing a cigarette and light from his pocket, apparently wandering aimlessly in the car park.

But the guy just thumped his head against the fence, the discoloured skin of his forehead showing this clearly wasn't the first time. Jason winced and looked away.

A few minutes passed, the cigarette crumbling between his fingers as he grew less and less convinced that hiding in plain sight was a good plan after all. Thick drops of rain started to pelt down, a distant rumble of thunder coming from across the water.

Jason turned to look for shelter, but just caught sight of someone hurrying towards the fence. The man dropped to one knee, as if to tie his shoelace, but instead scrabbled in the dirt beneath the shrub where Jason had found his package.

Jason tapped on the plastic above his head. "Looking for something?"

The man's head shot up, wary but taut. "What do you mean?"

Jason slid the tip of the package out of his pocket, so it was just visible. "I need a favour."

"That's my property," the man huffed, as Jason watched his fine-tailored trousers soak up the mud from the grass like a sponge.

"Not sure the nurses would like it though, would they?"

The man scowled, running a hand through his neat but greying hair. "What do you want?"

Jason removed the small mobile phone from his other pocket and pressed it against the bloke's package, crouching down so they were at eye level.

"My friend Amy's in there. You know her?"

A strange gleam entered the man's eye. "I know her."

"Get her this phone, I'll give you your package, and the staff inside need know nothing about anything."

"And if I don't?"

Jason smiled, the cold, dark smile that had frightened many gang boys into running home to their mothers. "I'll know."

Chapter 17: Under Pressure

Bryn hated everything today, but especially the criminal bastards, his incompetent colleagues, and Jason bloody Carr.

Why couldn't the boy just stay hidden? Though, from the speed with which he had arrived, the stories about "The Bristol Bat" were beginning to make a lot more sense. Even when supposedly lying low, the boy couldn't stay out of trouble.

Bryn was also adding Dr Al-Dosari to The List. After finally giving way and permitting Bryn to interview his patients, he had selected only one who he felt fit to be questioned on that day. The banker Tony Rogers had heard nothing and seen nothing, therefore rendering the whole trip pointless. He hoped Jason had fared better.

He stopped at the Heath Hospital, deliberately leaving the boot unlocked and hoping Jason could find his way home from there. The Carrs had Cardiff in their bones, and Jason knew his way about better than even Bryn did.

Pushing his irritation with Jason to one side, Bryn entered the hospital for another unpleasant task. The last time he had been here had been to chase down a serial killer before he snatched another victim. They had failed, and Bryn felt as if the hospital was silently judging him for it.

The door to the ward was no different to any other, and Bryn was admitted via the buzzer. He asked to speak to a nurse, but when he confessed that he wasn't a close family member, the staff grew reticent. Instead, he had to visit in his official capacity as a detective. This did have the advantage of upgrading him to a chat with the consultant.

"Dr Bharani is in theatre," he said. "We'll know more after the surgery."

Bryn stomach dropped. "What happened?"

"The pressure in her brain was increasing, so we're removing a portion of the skull."

"Can I take it as evidence?" Bryn asked, feeling macabre.

The consultant looked at him strangely. "Dr Bharani will be keeping hold of it, in case we need it in the future. Anyway, enough about that - what else did you need?"

Bryn was very grateful for the reprieve from the bizarre conversation. "When do you think she'll regain consciousness?"

The doctor's expression was carefully neutral, his voice gentle. "I fear we're still in the 'if' stage, Detective. I can call you if there's any change?"

Bryn nodded dumbly.

"Your colleague has already collected samples and Dr Bharani's clothes, but I don't believe they'll tell you much. Our priority was her health, not your evidence."

Bryn mumbled his thanks and moved swiftly towards the exit. He didn't stop until he reached the front entrance, walking straight out of the doors and out onto the sodden grass in front of the hospital.

He needed to breathe, he needed to see past the red mist of anger clouding his eyes, or the bite of grief in his chest. She couldn't die - but what if she lived? Bryn knew there was a big difference between "conscious" and living as a functional human being. He didn't want to think about that, but avoidance didn't make it less of a reality for Indira.

"Detective?"

He turned towards the voice, and it took a moment to see her. The slight teenager was awkward in her oversized clothes and, for a brief flicker, she reminded him of Amy. Then she resolved into a memory, a frightened little girl hoping her best friend - her something more - wouldn't die in surgery. That had been almost two months ago.

"Heddwen," he said.

She smiled, a quick, nervous quirk of the lips. "Corelia is doing much better now. They say she can leave rehab in a month or two."

Bryn realised that, in the chaos of Amy's arrest and Jason's flight, he had forgotten all about the wannabe-hacker known as Corelia. She had been caught up in Amy's investigation, an eager, young solver of puzzles. But she had been found by the killer, and brutally injured. He felt a flush of guilt that he hadn't bothered to find out whether she was dead or alive.

Heddwen continued, oblivious to his pain: "If Amy needs anything, Corelia would love to help. She's so bored on the ward all day, and they let her have her laptop. I can do the legwork."

As he watched her cringe at her own words, Bryn saw the girl behind her, staring sightlessly out over the pond, slumped forward in her wheelchair. One hopeful duck was quacking beside the chair, but Corelia didn't seem to notice or care.

He meant to say no, that Amy had clearly caused enough trouble in these girls' lives, but he couldn't bring himself to smack them down like that.

"I'll see what I can do," he lied.

The girl fished an artist's sketch pad from her satchel and tore out a page, carefully printing out an email address and phone number before handing it over to Bryn. He awkwardly stuffed it into his pocket, intending to lose it at the earliest opportunity.

Heddwen held out her hand for him to shake, the floppy sleeve falling over the palm. Well, shit. She'd seen straight through that.

He took her hand anyway, shook it, her grip surprising him. She met his eyes for a second, full of trust and hope, before returning to her friend's side.

Bryn couldn't stay there anymore. The hope, and the crushing of it, was far too much to bear. He headed back to the station, no further forward in deciphering this murder or anything around it. Someone killed a mad old lady, and then stole her body, injuring his pathologist. They had no evidence of means, motive or opportunity for either incident.

He had his officers trawling through Ffion's life and running background checks on every staff member at the facility, to see if their paths could ever have crossed. The visitor log had consisted almost exclusively of care staff from Ty Coch, with a total of three visits from her remote daughter. So far, they'd uncovered nothing more interesting than the administrator who lived three streets away from Ty Coch, a nurse who'd worked in Australia on an expired visa, and a chef with three unpaid parking fines.

Though there was one person, one team, who could shed light on the kidnapping of the body. Bryn did not want to go there, but he didn't see that he had any other choice. He would have to learn to play nice with Owain if they were both to continue working on the same police force.

The door to the Cyber Crime Unit was ajar, the gentle clacking of keys and whir of computers the only sound. Bryn pushed open the door to the tiny office, barely enough room inside for its two desks and two occupants.

At his arrival, Catriona Aitken abruptly stood and headed for the door, mumbling something about coffee. Clearly, the detective constable knew when to steer clear of a storm.

Owain, however, continued to type. He glanced up once or twice at Bryn, but his fingers continued to move over the keys, faster than Bryn could ever hope to achieve. He grudgingly conceded that the boy might come close to Amy's top speed, though she was now out of practice, locked away.

Where Owain had helped put her.

Eventually, he stopped and looked up, though he didn't meet Bryn's eyes. "What?"

"CCTV - where are we?"

"I put our best images up on the board - average height, all in dark colours, nothing distinctive." He nervously fiddled with some printouts on the desk. "Fast, though. In and out in less than five minutes."

"What about the van?"

"No distinguishing marks. I did some digging on the white van man and he reported his number plates stolen about six months ago. He was in Newport at the time, doing up his cousin's place."

Bryn immediately thought of Jason. Even out of the loop, he would know who might be involved in number plate theft in South Wales. Bryn was torn between his reluctance to encourage him further and the advantages of diverting him onto harmless side tasks that would prevent him stumbling into the main investigation. Not that there was much to that investigation at present except a hundred blind alleys.

"Is he helping you?"

The comment came out of nowhere, but the biting tone made it clear exactly who "he" was. Bryn wasn't surprised that Cerys and Jason had gone to Owain, but they could hardly have expected a warm reception.

"He's around." Bryn saw no point in denying the facts, even if it technically made them both accessory to hiding a fugitive from justice.

"Then stay away from me. I want nothing - "

"You are part of this investigation!" The shout came out of the blue, and a hush fell over the surrounding offices. "I am the lead officer, so you will play nice with me. Are we clear?"

Owain scowled and looked away.

But Bryn wasn't relinquishing control so easily, even though he despaired that it had come to this. "Are. We. Clear?"

Owain nodded, once, short and sharp.

Bryn didn't push him, couldn't force him to budge, and instead left him behind. He would have no joy in soliciting Owain or Catriona's assistance with this case beyond the bloody obvious.

The folded piece of paper burned a hole in his pocket. He reached for it, intending to cast it in the rubbish, but he couldn't quite let it go.

He reached for his phone instead: *I have something for you.*

And if Cerys Carr shared that information, then it was out of his hands entirely.

Chapter 18: Lifeline

Amy didn't want to live anymore.

The thought had entered her brain fully-formed, without any fanfare or creeping sense of dread. She had just closed her eyes, for a moment, and there it was. But the reaction was immediate, instantaneous - she would fight it, she would rail against it. And Jason would -

Jason was not here. Lizzie was not here. Her sanctuary, her beloved AEON - both were lost forever. What was there to fight for, really?

She would give anything to be back at home, with Jason and AEON. She took a moment to picture her - Ada, Enchantress of Numbers - the computer she had built up over a decade, constantly rebuilding and improving, until they could go anywhere and everywhere together without leaving her living room. As well as her eyes into the wider world, AEON was her protector, the guardian of her fortress. Every door and window had been alarmed, every external angle covered by a camera, and a sophisticated entry system and elevator separating her from anyone who might want to come calling.

She had been safe there. Until Jason had persuaded her that outside might be okay. Until a murder victim and a stolen painting had lured her to the National Museum of Wales, and away from that carefully-maintained safety. Until Frieda Haas had decided that her time was up.

Lois had returned her to her room with a cup of tea. A small box of chocolates sat on her bedside table, no doubt from Emma, whose brother brought her enough for a small army.

But she did not eat, could not drink - her stomach was threatening to turn itself inside out, and she couldn't throw up. Couldn't faint, couldn't fail. Her parents would never have that satisfaction again.

The threatened police visit came and went without disturbing her - evidently, Dr Al-Dosari had not thought her fit to discuss anything with Frieda. She was grateful to him for protecting her from the National Crime Agency, even though he had failed to protect her from her family.

The hours slipped away from her, sand running through her fingers, until it was dark and three successive cups of tea had been taken away, undrunk. She heard the sounds of lights-out, patients stumbling to bed past her door, and she made herself small, unnoticeable.

The door opened anyway. She looked up, because she didn't want it to be Tony. The terror flooded back then. She had almost forgotten the threat he posed - how could she forget?

"I brought you hot chocolate, and toast."

Emma had the two items precariously balanced, so Amy cleared a space on the bedside table. Her limbs were stiff from inactivity, but she could rally herself for Emma. How long had she rehearsed that sentence so that it came out whole?

Emma took one square of toast and Amy mirrored her, nibbling at it like a small rodent. The silence stretched, as Amy waited for Emma to find her words, but it was not uncomfortable.

"The police came today. But only Tony saw them. I wasn't well."

Despite her own shrunken world, consisting only of her hurts and fears, Amy had heard Emma's distress throughout the night. "Bad dreams?"

Emma stared at her toast square as if it held answers. "Lots of numbers. Too many to count properly."

The sentence didn't exactly make sense, but Amy could imagine that counting was a big deal for Emma. "What did you do?"

Another silence, the toast still untouched. "Nothing. Waited. Cried."

"What did your therapist say?" Amy realised the hypocrisy of such a statement, as she had mostly ignored every word her therapist said. If she hadn't managed to figure out her own brain after over ten years of study, what could this woman do in six weeks?

Emma finally bit into the toast and, to Amy's surprise, spoke with her mouth full. "Distraction. Talking while eating. It doesn't work at night."

Amy dutifully finished off her bit of toast and, as her stomach griped with the entry of food, reluctantly picked up another square. "Does it work at all?"

Emma shook her head. "She doesn't really help, the therapist."

Amy nodded, feeling vindicated in her dislike of the woman. "She doesn't help me either."

"Do you…do you ever think that, maybe, they don't want us to get better?"

Amy hadn't thought about it. Now, though, in this quiet room with another wreck of a woman, she too wondered if it were true. There was money to be made in their sickness, in their ineffectual therapy, their rattle of pills. Frieda was presumably footing the bill for her stay, and Emma's family paying for hers.

She had never seen Emma's mother or brother, but from what little Emma had said, she knew they came from money. Her dead father had been very successful and, unlike Amy's family, he had provided for his children.

Emma's hand came up, hovering in mid-air, fingers twitching. Then she reached into her thick, woollen cardigan and pulled out something, tucking it under Amy's blanket. "For later."

Amy didn't have the heart to turn down Emma's chocolate gifts, so she merely smiled and ate her toast.

Emma wasn't smiling. "You had a bad day."

The ugly weight of it fell across Amy's shoulders. "Family."

Emma nodded unhappily. "I…I…"

Whatever she was going to say was lost in a series of movements of her hands, tapping at different parts of her body so fast that Amy couldn't follow, and then she looked worse than when she started. She tried to speak again but merely shook her head, before leaving the room and closing the door behind her.

Amy understood all too well. Her own family sent her into a similar state of nervous energy, though hers was directed inwards instead of trying to appease mystical forces of fate.

She sipped at the hot chocolate, feeling its warmth trickle down to coat the inside of her unsettled stomach. The nurses flashed a torch into her room and then wandered on, so she crawled into bed, something thumping onto the floor as it was dislodged from the blanket. Emma's gift!

Amy fished around for it on the floor and her fingers caught on cool plastic rather than shiny cardboard. She brought it under the covers and sunk down with it, turning it over with dawning realisation. Her thumb grazed a button and it lit up with a faint glow - a mobile phone.

It was basic, true, but it would have a long battery life and perhaps even an internet connection. Who was it from? How had it reached her?

She looked at the contacts and her heart leapt with a joy she hadn't felt in days. For there was only one name: J.

The number was unfamiliar, but that was to be expected. While she hated that he was back in Cardiff, she also revelled in it. He was home - he had come home for her, even though it could lead to imprisonment and Frieda Haas and a hundred terrible things.

The little envelope on the screen told her there was one unread message and she clumsily navigated to it, out of practice with phones like this. It was from Jason, and it said: HOLD ON X

That was all she needed to live another night.

Chapter 19: Friends Like These

Jason had been lying low at his mam's house, drinking her tea and hiding from her disappointed looks. He hated waiting, hated the inactivity, the feeling of being trapped by four walls. It reminded him of those few months after prison where he was desperate for a job, any job, and had wound up cleaning for pennies. And meeting Amy.

The uncertainty was also slowly killing him. Was Amy okay? Would she get the phone, or would this bloke at the hospital withhold it? How did she fit into this wider problem of a murder at this hospital, and the missing body?

He couldn't do anything. He'd thought about trying to see Indira at the hospital, but it was likely crawling with police. Their brief investigation into Ffion's life hadn't yielded anything significant and he had nothing else to go on. Owain had denied them his help, and Cerys had to go to cop school. He couldn't even go down to Dylan's garage to tinker with a motor, for fear his mate might turn him in.

Life was shit. Except it was worse for Amy, and Indira, and Ffion. That was the only thing that stopped him feeling sorry for himself.

The front door banged, rousing him from his stupor. Cerys was upright and stiff in her probationary constable uniform, still pressed and polished after a day at college. She didn't speak to either of them, walking through the kitchen and upstairs to change. Jason went back to staring into his mug. Great - Cerys wasn't talking to him either.

Dinner passed in mutual, moody silence, despite their mam's half-hearted attempt at chit-chat. Yet, with a mouth full of peas, Jason saw Cerys deliberately tapping at the screen of her phone while looking significantly at him. He swallowed and then mouthed "what?", but she had already slid the phone under the table.

"Something funny, *bach*?" Gwen asked.

"Just Twitter, Mam," she said.

"My chapel book club are all on the Facebook now," Gwen said proudly, and they both nodded like dutiful children should.

When Gwen retired to the living room to watch some soap or

other, Jason gestured for Cerys to hand over her phone. She merely smiled at him.

"Do you remember Corelia?"

The name was unforgettable. "Is she - ?"

"In rehab at the Heath. Her girlfriend reckons she's bored senseless - wants to work for Amy again."

Jason looked at her incredulously. "But it was Amy's fault she... y'know..."

"We are not turning this down. We need help, computer help, and if this girl knows what she's about, we need her."

It was awkward, no doubt, but he couldn't let awkward get in the way of helping Amy and solving this case.

"How did you find this out anyway?"

"Got it from a friend," she said casually. Too casually.

"Owain?"

She scowled. "Bryn."

That made more sense, though not by much. "Is he on our side or not?"

"I think he's on the side of keeping his job and solving this murder."

"Let's do it then." He said it quickly, before either of them could change their minds.

"I'll email her," Cerys said.

"Saying what?"

"'Can you help us, pretty please?'"

"With a cherry on top? What are we asking for, exactly?"

They both thought on that question for a good few minutes. Jason fetched them a couple of beers from the fridge, Gwen's concession to the fact Cerys was now an adult, and they mulled over it together.

"I'll get the laptop," Cerys said.

While she was upstairs, Jason took a pull of his beer and leaned back in the chair. Maybe the reason they couldn't work out their questions was that they had no idea what they were doing. Amy was a self-taught detective, but Jason was only her minion. Cerys was just starting out with her police training. What if they were deluding themselves that they could do this? What if Bryn and Owain were right, and they were just getting in the way?

Cerys set her laptop on the table and they waited for the ancient machine to start.

"Cerys - "

"I think we just outline the situation, for now," she said. "We can think of the questions as we find them out ourselves."

"If you 'outline the situation', she might run a mile." Clearly, Cerys had been spending too much time in lectures if she'd started talking like that. Like a proper copper.

"Total disclosure. It's the only way we work now. Reduces the chances of us getting arrested without knowing what we're getting into."

Jason shifted in his chair. "When are you next meeting with your... supervisor?"

"Friday," she said, opening up a browser window. "Hopefully we'll have made some headway by then. Wouldn't want them to be worthless lies."

Jason wanted to apologise for putting her in this position, but that's not what they did. She may be a probationary constable with Cardiff Police, but she was his baby sister first. Instead, he punched her in the arm and she tried to shove him off the chair, and then they settled back into work.

Cerys opened her email and carefully typed out Corelia's email address. "How do I start this?"

"'Hi, I'm the girl who stalked you at your school'?"

Cerys typed out the words verbatim.

"I wasn't serious," Jason said, trying to hit the backspace key.

"Nah, it works. Maybe you're just in touch with your inner teenage girl."

Jason winced. "That sounds wrong."

Cerys paused in her typing. "Ew. Yeah."

"Explain the case a little, and that Amy's...unavailable."

"Dead old woman...mental hospital...got it."

"Tell her we need her."

Cerys typed that bit out in capital letters and attached an image of that old US Army Poster with the posing girl and the slogan "We Can Do It!". "Sent."

And they were back to the waiting. Jason loathed waiting.

"You find out anything today?"

"Nothing but dross. Did you see Amy?"

"Nope. Saw her sister though. And her parents."

Cerys whistled a low note. "Damn. That's shit for her."

"We're more family to her than they are," he said, vehemently.

"*You are*," Cerys said.

Jason didn't know what to say to that, what to think, so he ventured back to safer territory. "What do we know then?"

After an hour or so of thought, they had very little to show between them. Cerys read back the hastily-typed notes, correcting them as she went.

"'Ffion Edwards died on 31st October 2014 at Cliff House Mental Health Unit in Penarth. Cause of death unknown' - therefore methods unknown? I'll write that. 'Body stolen from Cardiff Police Station on 1st November with injuries to Indira Bharani, pathologist.' That is how you spell her name, isn't it?"

Jason shrugged and Cerys moved on.

"'Motive - Ffion accidentally killed a child nine years ago, but the family seem legit.'"

"You're writing 'legit' in our investigation notes?"

"Fuck off, Jay Bird," Cerys said, mildly. "'No other motives known. Opportunity - someone in the hospital has to be involved.'"

"What about visitors?"

"Mared from Ffion's place said she and the other carers were the only ones who visited and they hadn't been for ages. Unless you want to put them on the suspect list?"

"Who've we got on it so far?"

"The kid's dad."

"Yeah, put them on - why not? Maybe one of the other residents put Mared up to it." Jason drained his third bottle of beer and went back to the fridge - all out. "Where's Mam keeping the gin these days?"

"Nowhere you can find it. Are we saying this was an inside job then?"

Jason took his cheap mobile phone out of his pocket. "Only one way to find out."

Chapter 20: Nevermore

Amy wasn't asleep, but it was nervous excitement that kept her awake, not the dread and despair of previous nights.

She wanted to text Jason, to tell him she was okay (a white lie) and check if he was well (a necessity). Though he was probably in hiding and she didn't want to risk his discovery for one single text. He would contact her when he was safe to do so, she was sure of it.

She hadn't felt this good in weeks, an aura of calm over her that was better than any little blue pill could give. But she was worried about discovery - the nurses seemed to be passing by very frequently, the light through the slatted window of the door brighter than usual. Were they keeping the lights on deliberately? Were they, too, afraid?

Beneath her pillow, a soft bzz reached her cheek and she slid her hand underneath. She ducked her head under the covers again and eagerly opened the message:

SUSPECTS IN THERE? X

No "hello, how are you, how's that breakdown going?". Jason wanted to know if she was making progress, assuming that she had an investigation underway. He had always believed in her, too much. It would be the ruin of them, this misplaced faith.

No leads. Tony odd. Nurses kind. @

She agonised for a moment or two before adding a small x of her own to the end of the message. No big deal, friends did that all the time. Sure, they never had, but she would go with it, see where it took her. She was feeling reckless this evening.

He replied within a minute - he was obviously waiting on her words.

CORELIA HELPING WITH IT TIPS? X

At that name, Amy froze, but only for a second. If she was helping, she must be all right. She felt guilty that she hadn't thought of her before now, but depression made her selfish, inward-staring. She should've thought to find out before now, but she hadn't. Not that anyone would've told her.

She returned to the text. After figuring out that Jason meant 'IT', not 'it', she couldn't imagine any "tips" that would allow Corelia to help the investigation while keeping her safe. Well, except one.

She turned off predictive text and painstakingly typed out the URL for her gateway site, along with one of the limited access usernames and passwords. From there, Corelia could access the files on her Polish server - a resource Amy had liberated during a previous investigation - and, if she had any affinity for it, Corelia could use Amy's less potent hacks. It also opened a window into Cardiff Police's files, unless Owain had sealed that particular gate - long after the most important horses had bolted.

She sent the message and waited. The nurse outside was pounding her feet along the corridor, and Amy clutched her phone beneath the covers as the torch shone in, near-blinding in its intensity. It was torture, that bastard little light.

She thought she could hear Emma moving next door, tossing and turning and moaning in her sleep. She wanted to comfort her, but the nurses would have none of it. Even if she could reach out to her, what then? She had no skills in that area, had proved it time and again.

Shadows played across the ceiling like dark, oily clouds, and she started to imagine faces in them, like a game she was playing with herself. She felt the phone vibrate in her hand but she was too lost in the clouds. Perhaps her insomnia was finally catching up with her, though she felt wide awake.

The torch flashed a couple more times through the window before she vanished beneath the covers and looked at the phone.

EMAILED BY C 2 C SLEEP NOW X

C2C? Was that a new email client she hadn't yet heard of? Her tired brain spat out Cerys and Corelia eventually - she really needed to sleep, to rest. If she was now heading up an investigative task force from her sickbed, she needed to be at her best.

She shoved the phone down the side of the bed and closed her eyes. Her blood was thrumming in her veins, a near-constant hum of transit like a vast motorway or an electric current. Her temples throbbed in time with it and she scowled into her pillow. Sleep had always been elusive, and tonight her body was determined to betray her.

Clink.

The sound was faint, like a faraway bell made of tin, but her ears smarted with it. Where was it? Was it coming from Emma's room? No. It was not within the building. It was elsewhere - perhaps even otherworldly.

Clink. Clank. Clink. Clank.

There were chains rattling outside her window. Small ones, large ones, chains of every size - waiting for her. She was suddenly reminded of The Muppet Christmas Carol, the singing lockboxes, the certainty of chains for crimes. Had she kept Christmas all the year round? No, she had wronged many, hurt them, crippled them. She was doomed for all time.

A dark shadow passed across the window, breathing harsher than Darth Vader. Amy huddled beneath the blankets on her bed and watched the curtains, the darkness beyond, the reaper passing through.

Clink. Clank. Clink. Clank.

If she hid here, maybe he would think she was asleep. Did Death allow you respite if you slept? She was mixing him up with Father Christmas, which was so absurd that she almost laughed out loud, an hysterical bubble rising in her chest. But she wouldn't shout, or pout, or cry - Death was coming to this town, to this hospital, to finish what he'd started.

She heard the Angels of Death whispering, too close and too loud, about rewards and just-dues and one poor sinner thanking the Angel for his respite. What would she say when he came to her window? What could she possibly say that would save her?

The shadow passed over again and Amy muffled her cry with the pillow, squeezing her eyes tightly shut and willing her tears not to fall. No sound, no movement - nothing to tempt the Reaper outside the window.

Then…nothing.

After half an hour of lying in terror, Amy slowly eased her body up and twitched aside the curtain. The glass was steamed up and she slowly moved her hand over it, her heart thumping with what she might see on the other side.

Nothing but an ill-tended scrap of grass and a hedge beyond. No chains, no Angels, no Death.

She was losing her mind. This place, it was infesting her, turning her brain to mush. Maybe her parents were right after all - she was just a crazy child, who had never achieved anything and never would.

Scrabbling for the phone, Amy read Jason's messages again, imprinting each one into her mind. Drawing the words to her, rebuilding her fortifications, shoring up her defences against this place and its infectious madness.

She would not break here. She would not let Death in. She would hold on, for Jason. For herself. And she would find out why Death had visited this place, and how Ffion Ellis had met him. To prevent them all from joining her.

Chapter 21: The Cuckoo's Nest

Leaving the countryside reminded him of just how much he hated outdoor Britain. The ceaseless rain, the damp that never shifted, the creatures that were merely ugly and never fascinating. A boring, grey country full of boring, grey people.

Finally dry, he had set aside his work in favour of viewing the media's response to whatever crumbs the police had left for them. The mainstream media were still faffing about, thank God, so he had a little room to play with. Find out what the law actually knew and what they didn't.

That was where he could've used an inside man. He'd already learned the value of immediate proximity up at the mental hospital. You had to keep an eye on the place, closer than close - and you had to find a way in if you wanted to get something done right. Of course, it wasn't exactly "right" yet but he still had some leeway there. By all accounts, it was getting there and patience was definitely among his virtues.

The police were a different matter. How did one get cops to turn? They didn't earn a whole lot, so there was always money. But they had that whole duty and honour thing going on and he couldn't just walk up to a beat cop and bribe him. This would require a more delicate hand.

If he couldn't find an inside man, maybe he just needed to find a back door. He didn't need access to a person so much as he needed access to records. It wasn't as simple as a folder going missing - everything was backed up, and networked. Which played to his advantage, because what he really needed was a hacker.

He was good at making connections, finding the right way. He could find a contact and get the access he needed. It would be a piece of piss compared to what he'd just been through. He could squeeze every last drop of blood from a stone, if that's what it took.

He would get into the police and he would find out what they knew. Then he'd make it disappear. Or, failing that, he'd make the cops disappear and the witnesses and every fucking thing until he was home and dry.

What had happened to that woman he'd hit about the head? Was she dead? A vegetable? He needed to know. If there had been any chance she had seen him, he'd have to take care of it. He was getting good at taking care of things.

He would find out who he was up against, who he could target if the shit hit the fan. What was that trite phrase - 'hope for the best, plan for the worst'? He was your man for that. Planning for setbacks was his thing. He'd had enough of them to practise, that was for damn sure.

Why should he be punished for his resilience? He kept bouncing back, his wallet a little lighter and his reputation a little muddier, but he survived. Nobody valued that shit any more. They expected a rising star, not a stop-start meteorite crashing back to earth.

But he wasn't crashing. He wasn't. This period of his life was a temporary problem - just another trivial setback - and he would soon be on top again. He'd worked hard for this, worked fucking hard, and he wasn't going to see it all go up in flames. He hadn't just been handed all his shit on a plate like some people. People who could just sit around at an all-expenses-paid life camp on the cliff tops.

Rich fucking nutcases. He'd had his start, sure, but why did some fuckers hold his sanity against him? They couldn't all get the crazy reprieve. Sure, he'd seen things and heard things and found himself at the end of a joint - who hadn't? Did that mean he could go ga-ga and freeload for the rest of his life?

Calm. He needed to be calm. He turned off the TV, ignored his work, and rolled a slim one. There would be time for anger. Now was the time to be calm, to be patient. He was versatile, he was a rising star, he was on his way to the top.

Fuck anyone who stood in his way.

When Amy finally slept, it was in fits and starts, too hot and too cold, the nurses outside unable to keep quiet for even half an hour. She rose just before breakfast, aching for no good reason. Was she coming down with something? Did that explain last night's bizarre experiences? The advantage of all those years without proper human contact was that she had rarely been ill. She'd made Lizzie decontaminate every time she came back from the hospital before entering her part of the house.

When she met Emma in the dining room, she looked even worse. Her eyes were red and puffy, as if she'd been crying again, and the circles beneath them were deep as bruises. They ate breakfast in silence, sharing their toast and drinking down two or three cups of tea apiece.

If Amy was to make a true list of suspects for Jason, she had to start taking this investigation seriously. Tony sat in the corner with a newspaper - her eyes deliberately avoided him - while Ron just stared at his bowl of porridge as if it were a crystal ball. Mordecai was nowhere to be seen and Carwyn was also absent.

As Bryn had already interviewed Tony, Amy could leave him alone for now. Besides, she didn't want to spend any time with him by herself, or at all. She didn't trust him an inch and that had already placed him top of her list. Ron would be difficult to broach any subject with and she had already tried and failed with Emma.

That left Mordecai and Carwyn. She felt she could get information out of Mordecai easily enough - he loved to talk. Whether any of it was true was a different matter. She had attempted to find Carwyn before but Tony had thwarted her. Maybe the nurses would let him out of his room today and she'd have better luck.

While they both remained out of reach, her only other option was the nursing staff. She needed to make a list of those on shift that night and speak to them all. She remembered sensible Scottish Sandy being there because she had matter-of-factly dealt with her panic afterwards. The name of the healthcare assistant escaped her, and her brain felt very slow and stupid that morning. Perhaps she was sickening, but she didn't want that useless doctor to examine her. She longed for access to the internet and, with it, every pill she could imagine.

The nurses tried to persuade her yet again to take some antidepressant and she respectfully declined. She also turned down the chance for therapy, electing instead to sit in the largest chair in the communal area and pretend to read a book on British birds.

It was gone eleven by the time Mordecai flung himself dramatically onto the sofa. "My head is killing me," he mumbled.

Amy called over Darren, a towering giant of a nurse who had evidently just returned from his holidays or a midweek bender, judging by the tan lines and dark circles vying for dominance of his face. He gruffly offered Mordecai some paracetamol, and Mordecai sipped at his water like a dying invalid. If Amy hadn't known better, she would say he was hungover - this is what Lizzie had looked like after her nursing socials, and what Jason had embodied after one particularly disastrous night out with Dylan.

Maybe he was. If Jason could smuggle a mobile phone in to her, who was to say that Mordecai wasn't getting alcohol or whatever else he desired? Her mind returned to that little strip of pills she'd found, now safely hidden away in her room. But if Amy's untrained eye could suspect a hangover, couldn't the nurses also point the finger? Surely they had tests for that?

When Darren had gone, Amy decided to just come out with it. "You're hungover," she blurted.

Mordecai turned his head slowly and smiled at her, like a languid cat. "You want some?"

She leaned in a little closer. "How'd you get it?"

He touched the side of his nose. "Gin or vodka?"

Clear spirits. Not the most difficult things to conceal, if sufficiently motivated.

"We'll get caught," she said.

He shrugged. "Look at Darren over there - he's hanging worse than me. They just want my management's money. What do they care?"

There it was again: that suspicion that the hospital might not want their patients to get better. How much was Frieda Haas paying for her stay here? Why was she here and not a prison hospital, or even a normal NHS ward? Did it suit Frieda to keep her mad and was Dr Al-Dosari willing to facilitate that?

She knew nothing about the good doctor except that he was her doctor and that accent wasn't British. Where was he from? Where did he train? Was there some reason, some incompetency or disgrace that meant he couldn't work in the National Health Service or his country of birth?

Her fingers itched to text Jason the doctor's name, but she had left the phone in her room, hidden at the base of an ugly fake plant pot on the windowsill alongside the tablets. She didn't want to risk carrying

it in case they searched her - Dr Al-Dosari had been making noises about it since she'd started outright refusing her regular medication, and she'd seen Mordecai patted down regularly enough. She just
hoped they had no cause to turn over her room.

"Do you think they didn't care about Ffion either?"

"'Course they didn't. She was a crim, wasn't she?" At this, Mordecai
leaned in a little closer. "My man Tone reckons that's how they make
most of their money - government pays them to take care of the loopy
ones that can't stay in a real prison."

The loopy ones. She hadn't considered it before, but a history of
crime linked both Ffion and herself. Was it mere coincidence that they
had both ended up at Cliff House?

"What else did Tony say?" she asked warily.

Mordecai wore a smug smile as he settled into the sofa cushions. If
Tony was hoping for discretion in his confidant, he couldn't have chosen a worse man. "He reckons there were at least two more here. Me
and him - we're here voluntary, so it can't be us. So that leaves Carwyn,
Ron, Emma - and you."

Amy laughed, but it didn't sound as convincing as she'd hoped.
"Emma and me?"

"My money's on Ron and Carwyn, naturally. But Ffion was an old
lady - a barmy one, sure, but looked innocent enough. See, you never
can tell."

Amy had the advantage of Mordecai, because she knew she was
one and that Tony knew that too. But who was the third? Could they
be a murderer? If so, had they murdered Ffion?

Surely, though, the police, or someone, would know their crime
and question them first? Would they not be top of the list? Unless they
didn't know. Maybe Dr Al-Dosari hadn't received her rap sheet with
her police transfer documents. Maybe they were looking for objectiv-
ity and that's why criminals came here.

"How does Tony know all this?"

Mordecai tapped his nose again. "Privileged business. Need-to-
know."

Which meant that he had no idea, and didn't care to find out. Mordecai didn't strike her as a naturally curious mind, but neither did
Tony seem like a fool. Why would he confide in such a loose-lipped

moron?

"I think I'll pass on that gin," she said. "I like my eyesight."

Mordecai shrugged. "Suit yourself. But my door's always open... always..."

He turned his head towards the sofa back, ostensibly to nap, and Amy stared at the back of his head. *My door's always open...?* Was that a come-on? Was the little rock star trying to pick her up? Admittedly, the prospects weren't great in here, but the boy had his hand. Maybe he just wanted someone to drink with.

Amy was not attractive. She had never been attractive, not by any definition. She'd even downloaded the software to prove it and, in the Hot or Not stakes, she was definitely a Not. Jason seemed to see something in her, though that was friendship and he had his prettier girls for everything else.

Focus, Amy. Mordecai's nonsensical statement had thrown her from the point of her investigation. With a slow, sinking feeling, she knew she had only one choice: she had to find out what Tony knew, and she had to do it fast.

Chapter 22: Gather Ye Daffodils

Jason had never been great at sneaking around. He was much more into striding into a place, making his mark, shouting folks down - the "all guns blazing" approach. Except without any guns, apart from those half-dozen times.

Cerys, on the other hand, was a born sneak. Her lithe frame was built for it - when they were children, he had used her to climb through tiny windows so that he and his mates could clean up inside.

It was a different world now. Most of his mates were in prison, including his best friend Lewis. Cerys was almost a police officer. They would never rob a house together again, and truth told, Jason wasn't entirely sure how he felt about that.

Illicitly accessing a hospital was a different kind of wrong. From Corelia's reply to their email, she was admitted to a specialist spinal injuries unit and awaiting transfer to a rehabilitation hospital any day now. She could only take time outside when Heddwen visited, as her father felt she was too fragile for the outside world.

Cerys might be able to get access - taking a follow-up statement for the original crime that had landed her in hospital. The doctors had so far been reluctant and they would demand her father or another appropriate adult be present for such an interview.

They could continue to correspond via email, of course, but Corelia was already concerned that they had shared too much. She went on about unencrypted data flow and secure servers and all the other things that Amy used to waffle on about. Jason had read the email with a great sense of loss.

He'd decided to text only at night, so that Amy could save her battery and to minimise their risk of discovery. It wasn't enough, not nearly enough, and Jason spent almost every minute thinking about her like some clucking mother hen. He needed to see her, support her. He was nearly mad with it. Perhaps if he tipped over the edge, he could join her?

Eventually, they had agreed to meet Corelia at the front of the hospital. It was an exposed location but Corelia could get the nurses to agree to leaving her there for half an hour. That would be plenty of time to exchange information and get out.

Cerys wanted him to stay indoors like a good dog, but Jason was fed up of waiting. He needed to be part of this, even if it was only meeting schoolgirls in hospital gardens. As the arranged time ticked closer, the pair used the footbridge across the busy A48 dual carriageway and into the back entrance to the hospital. Moving around the edges of the building, they came at the hospital from the side, blending in with the dozens of people making their way to appointments or to visit loved ones.

Jason spotted her first. She was hunched over in her wheelchair, a clanky ancient thing that relied on others to push her around, next to an old wooden bench. But she wasn't alone - a tall, blonde woman sat beside her, dressed neatly in a dark tailored suit. Jason would've recognised her anywhere.

Frieda bloody Haas.

He halted Cerys with a hand, and she took a few moments to recognise Frieda, having met her only once or twice. Cerys started hauling him backwards, clearly intending for them to run, but Jason wasn't abandoning this opportunity because of that woman. They needed to find out what she was saying to Corelia, and make sure the National Crime Agency hadn't got to her - and, through her, to Amy.

Cerys fumbled in her ragged satchel before pulling out a crumpled but familiar daffodil pin badge. Jason had last seen it when they were interviewing a suspect together and knew it concealed a camera of Amy's design. However, it sent its pictures to Amy's now-deceased computer AEON - how were they to use it?

"It goes through my phone," Cerys said, reading his mind. "We can see the stream there before it's sent to…wherever."

"How do you know this?"

"I used it for - you don't want to know. Really, no."

Jason agreed: he really didn't want to know. While he lurked behind a high fence, Cerys idly strolled by, threw an old crisp packet in the bin, and dropped the little daffodil by the back of the bench. The video would be non-existent but the audio should be prime.

Cerys hurried back to him and handed over one earbud for his listening pleasure. Jason stooped to listen with his short-arse sister, the unwanted voice of Frieda grating in his ear.

" - best facility in the country, not this provincial place. Your father's military - I can get you military-grade rehab. The best this country has to offer."

Cerys' face screwed up in revulsion. Frieda was bribing a paralysed teenage girl to get her way. Was there nothing the woman wouldn't sink to? Bloody hell, how had Jason ever fancied that?

"All I have to do is turn rat." Corelia was making it abundantly clear what she thought of Frieda.

"You're avoiding trouble with the law, Miss Martinez. You just happened to receive a web link from a criminal hacker and used it to... what was it again? Claim an iTunes voucher?"

"Too bad you missed out, Agent." Corelia was smug, gloating. *Careful...*

"Well, now that my people have a direct link to the hacker's online space, it won't be difficult to break through her defences. Miss Lane always thought more of her talents than could be proven. Hence why she used an underage girl to do her dirty work - and look how that ended."

"I was stabbed in the back by a murderer. Who you failed to catch. So I'm pretty clear on who fucked me over there."

"Language, Miss Martinez. Or will I need to involve your father?"

"Go right ahead. You're not meant to be talking to me at all. I'm sure he'd love to get you fired for this. In fact, let me go right ahead and call him."

Frieda's voice turned low, dangerous. "Why don't you call your friend Miss Carr instead? She's late for your little meeting. What exactly were you going to tell her that couldn't be shared by unencrypted email?"

"Top ten beauty secrets for blondes," Corelia said, deadpan.

A slight pause.

"She's winning," Cerys said, gleefully.

Jason wasn't so sure. He knew that pregnant pause. He had seen Frieda use it to her advantage in an interrogation. She was about to play dirty.

"It's a shame about your *friend* Heddwen, isn't it? She was doing so well at school, before…well, before she met you. Now she's missing so many lessons - I expect that soon she'll have a warning, maybe even a suspension. If she were to be linked to a criminal enterprise, I should think the headteacher must consider expulsion."

"You're a bitch, you know that? If you think that will make me help you, you are fucking deluded. I trust Amy to fix things - to make it right. She got her friend out and she'd do the same for me and mine. So kindly fuck off, would you, and leave a crip in peace."

"As you wish, Miss Martinez. But remember: you are so very young, with your whole life ahead of you. You could spend that life consorting with criminals. Or you could build a promising future at GCHQ, or even the National Crime Agency. You don't have to be another Amy Lane - you could be so much better."

They watched from behind their fence as Frieda stole the last word, her face a mask of terrible ice.

Corelia started off towards the main entrance, clearly done with her "relaxing" outdoor time. Jason gestured silently for Cerys to go forward, and his sister, naively, thought he was going to stay hidden like a good little lamb. But as Cerys approached Corelia, Jason quickly dived behind the bench, grabbed the daffodil and went after Frieda.

He didn't have a death wish but he did hold a grudge. He wasn't going to let that excuse for an NCA agent hurt Amy's friends, not when they were putting themselves in the firing line for her. He had to strike first.

Fifty yards ahead of him, Frieda swung into her ridiculous 4x4, more fit for a city jaunt than a real cross-country mudfest - and Jason made his move.

Sprinting up to the car, he jammed his leg into the door before it could close. "You miss me?"

She gawped at him, looking inelegantly like a fish as she stared.

"You're…you're wanted!" she stuttered, eventually.

"Yeah, what crime was that? Harassing teenage girls, was it? Fucking up NCA investigations?"

She looked unnerved, as if this was some kind of trap. But her eyes were fixed on his face, his body. Not his hand casually dropping the daffodil into the driver's door map pocket.

"I could arrest you. Right now."

"You won't. Because you quite like me, even though you screwed me over."

She didn't deny it, which surprised him. He had thought her games were purely to reel him in so she could get to Amy, but maybe not. He could use that. He needed to use something because he hadn't thought of much beyond dropping the daffodil into Frieda's car door.

"What do you want?" she said.

"I want you to leave Corelia alone. You've already got your claws into Amy - what do you care about the girl?"

"I don't need to explain my methods to you, Mr Carr."

"Is Amy going to prison? Are you going to send her there?"

Frieda's eyes flashed. "Of course, this is really about Miss Loach. Still defending her honour. But then I suppose you have her to thank for your vanishing act - one more crime to add to the list."

Jason wasn't going to implicate Amy so easily. "Prison - yes or no?"

Frieda sank back into her car seat, folding her arms under her breasts - probably to emphasise them, but Jason wasn't falling for that. Not this time, anyway. "No. Not if she…cooperates."

"What does that mean?"

"All in good time, Mr Carr. As a show of good faith, I will withdraw the warrant for your arrest. Maybe, when the time comes, you might want to do me a favour."

Jason didn't trust her as far as he could throw her, but he wasn't going to turn down a deal like that. He held out his hand for her to shake.

She took it solemnly. "You can check, of course, with your little police friends. If they know you're in town."

Again, no comment. He merely smiled at her, and she laughed.

"The boy can be taught. Now, if you'd move your thigh…"

He withdrew his leg and she slammed the door shut. He stepped back a pace, watched her reverse and drive away, smiling to himself. It was true - *he who dares, wins.* Amy would be pleased. After she had finished bollocking him for taking such a risk.

He had freedom of the city once more. Now - how to put it to use?

Chapter 23: No Smoke Without Fire

If Amy wanted to conduct a clandestine interview, she had to pick the right moment. So far, she had been interrupted no fewer than four times when trying to speak to Tony and she was beginning to lose patience.

It wasn't as if he was avoiding her. In fact, she almost thought he was seeking her out, which was really disconcerting - frightening, even. Yet every time they exchanged more than two words, a nurse or another patient stumbled across them and that was the end of that.

"Why are you interested in Tony?" Emma asked over lunch, after three failed attempts to form words.

"I think he knows something," Amy said.

Emma was a good confidante. Even if she wanted to tell on you, it would take her too long to confess and her interrogator would move on. Amy felt cruel for thinking it, but there it was. She'd lived too long with her own issues to tiptoe around other people's.

"About Ffion?" Her face was pinched as she whispered across the table, the bags under her eyes like two deflated black balloons.

Amy leaned forward conspiratorially. "He's hiding something. I got it from Mordecai."

Saying his name aloud was ridiculous, but then Amy had spent her morning pretending to be interested in cross stitch in order to get close to Tony. The ward's occupational therapist had been delighted to see her, even when she repeatedly stabbed her fingers with the large, blunt needle.

"I don't trust him," Emma said.

It was unclear whether she meant Tony or Mordecai, but Amy felt they were both shady characters. She thought she understood Mordecai a bit - an addict smuggling in his fix, living a lie both inside and out - but Tony completely eluded her. If she couldn't get firm answers today, she was going to text Jason his full name tonight. It was a start, at least.

Texting Jason. She couldn't wait, her heart beating faster in anticipation.

"Thank you for my present," she said to Emma. "I really liked it."

Emma smiled faintly. She paused for a long time, her eyes darting around the room, but they were the only two remaining except for the domestic sweeping up around them.

"It's not from me," she said. "It's - "

"Good afternoon, ladies." Tony smiled down on them, turning to one then the other. "Miss Mason. Miss…Loach."

The pause was deliberate, designed to be intimidating. Amy was determined not to feel fear, swallowing down her anxiety, but Emma was immediately paralysed.

"Care to share my cigarette, Miss Loach?"

It seemed he was just as eager to speak to her as she had been to talk with him.

"Sure," she said, though she had never smoked in her life.

As she left the table, Emma gripped her hand and mutely shook her head, eyes wide. Amy prised her fingers away, sending her what she hoped was a reassuring smile, and approached the garden doors.

Amy hadn't been outside since she'd arrived at the hospital. She tried to tell herself this was an insignificant threshold, that this was still safety or as safe as she could get. The garden was surrounded by a glass fence and no one could get in or out.

Yet she couldn't help wondering if the glass was bulletproof, if there were monitored surveillance cameras, if the external gates were locked at night. Could she take a chance like this, stepping into the unknown with a stranger?

"Are you coming or not?" Tony's smile was taunting. He knew how hard this was for her, knew he held all the power in this encounter.

She was determined not to let her fear show. Swallowing down the bile rising in her throat, she stepped out of the door and into the garden. One step, two, and she was free of the building. From the dining room roof, a single camera winked down at them in the half-dark of an overcast sky. She found that oddly comforting, enough to slow her heartbeat a few degrees.

Tony lit up his cigarette and offered her a drag. She was tempted to take it, but who knew what was in that thing? She shook her head and he shrugged, smoking away in the silence.

Across the garden, Ron was pacing the perimeter, hitting his head against the fence every now and then. Amy winced and looked away, staring up into the clouds overhead as if they could yield her answers. When was the last time she had stared into the clouds, under an open sky? She shuddered and looked away, feeling suddenly exposed. *Deep breaths.*

"I met a friend of yours," Tony said. "I hope you liked his gift."

So that's why Emma had tried to warn her. Amy cursed Jason for a fool, but she couldn't entirely regret it - she had the phone now, and she didn't think Tony could've interfered with it before delivering it to her via Emma.

"How did you meet?" she asked.

"Oh, around." He fiddled with something in his top pocket. "A more interesting question - how did you meet him?"

Amy smiled. Despite his probing questions, she felt she was gaining the advantage. She knew his game, whereas he had yet to learn hers.

"He was my cleaner, and an ex-con."

Even though she was staring at the sky, she could feel him practically vibrating next to her.

"Interesting life choice. How did he become a criminal?"

"Sometimes you just fall into these things," she said, vaguely.

"I wouldn't know," he said. "But you do, Miss Lane."

He was showing his cards again. She found herself on firmer and firmer footing the more he talked.

"I think," she began, slowly, "that you would like to know what I know."

She turned to him and watched his cautious smile.

"I would," he admitted.

"What's in it for me?"

His smile turned sharp. "I keep your little secret about your friend."

Amy reached out and tapped his top pocket, feeling something solid and plastic. "What about your secrets?"

He took a step back. "What - ?"

"Turn off the Dictaphone and we'll talk."

Crestfallen, he sullenly touched it and lifted it out slightly to show the red light fade. "How did you know?"

"You don't belong here," she said. "You know too much. What's the story then?"

"Criminals' luxury healthcare on the taxpayer."

"How many of us are there?"

She wanted to avoid giving up Mordecai if she could. She might need him for later. Jason would be proud of her working her sources, just like he did on the streets. Except hers were all locked up with her - and possibly more dangerous.

"I came here because of Miss Ellis," he said. "Then I found..."

He stopped, perhaps realising he was giving away everything for nothing.

"I will tell you everything about me," Amy said, feeling sick as she said it. "In exchange, you will tell me everything you know about Ffion and any other criminals here."

"Can't stay away from a murder, can you?"

"There's nothing else to do."

"You drive a hard bargain, Miss Lane, but I'll take it."

"Tell me about Ffion," she said.

Chapter 24: Deputy Sheriff

When Jason walked into the detectives' office, Bryn nearly had a heart attack.

He was escorted by a nervous uniformed police officer but Bryn couldn't see handcuffs. Everyone stopped to stare, a hush falling over the office, as Jason grinned like a certified lunatic. Maybe he was trying to get locked up with Amy. Only possible explanation…

"He just walked in, sir," the young officer said, sounding gobsmacked. "Asked to see you. I looked him up on the system - *and it wasn't there.*"

Bryn looked between Jason's smug face and the officer. "What wasn't there?"

"The warrant for his arrest. The NCA withdrew it."

Jason kept on grinning. Bryn resisted the urge to smack him about the face.

"Come with me."

Bryn grabbed Jason's arms and hauled him towards the first semi-private room he could think of - the men's toilets.

Jason leant up against the wall by the hand dryer. "Miss me?"

"You talked to that woman," Bryn said. "Why would you do something so stupid?"

The grin faltered. "Uh…well, it wasn't exactly the plan."

"When has anything around you ever gone to plan?"

A detective constable walked into the toilets, saw Bryn's scarlet face, and promptly walked out again.

Bryn scrubbed a hand over his face, trying to rein in his temper. "Why are you here?"

"How's Amy?"

"You're risking everything to check up on your girl?"

"Have you seen her?"

Bryn felt a stab of guilt at that. He had been calling every day to try to persuade Dr Al-Dosari to let him interview more patients. The man was obstinate as a goat, but Bryn could've pushed harder, obtained a

123

court order, done something to make sure she was all right. He deserved that look of recrimination in Jason's eye.

He dodged the question. "Why are you really here?"

"To help."

Bryn stared. "Help? I have a whole station full of qualified police officers."

"You need me."

The boy was cocky, sure, but he had a point. Bryn had been thinking how useful he might be - how he wanted both Jason and Amy back on this case. If Frieda had pardoned Jason's sins, then who was he to look a gift horse in the mouth?

Unless it was all a ploy on her part to get them to incriminate themselves, replacing the evidence that had been wiped with fresh transgressions fit to hang them. Bryn wouldn't put anything past that witch, who seemed to have schemes within schemes ready to ensnare even the most honest of coppers. Look what had happened to Owain, and he had been on her side.

Still, he could use Jason's knowledge. He'd had a few plain clothes boys sniffing around the white van leads, but they'd come up empty. They didn't have the look or the reputation or the menace to play the part, not the way Jason could, as simple as breathing.

"You do exactly as I say," he said.

The gleam in Jason's eyes was already making him regret this.

"Exactly," he repeated, hoping the word might sink in. "If you do anything...I can't protect you. Do you understand? You have to play this one by the law."

"I won't let you down," he said, practically bouncing on the balls of his feet.

"And keep your sister out of this."

"Cerys? She's - "

"She's in enough trouble. They only kept her on because they've seen her potential. So have I. You can't fuck this up for her, boy."

Jason shut his mouth and nodded. He would listen where his family was concerned. Unless Amy was in immediate danger - in which case, all bets were off.

"Now, here's what I need you to do."

Jason's Nissan Micra had been impounded by the police at the crime scene he had fled. Thankfully, his beloved Harley was still at Dylan's garage, ready and waiting for him to take her out.

Dylan greeted him with a worried embrace but after Jason assured him he was free from cops on his tail, his mate gladly handed over the bike. Bryn had given him a mundane task, sure, but it was perfectly suited to his skill set - find out who was handling stolen number plates.

To start him off, Dylan noted down half a dozen names of blokes who might be into that kind of work. It was a difficult needle to thread, because Jason didn't yet know how deep these guys were involved. Fitting stolen plates to a legit vehicle was a different bag to stealing a van and then kitting it out with false plates.

Could he act like a buyer? Most of these lads knew him of old and wouldn't have trouble believing he needed a stolen ride. Was this exactly the kind of thing Bryn wanted him to avoid when he said to stick to the law?

His new phone buzzed in his pocket: Cerys. He ignored the call, mindful of Bryn's words about ruining her life, and started up the Harley for his mini-tour of the city's chop shops. The first three tried to stonewall him but relented at his persistence and inside knowledge of a mechanics' work - especially one working the wrong side of legal. All those hours tinkering in Dylan's garage were paying dividends.

The fourth guy was a different kind of customer. Out-of-towner, new to the scene, and reluctant to give an inch. He might deal in vans, he might not. Some might have papers, some not. He couldn't name any satisfied customers Jason could speak to - wasn't his word enough? Jason found the whole experience dizzying, and left dissatisfied with his work, mostly because he had avoided laying hands on the idiot.

At the fifth garage, he struck gold. They didn't do that kind of thing, no, but they knew a man who did. Dealing out of Bristol, specifically in vans, could get you a plate from anywhere in the country. He marked his territory pretty clearly, it seemed - anyone could deal in luxury, off-road, SUVs, but they left vans alone or he asked them to cease and desist. And he didn't always ask nicely.

It smelled like a trap to Jason. White vans were clearly the criminal's vehicle of choice - it would do nicely for the National Crime

Agency to get their teeth into a business like that. Or maybe he was just overly sensitive, now he'd been burned.

He did have one way to find out - but he'd have to face the music back in Bristol. Returning the borrowed bike would be a good start, but he could explain himself, come out of it with no more than a few heated words if he played it right. Of course, if he fucked it up, he'd probably end up with something broken, but that was the price of doing business. Lies had a way of catching up to you, one way or another.

He returned home for the bike, dropping off the Harley at Dylan's - he didn't want his beauty mixed up in this. It was outside his mam's front door that he caught the tail, the shiny black 4x4 completely out of place on a Bute back street. He could ignore it, try to lose it on the M4 - or he could take the bull by the horns.

Jason walked up to the car and rapped on the window. The startled agent dropped the tinted screen, watching Jason cautiously, reaching for something dully glinting inside his coat.

"I don't think Frieda will like it if you shoot me," Jason said. "Just keep your distance, yeah? Or you can tell Frieda the deal's off."

Jason returned to the bike and sped off before the agent could get his motor started. Frieda would try again, of course, and he might've driven her to dirtier tricks with that display. Still, it felt good to spit in her eye and he was laughing as the bike hit eighty on the motorway, the wind tasting a lot like freedom.

Chapter 25: Background Check

Now that they'd called a truce, Amy found Tony absolutely fascinating.

His was a mind that worked along similar lines to hers - meticulous research, all carefully documented on his iPad, and extensive audio recordings of the staff and patients within the facility. He had even attempted to bug the nurses' office, but had been thwarted by interference from the alarm system.

After dinner, they sat together in a corner of the lounge, while he ostensibly showed her the novel he was working on. Mordecai looked on the pair with jealousy, as if he knew that Amy had replaced him in Tony's confidences, but Emma wasn't to be seen at all. Amy made a mental note to seek her out later, to give the reassurance she so desperately craved.

But, right now, in this moment, all she could think about was the smooth plastic and glass under her fingers. Something inside her physically ached at being so close to technology and yet unable to make it sing in the ways she knew she could. She could barely concentrate on what she was meant to be reading, her whole body filled with nervous tension at finally having a tablet in her hands again.

"There's a lot of exposition in this section," he said, leaning over to open up a set of notes titled "FE bg". "What do you think?"

Forcing herself to concentrate, she skimmed over the sparse information about Ffion's childhood and early years, noting that her marriage had ended quickly in divorce, leaving her with a young daughter. From her medical notes - and where had Tony obtained those? - she learned that Ffion had her first breakdown shortly after, though the doctor suggested she had long suffered with post-natal depression that had never been recognised.

The child was primarily cared for by her grandparents, as Ffion slipped in and out of hospital over a period of thirty years. Things had settled for a while, with a period of stability from 1999 to 2005. Then, out of nowhere, Ffion Ellis had driven her car into a bus.

"It needs a clear link to what happens next," Amy said. "Your character's motivations are unclear. It also fails the Bechdel Test."

Tony laughed under his breath. "Thought you might say that, Miss Lane."

He opened another document, also marked confidential. To Amy's untrained eye, it appeared to be a report from a psychiatrist on whether Ffion could have leave from a specialist unit, the one Tony had alluded to when he'd first told her about Ffion's past. The information contained within it was detailed but essentially useless. Only one thing was of any significance - the other prisoners had hated her, called her names, branded her a child killer and treated her like scum. Had any of them carried over that grudge?

"Researching the…cultural context for this chapter was very difficult."

"You need more background characters to flesh it out."

"If only I could make them feel real."

"It's possible, but I can't help you with it."

"Not even with this?" He tapped the side of the iPad suggestively.

Amy felt a tingle of excitement shoot up her spine. He was offering her freedom. A powerful, internet-enabled piece of technology that could take her anywhere and everywhere. Her wings might be clipped, but she could still fly.

"Amy! You know you're not allowed to touch that!"

Busted.

Lois tore across the lounge space and lifted the iPad out of Amy's hands, two seconds after she managed to shut down the reading app. "Where did you get this?"

"It's mine, nurse." Tony smiled up at her. "I was showing Amy my novel."

Amy put on her best innocent eyes. "I'm sorry. I just didn't think."

Lois was not moved, as she handed the iPad back to Tony. "I will have to report this to the doctor. I'm disappointed, Amy."

"And why can't Amy use my iPad? It's my property, after all."

Amy watched Lois' face as she tried to come up with an answer that wouldn't offend a private patient, presumably paying out thousands of pounds to stay at this hospital. "Tony, the details of other clients' care plans are confidential. Amy knows she shouldn't use technology and she shouldn't have put you in such a position."

"I offered, nurse. Amy is not at fault here."

"You may have enabled her, Tony, but it was Amy who fell off the wagon. I will have to inform your therapist."

Amy blinked at her as she walked away. Lois was acting like Amy had an internet addiction, or some other compulsion. Did she really not know the true reason for Amy's stay here? What did the nursing staff think was going on with her?

"That was very enlightening," Tony said, casually.

"It was. It seems information is at a premium among the nursing staff."

"Does your therapist seem to know?"

It was a good question, but Amy merely smiled. "Client care plans are confidential, Tony."

Bryn was ready to call it a night. He had no new leads, no suspects requiring interview, no evidence that wasn't already being processed. Jason hadn't reported in since he'd given him his new task, but it would take time to sound out Cardiff's criminals.

At least Bryn knew Cerys had been in college that afternoon, after her morning's absence. He knew he shouldn't be keeping tabs on her like this, but there was something about Cerys that made him want her to get on. Not to protect her - God knew that Cerys Carr could handle herself - but to help her make something of herself, steer clear of the dark and rocky road that Jason had stumbled down. She was about the same age as his eldest daughter, and he couldn't help seeing the differences between them. How Cerys' life had moulded her into someone serious and intent, yet also a risk-taker who loved the chase.

Leaving the detectives' office, he saw that the lights were still on in the Cyber Crime office. He came a step or two closer, the murmur of voices filtering through the ajar door. He'd seen Catriona leave a few hours earlier, so who could be keeping Owain company at this hour?

"Are you mad? How can she hack your precious computers from inside a hospital?"

Bryn stopped. He knew he should turn around and walk away, leave the former lovers to their argument. Yet he felt a morbid fascination with this conversation - would she be able to get a rise out of

Owain? Eke something out of this sullen, passive-aggressive shadow that haunted the station?

He couldn't hear Owain's reply, but Cerys wasn't about to back down. "How could he help her? He doesn't even have a credit card - not since your *best friend* stuck a warrant on him."

No prizes for guessing who had earned that title in Cerys' mind. Frieda Haas had some kind of hold over Owain, though Bryn had no idea what it might be. He'd originally been charmed by her advanced techniques and "big city" veneer, but after she'd been responsible for investigating him and his colleagues? After she'd condemned their friends?

"She's not my friend!"

"Then what is she, Owain? Because she's clearly more important to you than me."

The silence was thick, dark and pregnant with emotions that Bryn could feel even through the door that separated them. He knew he was intruding now, and he turned his back, heading away from the door.

Owain's voice was a broken murmur, but Cerys was Jason's sister, all fire and passion, emotions all hung out on the washing line for anyone to see.

"And I don't get a say, do I? I wanted to be there for you! You're such a prick."

Bryn heard the door slam and Cerys' barged past him in the corridor, blinded with rage. He hesitated, half-turning on his heel. He knew his presence wouldn't be welcome; that the last person Owain wanted to see right now was him.

How can she hack your precious computers from inside a hospital?

Bryn felt a stab of guilt. If the police computers had been infiltrated again, it was probably the work of Corelia. Bryn had been the one to put her in touch with Cerys - had she used Amy's tricks of the trade to get exclusive access?

Yet while he knew the Carrs to be skilled in deceit, Bryn couldn't see an advantage to Cerys causing a scene over this. If it was Corelia using Amy's access methods, Owain would find out soon enough. If Cerys did still care about him, why would she not tell him the truth and brazen it out instead?

Deciding that he needed to know what was going on - for purely professional reasons - Bryn walked back down the corridor and opened the office door.

Owain was sitting at his desk, clutching at his forehead, brown tufts of hair visible through his fingers. "Cerys, I can't - "

"What's this about a hack then?"

Owain started, jerking upright and releasing his hair. He looked like he hadn't slept for days, eyes hollow in his pale face. "What do you want?"

"If someone's broken into our computers, I need to know about it."

Owain scowled, as he returned his attention to his computer, shutting Bryn out. "You know exactly who it is."

"What have they accessed?"

"Nothing - yet." His fingers danced across the keyboard. "I have IT trying to keep them out, but the attack's coming from multiple sources."

"Attack?"

"They're not politely knocking on the door. They've got a battering ram at every entrance while flinging stones at the windows."

"It's not subtle enough for her," Bryn said.

Owain gave half a shrug. "Desperate times."

His computer beeped at him. Then again. A litany of beeps and alarms all went off at once, deafening in the small space.

"Shit."

"What? What is it?"

Owain's computer monitor was a mess of little windows, all popping up to scream something at him. Antivirus alerts were stacking on top of each other in the bottom right-hand corner of the screen, trying to be heard over the cacophony of errors.

Then the screen went black.

An image of a dead-eyed cartoon boar appeared in the middle of the black, with the words beneath: THANKS PIGS.

And then all was black again.

"What the fuck just happened?" Bryn asked.

The phone started ringing and Owain answered. "Cyber Crime."

Bryn heard the tinny sounds of panic filtering through the receiver.

"Yes, I'm down too. What did they get?" He paused, listened. "Shit."

After a few more seconds, he hung up the phone. "It's gone. The whole system's infected."

Bryn gestured at the computer. "How quickly can they replace it?"

But Owain shook his head. "Not my system. The system. Every computer connected to the South Wales Police network has been infected with a virus and crashed. IT aren't even sure what data they grabbed before they killed the computers."

He looked at Bryn then, his dark haunted eyes filled with shock. "We're all in the dark now."

Chapter 26: Poison Pen

Amy was in need of caffeine.

However, the nurses cut off her supply of tea after six o'clock, so she'd have to settle for hot chocolate. She could bring one to Emma and they could eat toast together before bed. It was almost cosy, if you could forget the nurses and the pills and the therapy.

Amy approached the office to ask for the hot chocolate, the boiling water kept away from patients in case they should start flinging it in their disturbance. The fishbowl was empty, all the nurses busy elsewhere. She thumped at the glass door in frustration, and saw something vibrate next to the door. A few letters were leaning against the glass, facing out so that patients would know they had mail. Amy's only correspondence had been about the Mental Health Act, but she had been too depressed at the time to pay much attention to it.

What struck her was that one of the letters was clearly marked for Ffion Ellis. The address was handwritten and the postmark was from Newport, the envelope bulging with the contents. The nurses had clearly forgotten all about it, but now all Amy could think of was obtaining it. Maybe it was from a relative, or a friend? Or, perhaps, it was from someone who hated her, perhaps even the killer?

She had to get to that letter.

Crossing the communal area, keeping her eye out for nursing staff, Amy saw that the top part of the stable-door of the clinic room was slightly ajar. It was the counter at which they were meant to receive their regular medication, with the bottom part of the door preventing the patients grabbing handfuls of drugs - or the nurse. Yet it wasn't time for meds for another couple of hours.

She checked the communal space for curious onlookers. Tony had just retired to his room with his iPad, and Ron was engrossed with a set of dominoes, turning them around and around on the table. Everyone else was absent. *Perfect.*

Approaching the door, she peered through the slight gap and saw Darren the nurse next to the open drug cupboard. In front of him, a register was open and a dozen boxes and bottles were arranged about it. He removed the strips of tablets from a box and checked something in the register. Then, he took up his pen and turned the page back, altering one of the columns. He then returned to the current page and changed another number.

Before pocketing one strip of tablets.

Amy watched him repeat the exercise with two more boxes, before removing a couple of loose tablets from a brown glass bottle. They all joined the collection in his deep pockets. What was he up to? Was he the source of the tablets she'd found in the corridor? Amy didn't know much about what drugs might be available on a psych ward, but surely the chances of them killing a person skyrocketed if used in combination.

She racked her brain, trying to remember if Darren had been on shift just before Ffion died. She couldn't quite remember, but she recalled that the nurses' rota was pinned up in the office. If she could just get a glance at it, she could warn Bryn that there was one nurse in particular who needed checking out.

Belatedly, she realised that he was returning all the boxes and bottles to the cabinet and she would soon be discovered. Slipping away from the door, she flopped down on the nearest armchair and pretended to be captivated by the state of her fingernails. She heard the door open and close, before he passed behind her chair.

"You bored, Amy?"

She nearly jumped out of her skin at Darren's voice, fingers grasping at the arms of the chair as if she were about to be launched into space. "M'fine."

"You could play dominoes with Ron."

They both looked at the table, where Ron had started stacking the dominoes in odd piles of three and four, making a pattern that only made sense to him.

"Yeah, maybe not. He's a proper crazy. Not like you."

Amy flinched at his words. "Proper crazy"? What exactly was that supposed to mean - and what did it mean that Amy wasn't in the group?

"Like Ffion?" she said, voice quavering.

"At least she's at peace, eh?"

He moved away at last, and Amy took a few deep breaths. Was that a motive - mercy killing? Did the killer view himself as a method for removing a soul from suffering, a murderous angel? If that were true, whose suffering might he want to remove next?

Amy looked up at Ron, who swept aside his piles of dominoes and headed out into the garden for a cigarette. She wished she had access to surveillance in here, the ability to watch everyone and everything. To monitor the situation in real-time - and intervene before it was too late.

Would Corelia be able to do that? If Amy could somehow hook her up with access to the network, could she be the "eye in the sky" they needed? But how would she get access to the office and its computers for long enough to establish a connection and inform Corelia of the access route?

Everything she needed was in that office. How was she going to get inside?

Standing up from the chair, her legs shaking, she tottered towards the goldfish bowl. Darren was kneeling on the floor, stuffing something into a rucksack. Most likely his haul from the drug cupboard. While he was distracted, Amy craned her neck to view the rota pinned up on the wall.

On the 31st October, Darren was listed for the day shift. Shit.

Darren looked up. Without thinking, Amy clapped her hand to her chest and urgently gasped for breath. Darren flung open the door and took hold of her arm, supporting her weight.

"I need Lizzie," Amy cried. "I want my sister."

Amy listed into Darren with all of her weight, forcing the man to take a step back into the office. She was inside now. She could make a grab for Ffion's letter, and then find her way back in somehow. *Somehow.*

"Just breathe, will you? Don't panic now."

Amy screwed her eyes up tight and blindly sank backwards, hitting the edge of the nearest desk and bouncing it against the wall. She felt the letters shower down, pelting her neck and shoulders, and she let her shoulders shake with imagined sobs until the letters all fell conveniently to the floor.

She sank with them, as Darren impatiently tried to hush her, shaking at her shoulder as if that would somehow make her stop crying. Lois soon arrived, and took over the comforting role.

"I'm sorry," Amy said, looking at Lois. "I didn't mean to do it."

Lois pulled her in for a brief hug. In the press, Amy's fingers closed around the thick letter and shoved it into the front pocket of her hoodie. Lois' badge caught on her subtle fingers and the lanyard broke, falling to the floor and spilling its cards. A swipe card. That was what she needed.

"Oh, these things are always breaking," Lois said, quickly gathering her cards before Amy could blink.

Another time. She would have to be patient. After reassuring the nurses that she felt a little better and could they ask Lizzie to visit tomorrow, she requested her pair of hot chocolates.

But Emma wasn't well, they said, and she needed to rest in her room. The guilt kicked at her like a mule - how had she not noticed Emma's absence was significant? Darren told her not to disturb Emma under any circumstances, and it was with an uneasy churning in her stomach that Amy headed for her room.

Emma's door was closed, the small blind shut, and Amy drank her hot chocolate with a feeling of loss. She had the letter and she had leads to follow, but she had let down Emma. Like she'd let down Jason, Owain, Bryn, Cerys - and even Lizzie.

Tucking the letter down the side of the bed, Amy settled under the duvet and waited for lights out, the hot chocolate making her drowsy despite the thrumming of anxiety and bad feelings throughout her whole body.

Had she done the right thing by getting into bed with Tony, metaphorically speaking? She understood his motives now, but she had signed away her privacy to get to the bottom of Ffion's murder. Could she trust him after the way journalists had hounded Jason? She didn't know what the coverage had been like after her arrest, but she couldn't imagine it was flattering.

That air of malevolence had gone from him, now she saw him clearly. She no longer feared him, even if she didn't feel entirely easy with him. He wasn't the source of her discomfort, that griping and twisting in her belly.

Was it Darren and his theft of medication? Did she think he would

136

crush tablets and hide them in her food, an Angel of Mercy swooping in to claim her life? She could feel a dread around him, but no, it wasn't that either.

It was Emma. What could she do about Emma?

Amy's anxiety and low mood had been effectively chased away by the renewal of her investigation, though she felt their presence just beneath the surface. Activity and purpose had always been her most valuable weapons against their threat. What were Emma's strongholds? Was one of them spending time with Amy, as unlikely as that seemed to her?

In the morning, she would forget the investigation for the day. She would spend time with Emma, soothe her, tend to her, and then she could get back to work. She had a creeping sense that this might be how Jason felt on her bad days, that he needed to stop his tasks to take care of Amy. Though that was his job, wasn't it? Even if he went far beyond his duty. She hoped he didn't see it as a duty at all, but she knew that hope may well be in vain.

When finally the lights went out in the corridor and the night nurse passed by for her checks, Amy brought the letter and the phone under her covers. The light from the phone was faint, but it allowed her to make out the date on the envelope - 29th October 2014. It had been posted only two days before Ffion's death.

Amy opened the letter, taking care not to tear the envelope or the pages within. She had some notion that she should hand this over to the police at some point in the future, but for now, she was only greedy for every last scrap of detail she could glean from the paper.

The letter itself was handwritten, with no address or date. It began: "Dear Bitch".

Amy read the letter with increasing dread:

your not fit for life
you shud of died in that car
I hate you and Ive always hated you

The vitriol in the letter left Amy's hand trembling, three folded sheets of A4 paper, covered both sides in furious black scrawl. While it made no specific threat, it was clear the writer held great animosity towards Ffion. Who had sent it? Was it the first such letter sent to her, or had there been more? Had she received them before she died?

Amy's lasting memory of Ffion was her muttering, over and over again, that the demons were coming. What if the demons were real and sending their intentions via letter?

Amy had to get this letter to Bryn, to the forensics department, but how? She fumbled with the phone and carefully composed a message for Jason. Perhaps he could ask Cerys to send Bryn to the hospital. It would alert the police that she was somehow communicating with the outside world, but it was worth the risk to bring this letter to their attention.

She hit send before she could change her mind, hiding the letter again and clutching the phone like a talisman. How long would it take Jason to reply? Was he all right? Did he miss her like she missed him?

The phone rumbled against her palm.

WILL TELL HIM FREE MAN NOW DON'T WORRY X

Amy stared at the words, struggling to comprehend them. Until, with slow-dawning horror, she realised exactly what they meant.

Jason Carr had made a deal with the devil. And it wouldn't take long for Frieda to collect.

Chapter 27: Secret Handshake

After replying to Amy's text, Jason safely stowed his phone in his jacket pocket and resumed his surveillance of the scrapyard.

His ex-boss hadn't exactly been thrilled to see him. "Where the fuck you been, Taffy Lee?" he'd bellowed across the garage, causing every mechanic in the place to suddenly find somewhere else to be.

Jason had buffed up the bike before bringing it round, so that the boys couldn't fault her condition, but the man was still unhappy.

"You can't just fuck off whenever you please. I employ a man, I expect him to work - and not to nick my fucking bikes!"

Really, "unhappy" was an understatement - the bloke was red-faced and fuming. Jason had let him rant for a good while, before finally explaining that he'd needed to leave town in a hurry because his girl was in trouble.

The boss had softened a little at that, while Jason nursed a strange feeling in his chest at calling Amy his girl. When he'd added that her trouble was related to some bastard in a cloned white van, the boss got very interested indeed.

"You're talking about Beaumont," he'd said, with a snarl. "Fucking Beaumont."

Which is how Jason had ended up outside Beaumont's place, the place old vans came to die - D.R. Beaumont & Sons, the breakers' yard to end all breakers' yards. Funny, though, how most of the vans inside didn't look broken up at all.

From what his old boss had told him, Beaumont hated middle men but loved the internet. Which meant he took anonymous orders online or dealt with folks in person. With the crime happening in Cardiff, the bodysnatching van could've been obtained by either method. Jason would pass the website on to Corelia to see what she could see, and handle the in-person work himself.

He missed having Amy in his ear, prattling away, running her elite hacking tools while he was taking care of business. They were a team, and he felt bereft working alone. He'd never been good at running solo. He wanted Lewis and the boys at his back, or his boss - his partner - calling the shots through his Bluetooth headset.

Right now, though, he had to find a way in. His way was usually walking straight up and knocking until his knuckles bled, and then knocking heads. That might be what Bryn called illegal, but it got the job done. This might take a finer approach, though.

As Jason approached the fence, the security light came on and a pair of dogs started barking. A middle-aged man in a pair of blue overalls came up to the gate, the snarling mastiffs at his heels.

"What you want then?" he drawled in a heavy country accent, more suited to a farmer than a car breaker.

"I'm looking for a van," Jason said.

"Are you now? Well, I don't know about that."

"I need it tonight. Stuff to be moved tomorrow. Quick, like."

The man's eyes gleamed. "You'll be wantin' to talk to Beaumont but he's not 'ere tonight. Come back tomorrow."

"Tonight." Jason leaned into the fence.

The dogs started to growl louder, a deeper warning tone. Jason had never been a big dog person, but he knew how to look hard and intimidating even when faced with these two creatures.

"He won't be 'appy," the man warned, but shuffled back to his small shed nonetheless, the dogs slinking after him.

Jason waited only a couple of minutes before the man returned, opening up the gates.

"You'll be paying cash, o' course."

"I'll see if I like what you're selling first, mate."

The man shrugged. "It's all the same to me."

The gate swung closed behind him - but the man didn't lock it, the chain trailing loose on the ground. As he shuffled off towards his cabin, Jason picked up the nearest thing he could find - a cracked, plastic hub cap. The dogs' eyes were instantly on him.

Yanking on the chain, Jason threw the cap like a Frisbee straight out the gate. The dogs bounded after it, barking into the night. With a cry, the man poked his head out of the hut and gave chase, calling after them as he ran across the street.

Jason slipped inside the watchman's hut and started his search. Most surfaces were filled with fast food containers and soft porn mags. An ancient computer sat in one corner, silent and gathering dust, but that couldn't hold what he was looking for.

Stuffed in the top drawer of a broken desk was a much-abused ledger, three-quarters full with a fraying spine. He shifted it open and, from the faint street light outside, skimmed down the columns. He should've asked Bryn for the bloody number plate, as each one was recorded next to a date and an extortionate sum of money. Instead, he took photos of the last six months' accounts - business was brisk, and they filled four pages - hoping that would contain the plate they needed. Failing that, Bryn could always show up with a warrant.

Shoving the ledger back in the drawer, Jason turned for the door - only to find it blocked by a large dark shadow.

"Who the fuck are you?"

Jason tried to brazen it out, offering his hand to shake. "I'm Bradley Thompson, mate. I've come for a van."

The bloke wasn't having any of it. "Step outside. I hate to have blood on my things."

Jason stepped slowly through the door, raising his hands in a non-threatening gesture. "No need for that, mate. Just wanted to do some business."

"Business in my drawers?"

A snicker came out of the darkness behind the man, and Jason counted three heavies shadowing their leader. This must be the legendary Beaumont then, and these goons either his body men or the sons.

As Beaumont turned to cuff his man about the face, Jason seized his moment. He ran towards the still-open gate, his leather jacket slipping through the hands of the nearest minder. He cleared the gates and started pelting down the street, hoping to outrun these men who seemed to love a life of intimidation, chips and beer.

The vice around his calf stopped him dead, almost felling him as he turned to stare at his assailant. One bloody mastiff had locked its jaws onto his leg, while the other was prowling around him like a born hunter. The men had stopped running and were laughing, fanning out to surround him. *Shit*.

The distinctive roar of his bike suddenly flooded the street, accompanied by its blaring horn. The dog yelped in fright and released him, as the bike headed straight for them. The men threw themselves out of the road, as the bike paused for only a moment and Jason leapt onto the back. It raced off into the night, its petite driver mute behind her bright pink helmet.

"Thank you," he shouted, as Cerys headed straight back to Cardiff.

"Fucking idiot," she replied, and concentrated on the road.

The light was on in the kitchen when they arrived home and Jason could see his mam's shadow moving around inside. The walks of shame in recent years were worse than the ones of his teens, where he'd merely stumbled in reeking of weed and telling Lewis not to break any mugs.

Gwen merely sighed at him with disapproving eyes before going to bed with her camomile tea. Jason raided the bread bin and came up with scones. He served them up with black coffee while Cerys started up her laptop, as he limped to the table with the butter and jam.

"Do you need a doctor for that?" she said, not looking away from the screen.

The trickle of blood towards his ankle and fear of tetanus meant A&E was in his future, but he wanted to know what Cerys was up to first. "You talking to Corelia?"

"She thinks someone's spying on my computer. She was the one who told me you were being a moron in Bristol."

Clearly, Corelia had inherited Amy's tracking abilities. "Ask her about the daffodil camera - where is it?"

Cerys looked at him strangely. "What have you done with it?"

"Gave it to a friend," he said.

She glowered at the laptop screen. "I hate you. Why does Amy put up with you? You're a fucking liability."

"I love you too." He ruffled her unruly blonde spikes, flattened by her helmet, and she pretended to bite him.

"Corelia's going to take over the computer at midnight and find out what's gone wrong. When she's done, she'll tell us what she's found out. Why were you in Bristol anyway?"

"Bryn reckons the van was cloned. I took some pictures of that guy Beaumont's ledger, because he deals in old vans made new."

Cerys stared at him. "Bryn asked you? In person?"

"I went down the station," Jason said, as casually as he could, propping his throbbing leg up on the chair opposite. "Frieda withdrew the warrant, like she promised."

Cerys blew up. "You went after her, didn't you? That's why you were acting so fucking mysterious after I met with Corelia! Is that where the camera is? Have you got an actual fucking death wish?"

"Calm the fuck down," he said, which was the worst possible thing to say.

Cerys threw her spoon at him, spattering his Rock the Casbah T-shirt with raspberry jam. "You fucking calm down!" she shouted. "That woman won't be happy until you're in jail or dead, and you're a fucking moron if you think otherwise."

"Language, bach," filtered down from upstairs and they both took a breath, lowering their voices to something outside their mam's earshot.

"Bryn didn't arrest me!" he protested, but deep down, he knew she was right. "She did put a tail on me," he admitted.

Cerys just shook her head in disgust. "Fucking moron," she repeated, mostly to herself, and looked back at the computer. "She's doing it, whatever it is. Take yourself off to the fucking hospital and we'll manage Frieda later."

"My leg can wait." Jason craned his neck to look at the screen. "What's she doing?"

"Something with the code. I didn't know she was this into computers."

"Maybe it's a new hobby." One less likely to get her stabbed.

The computer shut itself down and then restarted. Cerys logged in again and a little black window appeared in the top right-hand corner:

All clear. Key logger sending data to someone behind a government firewall. Watch yourself. C#

"Cee-hash?"

"Like cash?"

They both shrugged, the significance eluding them.

More text appeared in the box:

Got a message today through PM. Someone contacting black hats to hack Cardiff Police. Friends of Amy sending a warning. C#

"What are 'black hats'?" Cerys asked.

"They're the bad hackers, the illegal ones."

"What Amy is?"

"I think they call Amy grey, 'cause she's in the middle. Ask Corelia or Cash or whatever to find out who sent it."

Cerys typed their reply and they waited.

Over my head. Only working with what I got and Amy kept me from the good toys. But try me on anything else. C#

"How did the key thing get on your laptop? Ask her that."

Cerys relayed the message, and the reply was almost instantaneous:

Too big for email. Probably from a USB stick or external hard drive. C#

Cerys sat back in her chair, her whole body trembling.

"What? What is it? You know who it is?"

"He gave me my files back, from his laptop. He said he didn't want me to...to..."

Owain. Owain Jenkins had planted this shit on Cerys' computer. He was still working for those NCA bastards.

"I'll fucking kill him," he said.

Cerys' eyes flashed. "Not if I get there first."

Chapter 28: The Pyre of Ambition

The van had to go.

He'd needed it for his little camping trip, but now it was just a liability. He'd removed the plates, of course, but the van still held all that lovely forensic evidence from transporting a body and he didn't want anyone to get hold of that.

He could sell it on, underground, let it get lost in the highways and byways of the used car industry. That was risky, though, and the only bloke he knew who'd be interested was that scary fucker from Bristol.

Destruction seemed like the best option, but how? Scrapping it would be suspicious. It was barely six months old, and maybe the police could find some little telling thing from a crushed metal cube. He wasn't taking chances this time.

He also kinda wanted to get something out of it. If you were going to lose twenty grand, you had to do it in style. This would be a Vegas Casino van dump, not a slow death on the stock market.

It took a few hours of planning, but this was a magnificent use of his mind. He lovingly crafted every detail and, after a tedious dinner which he couldn't even enliven with cactus Tequila, he set his plan in motion. Loading up the van with his basic equipment and an old quad bike he'd found in an outhouse, he set off down the coast, looking for a likely spot.

He didn't have to go far, sweeping round the bay, and looking over at a neighbouring farm with its fields flush against the cliff edge. Perfect place for a set piece. He'd have to leave the road at some point - but where? This was out of his territory now, the province of country bumpkins and naked ramblers.

He decided to brave the farmer's own lane, creeping past the dark and silent farmhouse. Good job this lot weren't night owl party animals, but then who would stay in this dump if that were true? The lane petered out into grazing land and he drove on, taking the van over the empty fields. He hoped the animals were shut up somewhere - a bull or two would ruin everything.

The cliff edge came up quicker than he expected and he needed to brake hard to stop the van plummeting over the edge. He should've thought of this earlier, really - then he could've dumped the body with the van. Two birds and one slingshot, that sorta thing. But he was a "no regrets" kinda guy and he needed to push on.

Removing his tripod and camera from the van, he set up about fifty metres back. He'd have to rely on the flames to light the shot, but he was confident it would work. His experiments always worked. He'd spent easily forty-five, fifty minutes sourcing inspiration for this project, and then he'd shrugged and said, "Fuck it, I'll do it my way."

Taking the camera remote, he lit a flaming torch he'd prepared earlier - because it looked damn cool - and stood at the side of the van, all in black. He clicked "record" and waved his torch in a glorious arc, before shoving it into the open fuel cap.

Then he fucking ran.

But the van didn't explode. It just sat there with a stick protruding from it, doing fuck all. What was this?

Then he saw the smoke, thick dark smoke curling around the end of his torch and out of the nooks and crannies of his van. It was alight, but it wasn't a Hollywood blockbuster explosion. Pity. Still, if he waited it out, he'd get some good footage. Maybe not twenty thousand pounds worth of footage, but something for YouTube. In, like, a year's time. He wasn't stupid.

He could see fire now, the van practically glowing with it, and flames licking the undercarriage like the embrace of red-hot fingers on a cold night. That was beautiful, poetical even. He should write that down and sell it on to someone.

Flames started shooting from the exhaust, slowly propelling the van towards the cliff edge. Then something inside the van exploded, rocking the whole structure from side to side. Shit! He'd only left the bloody quad bike inside. It would be a long walk home.

Something metallic went ping nearby, as if some tool was hitting the inside of the van. Maybe bits of the quad bike, rattling around inside. Then something whistled past his head, burning a hot line through the air, and a shout carried across the field.

Some fucker was shooting at him!

Fuck, farmers had guns, didn't they? And he was trespassing, with a van making a fucking beacon that could be seen for miles around.

He turned and fled, running as fast as he could, trying not to fall over the edge and into the sea. He was missing the show and he had lost his camera, but he felt free, like he was flying, like he could take on the world. The exhilaration of almost dying filled him, and he wondered if that old woman had felt it, just before the end.

Maybe he was doing his victims a favour after all. He was like a shaman, leading them to a depth of feeling they couldn't imagine, taking them to new heights - and then beyond.

He ran and ran, laughing as he went, filled with the joy of his powers.

Bryn woke to the news that their killer had left them a gift in the night. Unfortunately, it was smouldering at the bottom of a cliff.

The local uniforms had already cordoned off the farm and marked a designated route across the farmland for officers and vehicles. Bryn abandoned his car in the lane, not trusting it to manage the rough country terrain, and headed through the dew-damp fields to a stunning view over the Bristol Channel.

He didn't know the forensics crew gathered at the scene, and he felt the absence of Indira, still floating around inside her own head and possibly unable to ever get out. He approached the huddle, and realised it also contained representatives from the fire service, mountain rescue and coastguard.

"Detective Inspector Bryn Hesketh - what's going on then?"

"We're not sure of the best way to reach it," the lead Scene of Crime Officer said. "It's in one piece on the rocks - do we go in by boat, or do we go over the cliff? If we can't get at it properly, we'll have to remove it first and then mull it over in the lab."

Bryn decided to leave them to their wrangling, as he hadn't the faintest idea how to achieve such a feat, and instead crossed to the scorched patch of grass with the tyre treads leading up to it and then over the cliff. One SOCO was busily preserving a tread, though as they had the van in question, Bryn thought that was rather pointless.

What did catch his eye was the flame-red hair of one Catriona Aitken. What was the Cyber Crime Unit doing out here? He'd left Owain late last night, in conference with IT and the higher-ups, trying to work out how to resurrect their computer systems. Surely that was an "all hands on deck" operation?

Bryn made his way over to her, as she ducked inside a white forensic tent. Peering in, Bryn noted a camera and tripod beneath it that were slowly sinking into the mud.

She looked up at his entrance and grinned maniacally, as if she had just conquered the planet. "He filmed the whole thing."

Bryn felt his soul leap. "And he left it behind?"

"The whole lot. Equipment, recording, everything. Better still, it's an old card. It's got other files on it, and surely more deleted debris besides. He's handed his identity to us on a plate."

Bryn clapped her on the shoulder, one step away from hugging her. "Get this back to the station - get all your tech stuff together..."

He trailed off as he realised they had no way of transferring and processing this footage. The attack last night had crippled their ability to investigate.

"One advantage to being a workaholic is that my laptop was safe at home last night," Catriona said, with a grin. "Owain warned me before I connected to the network, so we have one working computer at least."

Her smile faded a little. "Have you, uh, seen him? Owain?"

Bryn frowned. "Late last night. Why?"

"He wasn't in yesterday - during the day, I mean," she said, clearly uncomfortable with ratting on her boss. "I thought you might've sent him somewhere."

Bryn grimaced. Owain was still on his team, even if it didn't feel like it. Maybe he should be keeping a better eye on him. However, they were also in the middle of a murder investigation and a technological apocalypse, with a key piece of evidence just fallen into their laps. He couldn't afford the time to babysit one wayward officer.

He was tempted to ask Cerys, but that could only make the situation worse. He could just imagine how he'd feel if his boss had sent his ex-wife round while he was on gardening leave. Bryn would just carry on with the investigation and touch base with his slightly illegal minions, telling them to back off a little way, now they were so close.

His phone rang in his pocket, some dance-pop nonsense that his daughters thought was funny. He glanced at the screen - an unknown number - before answering it.

"Hesketh."

"It's Jason. Amy found a threatening letter at the hospital, addressed to Ffion. You need to get it off her."

So they were definitely communicating illegally - and Amy had stolen a dead woman's post. Though that thought was swamped by the prospect of another piece of evidence, the killer now firmly in his sights.

"I'm on my way."

They were close now - he could feel it. He couldn't abandon the chase, not for anything. This was redemption, this was his second chance made whole. He wouldn't allow Owain or Amy or anyone to get in the way of that, but he needed them too. He'd felt lost and alone without his job, but also without his friends.

"I'm sending you some pictures from a place in Bristol. And Bryn? We have a source that says someone's trying to hack the police servers."

"Bit bloody late," he growled. "Who told you that?"

"Corelia. Someone contacted a mob of hackers to get into the Cardiff Police computers."

"I'll get Owain on it."

"Not Owain." His voice was harsh, immediate. "I don't think he's on our team anymore."

Jason was gone before he could ask what had happened, but Bryn didn't really need that answered. Something was badly wrong with Owain, either of his own making or carrying him away in a fast-flowing river. Bryn wanted to leave him to swim, but could he let him drown?

The case came first. His ex-partner would have to wait, and then there'd be a reckoning. One that would probably break the both of them, but Bryn had never shied away from tough calls.

The pictures came through, slightly out of focus but their contents legible - number plates, with date sold, buyer and cash laid down. Was their thief's record among them? His eyes scanned the ledger before finding the plate: "online" was all it said, but the price quoted was significantly less than some of the others. That meant he'd likely only bought the plate and not the van.

So the van sitting at the bottom of the cliff was his own, and could contain a wealth of evidence. They were closing in on their killer - if only he could keep Amy, and Owain, and the rest safe while he tightened the noose.

Chapter 29: Shifting Sands

As soon as Cerys declared she was going to Owain's house, Jason knew there'd be trouble.

They'd apparently shared their phones' location data with each other when they'd been going out - was this the new third date? - and Owain had never revoked his permission. That was how Cerys knew he was at home on this crisp Thursday morning, when she should've been in college and Jason should've been resting up in bed.

The A&E doctor had been alternately anxious and exasperated at his bite wound, cleaning it out and stitching it up before handing over a course of antibiotics with strict instructions to take every last tablet. After his brush with pneumonia earlier in the year, Jason intended to follow the doctor's orders to the letter.

He'd also cadged some strong painkillers, so he was practically rattling as he limped down the front steps. Cerys was already waiting impatiently beside the Harley, but Jason held up his hand. He needed to deal with his sister's problems today, but he wasn't going to forget his boss - his friend. His something-really-confusing.

He called Bryn and quickly relayed Amy's message, before sending through the pictures of the ledger. That they were too late with their news about the hackers was a blow. Jason should've called it in immediately, but he wasn't used to playing police liaison. It felt good to be working together again, as a team, but these little reminders only emphasised the absence of Amy. Jason felt like he kept fucking it up without her.

Cerys made it clear she was driving, as Jason awkwardly mounted behind her, his leg protesting every movement. She barely allowed him time to settle before she was off, racing off towards the M4, to Bridgend and the house she'd briefly shared with Owain. Riding pillion with a busted leg was not the best experience of Jason's life, but he'd rather the griping agony than leaving Cerys to face that bastard alone.

Jason was willing to give the boy a chance to explain himself

- he knew first-hand what a sly bitch Frieda Haas could be, and he wouldn't put it past her to plant the device herself, to spread to Cerys. Then again, Owain had willingly worked for her before and might well do so again.

Arriving at Owain's bland house in a bland estate in Bridgend, Cerys parked right outside the door. Without waiting for Jason to get off the bike, she marched up to the front door and banged her fist on it.

As Jason limped up the drive, his eye caught sight of a familiar Mercedes 4x4 and his heart sank.

"Cerys…"

Too late. The door opened, to reveal an unshaven Owain in a thick dressing gown, looking down at her as if she meant nothing at all. "What are you doing here?"

"Why did you bug my laptop?"

Something flickered across his face and was gone. "You don't have anything to hide."

"I'll just send all your secrets to Bryn then, shall I? I trusted you!"

"This isn't about Bryn."

"So, it's about us? What have I ever done to you that you'd hurt me like this?"

Jason needed to cut in, protect Cerys, save her from saying anything exposing - or revealing. "Was it a gift for your new girlfriend?"

Owain and Cerys both turned to him. Cerys was pale, trembling, but holding it together - his baby sister was made of tough stuff. Owain might as well have been a ghost.

"Well, where is she? Her car's parked outside. It doesn't take a genius, Owain."

A curtain twitched in an upstairs room and then fell closed. She wouldn't meet them like this, on her lover's doorstep, not unless it held a distinct advantage. Everything was a game with Frieda.

He saw the realisation dawn on Cerys' face, then watched her pack away all those emotions that could hurt her, turning back to Owain with only contempt.

"You did it for her. Not even for your career or an investigation - just for her. Open your eyes, Owain. She'll use you just like she used Jason. And then she'll throw you aside like so much rubbish. Good luck with it then."

She strode down the path, and she did not cry.

Jason looked at Owain, with pity. "It'll come back to bite you in the end, mate. Trust me - I know."

Amy was up early, showered and dressed before breakfast, much to the staff's surprise. She ate with Tony, both silent and intent on their toast.

She wasn't sure what time Bryn would arrive. The letter was safely hidden with the phone, beneath the fake spider plant, but she was anxious to place it into his hands. After breakfast, she haunted the lounge, watching her fellow inmates drifting in to eat. Ron seemed a little better, a little less vague, but Mordecai looked like utter shit. Perhaps he'd moved on from alcohol. Where was he getting his supply? Maybe she should take him up on that drink just to find out. She hated an unsolved mystery.

Just like Darren and the medication. She had watched him that morning, but he had stayed around the other staff, mostly avoiding the patients and visitors. He looked frayed around the edges, as if he were barely held together by cobwebs. Was this a man capable of plotting murder?

He parked Carwyn's wheelchair next to the sofa where Amy was sitting, and wandered off to make his breakfast. The only other person around was Mordecai, who appeared to be passed out in the armchair. Now was her chance for an interrogation, to confirm Tony's story independently.

But she didn't get the chance.

"She killed a child, she did." Carwyn said it quietly, slyly, like he knew he was sharing something illicit. "That's why they came for her. They'll come for all of us in the end."

"'All of us'?" she echoed.

Tony hadn't got round to sharing the list of criminals he'd found in the facility, but Carwyn was a likely candidate - him or Ron, or both.

"I knew it was a sin, but I couldn't help myself, see. All those lovely girls. Pretty girls."

Amy flinched away from him, but he just laughed, that terrible creaking sound.

"Oh, not you. Who'd want a scrawny thing like you? No, plump girls, raw girls - the ones unplucked. No harm in it, not really."

"When was this?" she asked, unable to look at him and equally unable to look away.

"Oh, a long time ago. When I still had my legs. Every girl likes a uniform, eh? But some only give over in the dark."

She'd heard enough, too much. She stood abruptly, trying to flee.

He grabbed for her shirt, his gnarled hand grazing her buttock. "Nothing there at all. Pity."

"Carwyn!"

A nurse headed towards them. It was Sandy, the one who had calmed Amy down after Ffion had been taken away to hospital. Amy hadn't seen her since it had happened, but she was glad to see her now.

"He touched me," Amy said. "He tried to…"

"He didn't mean anything by it," she said hastily. "Why don't you take a walk in the garden?"

Amy stared at her, suddenly riled. "You need to stop hiding the truth. You know what he is. You know what I am. Why are we pretending?"

Sandy blanched. "I don't know what you mean, love."

"He's a paedophile!"

The word echoed across the room. But Sandy's look of horror wasn't for her shout, but directed towards Carwyn. She'd had no idea at all. Was Dr Al-Dosari keeping everyone in the dark - and why?

"I'm not here for an internet addiction or whatever. He's lying to you - they're all lying to you!"

Mordecai had jerked awake at her shouting and was watching, transfixed. Tony had come in from the garden to watch the show.

"I think you need a little something to calm down," Sandy said.

Amy took a breath, lowered her voice. The last thing she needed was to appear hysterical. "I am here because I committed a crime."

She saw Sandy's face resume some composure. She had filed Amy under the psychotic umbrella - this, she knew how to deal with.

"I am not delusional," Amy protested. "Ask Dr Al-Dosari, ask Detective Bryn Hesketh - ask Frieda Haas."

"You're upsetting everyone, dear. Come with me to the clinical room - "

"No! Why won't you listen to me?"

Sandy pressed something at her hip and alarms started blaring.

Amy folded her arms. "Are you going to force medication on me for telling the truth?"

She had unnerved the nurse, she could tell. She had to stay rational, logical. They expected her to be erratic, to fire off wild accusations. She had to hold her nerve.

Other staff arrived from around the ward to form a gang by the nursing office. Amy noted Darren's presence. She could continue to creep around, or she could light a fire and see what rats fled the smoke.

"You can't see what's right under your noses. This place is full of thieves and dealers and fuck-ups!"

"What is going on here?"

Dr Al-Dosari was standing in the doorway to the ward, with Bryn at his side.

"You took your time," she said, accusingly.

"Amy is having a little crisis," Sandy said. "We'll take care of it."

Amy looked straight at Dr Al-Dosari, the first time she had ever done so. His eyes were pale green, lighter than hers - she hadn't expected that.

"I told them I was a criminal and now they think I'm delusional. What have you said to them?"

The doctor hesitated. For one terrible moment, Amy thought he would lie, deny the truth, consign her to antipsychotics and locked doors for the rest of her life.

"I am Detective Bryn Hesketh - I need to interview Amy about the ongoing investigation. That is why I'm here, Doctor?"

Her saviour in a rumpled suit. Bryn had prevented the man from committing himself to a lie, but it seemed he couldn't bring himself to tell the truth either.

"Very well. We will talk about this afterwards, Amy."

He started to walk away, but Amy shouted after him. "I want to see the detective in my room."

"You know visitors are not allowed in the bedrooms."

"I've never had a visitor," she bit back. "Bryn is a police officer - I have evidence I need to show him."

The psychiatrist looked rattled, and Amy realised she was bringing the whole establishment to its knees with only a few words. She felt powerful again, like she'd been with keys beneath her fingers and AEON to do her bidding.

"Sandy, escort her please."

That was the last thing either of them wanted, but Amy needed to show Bryn now. She took off at speed, Bryn keeping close behind her, despite Sandy's mute presence between them. Amy threw open her door - and immediately knew something was wrong.

"Someone's been here."

The blanket and sheet were twisted on the floor, her pillows falling off the bed. She ran to the plant pot to find her treasures, but they were gone, the letter and her phone. Shit. How could she have been so stupid? She should have carried them, protected them.

"They're gone," she said. "Someone has stolen the letter. The killer is here."

Chapter 30: You Can Still Be Free

After Bryn had calmed her down, he'd taken a statement from Amy, detailing as much as she could remember about the letter. Newport was a particularly nondescript postmark - close enough to Cardiff to be local, but also widening the field of suspects. He made particular note of the poor spelling and the nature of the threats.

"He knew her. The man who wrote the letter knew her." She sounded certain, convinced.

Bryn was pleased to see her with a little more colour in her cheeks - she had looked like a phantom when he'd last seen her. The investigation had lifted her out of whatever hole she'd fallen into, helped her claw her way out. Though he wished she hadn't shouted about her supposed crimes for everyone to hear - they had yet to learn the killer's motive. Perhaps he had targeted Ffion Ellis because she'd broken the law. There were too many unknowns.

"What else is missing?"

Amy shot a sidelong glance at Sandy, who was resolutely sitting in on their interview. "Nothing important," she said.

Which meant she wasn't supposed to have it, probably however Jason had been communicating with her. A mobile phone? He was glad, in a way, that it was gone, because it kept Frieda at bay. On the other hand, it gave the thief access to whatever information Amy had given her partner - and what Jason had sent to her.

While Bryn was sceptical that the killer was in the hospital, this did point to him having an accomplice on the inside. Amy's bedroom had been unlocked all morning - anyone currently in the hospital could've wandered in and taken the letter. Amy had been outside her room for hours and she couldn't vouch for a single person's whereabouts the entire time. However, Bryn suspected Dr Al-Dosari wouldn't allow him to interview anyone about the theft, just as he was still reluctant to let him ask witnesses about the murder.

"I need a cigarette," she said, suddenly. "Will you join me?"

Bryn stared at her. Amy didn't smoke - in fact, she hated it. She'd worked very hard to get Jason to quit, poor lad, though Bryn was sure he hadn't managed it. Still, he went along with it, walking with her down the corridor and out of Sandy's earshot.

"I need you to send a message to J," she said, a cool murmur with her lips barely moving.

He mumbled his assent, already regretting his agreement as it left his lips.

"Tell him I'm fine and not to…not to send any messages."

Well, that was harmless and would hopefully keep him out of more mischief.

"Tell him that C has searching abilities, the other C. He'll know what I mean."

Unfortunately, so did Bryn. "Take care with her."

"It wasn't me," she said sharply, immediately. "I would rather she stayed out of it. I would rather they all did. I don't get a say."

Amy had told Jason to run away for his own safety and to escape prison, probably even going so far as to forge him a new identity, and he had disobeyed her. Bryn could see how she would run into problems getting him to stop investigating this mess.

"I'll tell him to be careful. All of them."

"Have you seen Owain?" she asked.

Why was everyone asking him about Owain? "I'm not his keeper," he said, rough, too rough.

She picked up on it immediately. "You can't leave him alone, Bryn. He hasn't recovered, from the fire…when he was… Cerys needs to look after him. So do you."

They were in the living area again now, and Amy fell silent, leading him through the dining room and into the garden, with barely a hesitation as she crossed the threshold.

Once outside, Amy made a beeline for a man Bryn vaguely recognised as Tony Rogers, the only witness he'd been allowed to interview and who'd been singularly unhelpful. Saw nothing, heard nothing.

He handed Amy a cigarette, and she looked between him and Bryn.

"You're going to tell him everything you told me."

Tony's face fell, but Amy was obstinate and the worst kind of dictator.

"What about our deal?" he said.

"You can have your interview, but your little show is over."

Tony scowled at her, but relented. "I'm a journalist - newspaper, doesn't matter which. I was sent here to look at criminals being treated private using taxpayers' money. I found Ffion Ellis, and then I found Amy."

"He also found Carwyn, but I don't think he's important," Amy added.

"You have been busy, Miss Lane," Tony said, with a hint of admiration. "And all without a single computer."

"You have research," Bryn asked, greedy for information.

Tony nodded curtly. "A lot of research. And I've been watching this place. Something is rotten here. Amy has it right - the staff don't really know what's going on with their patients or why they're here. The doctor, however, he knows everything. I don't trust a man who keeps secrets."

Neither do I. Bryn removed his notebook from his pocket. "How did you find out what was going on?"

"Detective, that is enough." Dr Al-Dosari was hurrying across the garden towards them, alarm in his features. He was flanked by a bruiser of a man, who looked like he was more used to breaking people than nursing them back to health.

Bryn reluctantly replaced his notebook. "We will finish this later," he told Tony.

"You cannot harass my patients like this. I will speak to your supervisor."

Bryn rounded on him. "It may have escaped your notice, doctor, but this is a murder investigation. This man has information and I'm not jumping through any more of your hoops to get it."

The doctor looked taken aback, but held his ground. "Then you will have to return with a court order. This man is my patient and while he is within my walls, I will not allow him to be interrogated."

"You know what, Doctor? I think I'm all better now. Where do I sign to get out of here?" Tony mimicked signing his name in mid-air.

"Consider your treatment plan, Tony. All the work we've done together..."

Tony looked at Amy. "I got what I came for. Let's get this over with, shall we?"

He pushed past the dumbfounded psychiatrist and headed back into the unit.

"You will leave now." Dr Al-Dosari was trembling with rage.

Bryn held up his hands and walked back towards the building, turning to face Amy for a bare moment. "Stay out of trouble."

The smile she gave him was brave, but frightened. He knew he was leaving her alone with someone who might want to do her harm, who knew she was closing in on clues related to the investigation. Who was surely aware that the police had captured his camera and everything on it. If it had been within Bryn's power, he would've taken her away there and then, but it was all out of his control.

"Stay out of trouble," he repeated, and she waved her hand as he abandoned her in that place.

Chapter 31: Song for the Lovers

Cerys couldn't face going to college, not after that drama, so they went to Penarth for ice cream. Jason looked up at the cliff top, even though he couldn't see the building, and Cerys stared mindlessly at her phone.

He didn't have the right words for Cerys, the words of comfort she needed. He was a blunt, awkward instrument when it came to feelings, to lovers and their betrayals. He'd never been in anything serious, never wanted that for himself, so he couldn't tell others how to go about loving. He'd hooked up with girls in his youth, but he'd always come back to the gang, to his friends. Since prison, he'd looked for women with easy smiles who didn't want more than a night or two of fun. It was simpler that way.

Then there was Amy, who confused and tormented him. She was his friend and he cared for her, more than cared for her if he was honest with himself - and he was trying to be honest more and more these days. She had rescued him from a life of pointless cleaning, and he had brought her back from the brink of something unnameable - until she had been locked up and he'd been exiled, and there was nothing either of them could do about it.

But when she was free, when Frieda was finally out of their lives, what then? What could he possibly do with this confused mess in his chest that wouldn't let him alone?

They started for home before the chill sunk into their bones, Jason's leg aching and seizing with every step. He shadowed Cerys as she approached the kitchen door and, stepping through it, their mam took one look at her and enveloped her in her arms.

Jason looked away, not wanting to see his sister cry, and mumbled something about a walk. Instead, he sat outside on the pavement, carefully stretching out his leg and looking at everything and nothing on the deserted street.

If he'd ignored Frieda in the first place, shut her down, maybe none of this would have happened. She would've found nothing out about Amy and quietly disappeared. She wouldn't have manipulated Owain, used him, and he would've stayed with Cerys, maybe even made her happy. Jason would be living at home with Amy, making her tea and solving crimes and finding out what the fuck was going on between them.

A text came through and he took a moment before he read it, holding on to his dream for a few seconds longer.

Amy fine. New leads. She says take care and no messages. What source plates? Check online date 01/11/14.

Bryn was still relying on him, not knowing how he'd almost fucked up the number plates and needed to be rescued by his baby sister. Amy was relying on him too, to still be her man about town, finding out the things she couldn't. He wouldn't let them down, not again.

He would need to get in touch with Corelia, but he didn't want to disturb Cerys and Gwen in the kitchen, no doubt doing whatever girls do when someone's heart is breaking. It probably involved tea.

Instead, he emailed Amy's secure email address - the one he had previously used for bad smartphone photos and notes from crime scenes. If Corelia had access to Amy's servers, then she might be able to read her email too.

After two minutes, his phone started ringing. *Good work, Carr.*

"Who are you?" she demanded, her voice fierce.

"Jason, Amy's assistant. Cerys' brother."

"Oh. What do you want?"

"I thought a phone call would be better for - "

"No bugs, yeah. But hurry up - I have the gym in five minutes."

Because she was a sick girl in the middle of rehab for a severe spinal injury. Jason's enthusiasm for this call immediately sunk.

"Actually, don't worry. I'll - "

"Don't pity me. Just get on with it. I have a busy day."

"The number plate website. I need the name and address of the guy who purchased on 1st November."

"One sec…he used a credit card to pay, but the site doesn't ask for more than a username. His is 'shaman69'."

"Can you trace the card?"

"I think Amy has a thing for that. I'll also search for that handle and similar - email addresses, forums, et cetera. I'll email after PT."

She disconnected without waiting for his reply. He made a note on his clunky phone - *shaman69, credit card*. He hoped the guy was stupid enough to use his own card, a trail that would lead them right to him. Even without that, it was more than enough to go on.

The kitchen door abruptly opened. Jason twisted, looking at Cerys standing in the doorway, holding her phone out towards him.

"It's Catriona Aitken," she said. "She wants to talk to us."

Jason struggled to get to his feet and Cerys rushed down to meet him, putting the phone on speaker in the middle of the pavement.

"He's here," she said.

"We retrieved a camera from the site of the van dump," Catriona said, getting straight to the point. "It's slow going with just my laptop, but we've got a lot of footage that's concerning to us."

"Like what?" Jason said, his heart seizing in his chest.

"You, Jason. By a large plastic wall, talking to a man on the other side."

"That's the hospital," Jason said, looking at Cerys in panic. "We have to warn Amy."

"Bryn's on it," Catriona interrupted. "But you need to lie low. Someone is watching you."

"Someone is watching Amy," Jason said. "I can't just - "

"Thank you," Cerys said, and hung up. "Inside. Now."

Jason stomped up the path and into the kitchen, regretting his tantrum as his leg throbbed its protests. "What then? We just sit here?"

"The police will inform the hospital to look out for strangers. We're strangers, aren't we? This is the quickest way to get yourself arrested."

"We need to do something!"

"You need to stop and think! Stop running into fucking walls!"

"I am not leaving her there unprotected."

"You can't protect her! She's inside a locked box and you're out here, with no weapon and a busted leg."

Jason's mind leapt on the idea of a weapon, but Cerys' stormy eyes quickly derailed that train of thought.

"I can't just stay here," he said, though he'd said it about ten times now and no one was listening.

"You can and you will. When we have more information, we can move. But not before."

Jason nodded sulkily, but his mind was elsewhere. He wouldn't be kept away from Amy, not if she was in danger - not again. Damn Cerys and her caution. He wasn't going to be sidelined, not now.

First he needed to know what he was up against. He picked up his phone, and sent another email to Corelia.

I need to hack into a laptop.

Chapter 32: The Devil's Due

After her outburst that morning, Amy knew that all eyes were on her.

She felt the urge to run and hide, but she forced herself to stay in the armchair, feigning disinterest in her surroundings, turning the pages of a book at random. They were all waiting for her to erupt, to lose it. She would not give them the satisfaction.

The weather had brightened and the occupational therapist herded patients towards the garden, declaring it a perfect day for tending the plants. Everyone was drawn towards the sunlight, except for Emma, who had kept to her room all day. With one last suspicious glance in Amy's direction, even Sandy followed them out into the soft light of an autumn afternoon.

The perfect opportunity to hunt down the missing letter.

She couldn't rely on other people for this. If Bryn relayed her message and Jason understood it and Corelia acted on it - but that was far too many "if"s to hope that they would track down her missing phone. She should've risked a more explicit message to Bryn, but she had been able to sense the disapproval that even those words had stirred up.

Amy closed the book and threw it on the coffee table. Where to begin? Patient bedrooms were the obvious first port of call - if they had been left open. She'd have to think about the staff areas later -

The armchair was seized and turned around with brute strength. Amy yelped and tried to jump off, but her exit was blocked by Darren, arms stretched out to grip both arms of the chair.

"What do you know?" he hissed.

Her heart was pounding in her chest, but Amy forced herself to count to ten in her head. She would not break in front of him. She would not even flinch.

"Answer me!"

"I saw you," she said, a tremulous note in her voice despite her best efforts. "I saw you stealing from the clinic room."

He scowled at her. "You saw nothing. Nothing that anyone would believe."

"How many drugs did you steal exactly? Was it enough to kill an old woman?"

She had shocked him, she could tell. His eyes went from grim to startled in an instant, widening to reveal his bloodshot eyeballs in all their glory.

"You think I killed the Ellis woman?"

"I think you had the means to do it."

Yet, the more she looked at his reaction, the less convinced she was that he was the killer. She seemed to have inherited Jason's habit of reckless, impulsive and dangerous decisions, to even take that chance.

"Listen, I am no killer. I just have..." He seemed to remember himself then, and drew away from her, trying to look intimating. "I don't have to tell you anything."

"No, you don't," she agreed. "I'll tell my police friends that you had nothing to do with the murder. They won't be interested in your theft of prescription drugs."

He grimaced. "You are fucking mental."

Amy smiled. "Is that what you say to all the patients? Is that what you say to Mordecai when he comes for his fix?"

Darren shook his head. "You're talking bollocks. I don't deal. I don't share."

I don't share. Amy remembered the hoard of tablets Darren had placed into his pocket. All that was for him. No wonder he looked wrecked.

Amy glanced quickly at the doors leading into the dining room and garden. They didn't have much time before it started raining or someone got bored of flowers. She had to act quickly if she wanted to exploit this.

"I want to make a deal. I won't tell anyone about your little problem, and you'll leave me alone in the nursing office for five minutes."

"I can't do that," he said immediately. "There's confidential info - "

"You weren't bothered about ethics when you were stealing drugs," she said, impatient now. "I won't take anything. I just need five minutes."

He nodded, resigned, and strode quickly towards the nursing office. She leapt to her feet, glad that her trembling legs could carry her after that confrontation. With only five minutes, she wouldn't have time to conduct a thorough search for the letter - but there was something more valuable she could do.

Using his access card, he let her in and then reluctantly turned his back to watch for anyone who might discover them. Amy made a beeline for the nearest computer, which was active and logged on with Sandy's account.

She brought up a new browser window and navigated to her gateway website. The network probably had antivirus and firewall protection to prevent her doing exactly what she needed to do, but since when had that stopped her?

Once inside her Cave of Wonders, she ran a programme that mimicked an admin-approved software update and effectively disabled the network security. She then ran the installation of her favourite infiltration tool, a discreet programme that allowed remote administrator access and the ability to siphon off feeds of information. Like security camera footage.

Finally, she sent a notification to Corelia about her latest conquest, and checked the office clock. Four minutes down. She was disappointed - that was a two-minute-thirty task, at most.

Restoring the network security to its former state of neglect, she crudely covered her tracks and returned the computer to its resting state. If someone checked Sandy's account history, they would see exactly what she had done - but, by then, it would be too late. She would have all the evidence she needed of the thief and murderer.

Darren watched her retreat. "What did you do?"

"That wasn't part of our agreement," she retorted.

He closed the door behind her. "How do I know you won't betray me?"

She forced herself to look him in the eye. "You don't know, but you don't have a choice."

"Amy?"

She looked up, to see Dr Al-Dosari watching them from just outside the conference room. How much had he seen?

"A word, if you please."

He appeared diminished, flustered in his expensive suit - she had rattled him with her accusations, and Bryn and Tony had riled him further. Was he liable to slip up in this state? She decided to play it cool, letting him take the lead, as she joined him in the conference room.

"The police are worried about you," he said, nervous. "They think that someone may be…watching you."

The words evaporated her calm in an instant. "How do they know?"

"They have found video footage at a crime scene. They have asked that you stay indoors and away from the windows."

As if a sniper might shoot her. Maybe her years of paranoia hadn't actually been exaggerated. You weren't paranoid if they were really out to get you.

"Why me?" she asked.

He looked uncomfortable. "Perhaps because you have been looking at this murder. Perhaps because of who you are…what you have done."

Now was her chance. "Why didn't you tell the nurses the truth about me? They don't know about Carwyn either."

The psychiatrist sighed and rubbed at his forehead. "A few years ago, when Ffion first came here, they found out what had happened to her - with the bus, you know. They treated her like a leper, an outcast. She never recovered from their whispers and their looks. Those nurses are gone now, but the threat remains. I cannot have my clients mistreated because of what they have done in the past."

Amy swallowed against the lump in her throat, feeling her cheeks burn with shame. She had outed Carwyn to the staff. Would they see him differently now? Or did the doctor not even know his own nurses? Darren was evidence that he couldn't know the whole truth about them.

"What happens now?"

"I will move him to another facility. And you - we will ask the NCA about you. Despite fighting against my treatment, you seem stronger. The chase drives you, hmm?"

Amy shrugged, non-committal. She would not give away details of her investigation, reveal how much progress she had made. She would soon have all the information she needed.

He regarded her, coolly examining her with only his gaze, weighing up. "I thought you were too unwell for police, but perhaps I was mistaken. I will allow them to see you."

She had already seen Bryn. He didn't mean Bryn. "Frieda."

Dr Al-Dosari looked surprised. "You know Agent Haas?"

"She ruined my life. I know her."

His smile had a patronising air. "Agent Haas isn't responsible for you being here."

"She used my assistant to hunt me down. If anyone's responsible, it's her." How she loathed that woman. Her manipulation, her creeping flirtation with Jason, that one night in Bangor…

"Your assistant?" The psychiatrist frowned, as if rummaging through his mental notebook. "You haven't mentioned him before."

Nice try. "I don't trust you. You brought my…you brought *them* here."

He knew immediately what she meant, a hint of a knowing smile on his lips. "Your family are an important part of your recovery."

"My 'family' haven't been part of my life for many years. There's a reason for that." Talking about them made her feel flushed, agitated. She hated them, and the power they still held over her. She saw in his face that he had fallen under their spell. The well-spoken, fashionably dressed couple in their middle years would always trump their quiet, skinny daughter who was a little prone to panic.

"Agent Haas is visiting me, for an update on your condition. She may interview you, I think - if someone sits with you?"

"No, I'll see her alone," she said, firm on that point. Frieda needed to use all the weapons in her arsenal and for that she required an absence of witnesses. Amy wanted her to attack her - she needed her to show her hand, let her know what she was fighting against. What exactly Jason had given up for her.

Dr Al-Dosari stood, opening the door to the room and calling to Darren. "Is Miss Haas here?"

Back to the lies he was spinning for the staff - no hint of police visiting patients unescorted, to make their threats behind closed doors. No doubt that would be bad for business, bad for staff morale.

Yet, as Frieda walked in, no one could mistake her for anything other than the law. She strutted like the sheriff and she might as well be wearing a shiny star on her chest. She looked at Amy with a flash of glee, a look that was quickly replaced with disappointment - had she hoped she would crumble in this place? Amy was glad she'd made an effort for Bryn this morning.

Dr Al-Dosari left them without a word, and Frieda circled the room for a moment, as if scoping out a vantage point for an ambush. Eventually, she sat in the chair vacated by the psychiatrist, crossing her long, slender legs.

"Amy."

"Frieda."

Amy resisted the urge to look away, to fiddle with her hoodie sleeve. She thought of how Jason carried himself, how he spoke, and tried to set her shoulders like he did. With Dr Al-Dosari, her anger had been close to the surface, emboldening her, but with Frieda, she knew there were consequences. She had to tread carefully, and yet never be trodden on.

"I trust Jason has been in touch."

"I haven't heard from him since you arrested me."

Frieda looked scornful, almost playful in her smile. "I don't believe that."

Amy gave her a shrug in reply. She wouldn't incriminate Jason, not for anything.

"I understand you're still playing detective."

Playing detective. The words were designed to provoke, to needle her. Amy had to be on her guard for these cheap shots, before Frieda tried the big guns.

"If you mean that I happen to be living in a crime scene, then yes."

"How are you, Amy?" Frieda sat back in her chair, too casual. Her style of interrogation was different from Dr Al-Dosari's - he was the impartial professional, whereas Frieda pretended she was your friend, a confidante. Amy had never been that stupid.

"I'm alive," she said.

Frieda laughed. "So pessimistic - but then I guess that is your problem, isn't it?" She removed a letter from her jacket and made a show of unfolding it. "Moderate depressive episode. Generalised anxiety. Mixed personality disorder. What a fun place your brain must be."

Confirming Amy's opinion that Dr Al-Dosari was not to be trusted.

"How are your dear parents? It was so good to meet with them.

Your father is such a gentleman - and your "Mummy", so glamourous."

Amy held her face frozen, saying nothing, doing nothing. She was used to these old wounds paining her, though they were freshly reopened and festering.

"Your sister Elizabeth was most helpful."

"Lizzie would never speak to you."

Frieda leaned forward - her bait had been bitten. "She did. I have three or four pages of detailed statement from her, all about your lives together and your poor dear Gran. Such a tragedy. Yet she's doing so well for herself."

Amy finally looked away, unwilling for Frieda to see the tears in her eyes. Of course she had told. She was implicated in Amy's crime, after all - she would speak to save herself. Could Amy really begrudge her that?

Yes. I did everything for her. I gave us freedom - and then I let her go.

"Of course, you didn't have quite the same opportunities as Elizabeth. University, a vocation, travelling the world. A life of petty crime is hardly the same, is it?"

Amy sensed something changing in the room, a turning of the tide. Frieda was almost sympathetic - what was this new danger? She kept quiet, waited it out.

"I have no evidence of your talents - thanks to your assistant's work - but I've heard great things. Imagine if you used your powers for good. And not just as a policeman's pet."

Was Frieda hoping she'd acknowledge Jason's role in AEON's shutdown? Amy had given him the self-destruct code to her beloved computer, ensuring that they weren't incriminated by her own files. If Frieda could implicate him in the destruction of evidence, she would have more than enough to imprison him again.

"Imagine if you could catch criminals with the full backing of the law and every toy you've ever dreamed of owning right at your fingertips."

Something bizarre was going on here, but Amy couldn't quite fathom it out. She decided to go on the offensive. "What do you want, Frieda?"

"It's very simple, Amy. I want you to work for me."

Chapter 33: We All Fall Down

When Corelia failed to answer her email or her phone, Jason took matters into his own hands.

Ignoring Cerys' protests, he limped into town and then took a bus up to the Heath Hospital, just in time for visiting. He wasn't convinced the ward would let him in, but he was itching for activity - anything to avoid sitting at home with his sister for one minute more.

The key to this new threat was the video found at the van dump. Jason knew Owain and Catriona wouldn't just hand it over - his only way in was through Corelia. Amy had found her way into the police computers. Could Corelia access one lone police laptop? If he could see the footage, he could work out where the bloke had been hiding when he'd filmed them.

Then he could hunt him down. Jason was predator, not prey, and he was tired of hiding in the shadows.

As he approached the ward, halfway through visiting hours, his steps slowed. How was he going to blag his way to a teenage girl's bedside without getting flagged as a pervert? She had been all over the news - they must've had weirdos chancing their luck before now.

Still, he had come this far. He approached the nurses' station confidently, though his mind was comparing this to visits over ten years before, watching his father slowly fade away.

"I'm here to see - "

"Jason!"

He turned, surprised to hear his name. He recognised the girl because he'd seen her through a lens - Corelia's friend or girlfriend or whatever. H-something?

"We weren't expecting you. Corelia's just in her room - I'm going on a coffee run. You want anything?"

He shook his head and she led him round the corner to Corelia's room, deflecting most of the nurses' suspicion with her cheery attitude and her status as a familiar face. Jason knew next to nothing about Heddwen - yes, that was her name - apart from that she came with Corelia. As he was sure the police thought the same of him and Amy, he felt she might be a kindred spirit.

"Jason's here. I'm off for coffee now."

"Mm."

Heddwen smiled and left, as Jason took in the entirety of the little room with one look. The bed was far more complicated that any he'd seen before, with metal bars suspended above it. The chair Corelia sat in wasn't hospital standard, holding her in an artificially upright position that no teenager would adopt spontaneously. Her laptop rested on the kind of table that could be swung over her bed, but she'd adjusted the height to that of a normal desk.

After a minute of typing, she looked up - and scowled. "What are you doing here?"

"You didn't call back," he said.

She didn't look guilty or perturbed - just slightly harassed. "I do have other things to think about."

Her wheelchair was backed into the corner, a sketchbook resting on the handle and a multi-coloured cardigan over the back. Heddwen's seat of choice when visiting, it seemed. It also served to remind him of how badly he was intruding.

"Don't just stand here. The little camera's been destroyed, by the way. I'm guessing your friend found it."

It had been a long shot anyway. Jason wasn't even sure what he would've done with a record of Frieda's movements once he had them. "I'm not here for that."

"You want access to a laptop? I'm not sure I'm up to that."

Jason frowned, trying to think of a way round it. If the police servers were down, how would Catriona share evidence with the rest of the team?

"What about email?"

"It depends if Amy already has a way in. She sent me a link to a whole new computer system today."

Jason stared at her. "What computer system?"

"It looks like a hospital to me. I can get CCTV footage for the dining room, the lounge, even the garden."

"That's bloody brilliant," he said.

Jason stepped closer, leaning against the wall to get a good view over her shoulder. She clicked on a tab that brought up a desktop view that looked exactly like Amy's primary screen on AEON, her now-deceased computer.

"You recognise the interface? Good. It means I'm doing something right. Everything beyond this screen is a fucking Wonderland."

"Amy built this over years. It can only make sense to her."

Corelia looked at him curiously. "She let you all the way in? Huh."

Jason could feel her jealousy, but chose to ignore it. She was a young girl with a case of hero worship. Jason was Amy's friend, but he saw her flaws, frequently up close and personal. He missed them.

Corelia was silent for a minute or two, fingers skittering across the keys, navigating a series of folders and databases. "I've got an email account for a Bryn Hesketh - he's one of the detectives, isn't he?"

"He's also Catriona's boss."

She scrolled down the page, before clicking on an email from Owain Jenkins. "Link to a secure server. It looks like a temporary file repository of some kind."

Probably thanks to his friends at the NCA, Jason thought darkly. "Anything good?"

"Patience, virtue, some shit like that."

Corelia was eagerly scanning her new find, caught up in the same enthusiasm Jason had seen on Amy's face when the case had a breakthrough.

She opened a folder with several segments of video saved. "Someone's divided them by episode. It looks like read-only access, so I can't copy them out. Not sure if it's the police or Amy preventing me."

That sounded like Amy - a good dose of paranoia, even with her allies. It's how she had avoided being caught for so long. Even within the hacker community, Jason didn't think anyone knew anything personal about her.

"Did you hear from the hackers again?" he asked.

"No. I didn't reply - I can't get her voice down - and they didn't send further intel. Better to lose one thread then lose the link entirely. If they also got access to the email system, they could be looking at the same evidence we are."

She pressed play on the first video. It showed the hospital in Penarth, from a position across the car park. The footage was blurred, as

175

if it had been shot from far away or in dim light. Jason remembered his lessons well.

Someone was standing at the clear fence wearing a maintenance uniform - probably the man Jason had intercepted in the car park. On the other side, Jason recognised the man he had conversed with that day, standing slightly to one side, smoking. The maintenance guy slid something carefully through the hole, a large package, under the bush. When was this? Had there been a further drop since Jason visited?

"Can we see the date on this?"

Corelia brought up some details. "Originally shot…that's weird."

"October 16th. That's two weeks before Ffion's death."

"He's scouting out the scene of the crime. But what's that guy got to do with the dead lady?"

"I don't know." Why was the killer filming him? Did he not trust his mole? Was he wary of this other guy visiting him, or were they all in this together? Maybe he was gathering blackmail material so that he could help him later.

Blackmail. Someone had been sending Ffion threatening letters - was that part of the killer's MO? Blackmail and threats? It was one more thing linking that letter and the killer. Jason hoped forensics could find something useful in it, worth exposing his link to Amy.

Heddwen crept through the door, shoving the coffee holder on the table and slopping the coffee through the lids. "There's a man at the desk. He's looking for Jason."

"Jason?" Corelia asked, incredulous.

"He described him to the nurses, said he was a friend and he wanted to tell him where he'd parked. But he didn't know who he was seeing."

"You need to go," Corelia said, suddenly scared.

Jason was torn. He wanted to confront this guy, hunt him down - at least see his weasel face. But he had two frightened girls with him, one unable to run, and he had landed them in danger, just by being here. He kept fucking up and getting people in trouble, people he cared about. No more.

"We need to go," he said, quietly, urgently. "Can you get into that chair by yourself?"

"We can do it," Heddwen said, definite despite the look of panic on Corelia's face.

Jason closed the laptop and slipped it into the wheelchair's back pocket, handing Corelia a jumper because it was too bitter to take a girl out in a T-shirt. Especially one recovering from major surgery. Shit, was this a good idea? She'd probably be fine if he left her - but what if she wasn't?

"We're ready," Heddwen said.

The corridor was clear, but the nurses' station was just around the corner. The main lifts were out on the corridor and, while Jason could see something that looked like a service lift straight ahead, they would have to walk right by the nurses' station.

"There are stairs behind us," Heddwen whispered.

Jason looked down at Corelia. He was a strong guy, but he couldn't imagine lifting the whole chair with the girl in it. But Heddwen was already moving, pushing her towards the hidden stairwell.

Holding the door, Jason ensured they weren't being followed before closing the door behind them. Flights of stairs cascaded down for five floors. "Now what?"

"The physio said we tip the chair all the way back and bump her down. I can brace the front if you can pull her back."

"Why aren't we facing this bastard?" Corelia asked, anger overtaking fear.

"Because he's killed someone and put my friend in the hospital," Jason said. "I'm not taking any chances."

With Heddwen bracing the front of the chair, Jason carefully levered Corelia back until she was gazing at the ceiling and only the back wheels touched the floor. Slowly, too slowly, he eased her down the first step. After the first few, they found a rhythm, but it was still taking too long. Jason hoped the ward staff were calling security, stalling the guy, or sending him away. Would that stop him?

"This isn't exactly a speedy escape," Corelia said, dry as a desiccated bone.

"Nearly there," Heddwen said, not a mote of strain in her voice.

The second flight of stairs was quicker, but still sluggish. Heddwen tried the door on the next floor down - and it opened into a building site.

"We need to chance it," Jason said, and pushed Corelia through the hanging plastic sheets and over trailing cables, around deconstructed panelling and towards the door - and the open, public corridor beyond.

He headed instead for the service lift inside the door. "We need to stay out of public spaces," he said.

"You've done this before," Heddwen said, a little in awe.

"He's been on the run for weeks, H - you were playing hero in Bristol, weren't you?"

Jason stopped outside the lift, staring at her as they waited. "How did you know that was me?"

"Amy planted a tracker in your jacket. I was looking over your recent location data - either you were the rapist or the Bristol Bat, and I figured it was the latter."

Jason felt a little uncomfortable at the idea he had been so obvious over the past weeks. What if the NCA had accessed Amy's servers? He would've been an obvious target for Frieda. Damn his love for that old battered jacket - and Amy's love of covert surveillance.

The service lift arrived and Jason manoeuvred Corelia inside, with Heddwen on his heels. He chose the first floor, unsure what they'd find at the end of the line and hoping they could talk their way out of wherever they ended up.

They emerged onto a bustling ward, where a sister instantly fixed them with a disapproving glare.

"We took the wrong lift, didn't we?" Heddwen said, with big innocent eyes.

The woman shook her head and smartly showed them off her ward, with a warning to never do it again. Jason was delighted at their escape, and Heddwen's deployment of doe eyes. It was one thing missing from his effective assistant's arsenal, though he knew he had plenty of charm to wield when needed.

"We'll head out the side entrance," Jason said. While chasing a serial killer around the Heath Hospital, Jason had become familiar with all the exits and entrances. At this time of the evening, the exit opposite the dental hospital would be the least busy and led straight out towards the busy A48 road. Once he had got Corelia away from the hospital, he could work out what to do next.

"Bryn isn't answering his phone," Corelia said. "Should I try Owain?"

"You got these numbers from Amy?" he asked, surprised.

"She has a list. Owain?"

He really didn't want to call Owain, for many reasons, not least Frieda Haas. Also, his sister would kill him. However, they needed someone with a car and connections to the law, and Owain was that.

"Call him," he said.

As they emerged into the dying light, his own phone started to ring in his pocket. They lingered in the shadows for a moment, as he pulled it from his tracked jacket - Amy. Why was she calling him so early?

"What's wrong?" he answered, breathless.

"Who are you?" The voice was screaming, an eldritch sound that possessed no gender, no soul.

"What? Amy - "

"She sent you! Why did she send you? I've done nothing wrong!"

The voice was sobbing now, and sounded more human, like a woman in distress rather than a creature in pain.

"I don't know you," he said, slowly and carefully.

"Then why are you hunting me? Are you watching me?"

"I'm not. Look, I need to speak to Amy - "

"No!"

Something smashed, loud and close to the phone. Jason started, dropping the little device to the ground, its guts spilled out on the concrete.

"He's coming, but he's not happy. What have you done to your phone?"

"I have to go," he said, and ran.

Chapter 34: One Step Closer

Amy heard the shouting, and the smashing of glass. Sounds of destruction from the room next door.

She hit the alarm and then she ran, towards the noise, towards whatever horror she might find. "Emma!"

The room was empty, the window shattered - a double-glazed window, destroyed - and myriad shards coated in fresh blood. Amy surveyed the carnage for a horrified moment, and then she followed Emma's path.

The glass ripped at her, scraping up her bare arms, her cheek, but she was through in a moment. Their rooms backed onto a scrubby garden, guarded by a pathetic hedgerow. She saw Emma fleeing over it, even as she heard shouts behind her.

She ran, as if the devil himself was on her heels. She had recognised the anguish, the desperation in those shouts. She had felt them before, knew them more than she wanted to. Emma wasn't safe, and she needed someone to stop her.

Amy squeezed through the hole in the hedge, into the open paddock beyond - and saw Emma. She was heading for the cliff top, the ludicrously unprotected edge, and Amy tore after her. No…no…no…

"EMMA!"

She turned, at the last moment, an inch or two away from the sea below. "St-stay away!"

Amy tried to catch her breath, a few metres away - too far, but could she move closer? "Come back, Emma. Please, come back."

"It was you. You killed Ffion!"

The words battered her, stealing her barely-caught breath. "No. I didn't."

"I brought that phone to you, and you used it to bring them. Who are they? I can hear him! I can see him! He spoke to me - and he said your name!"

She had never been so fluent, and she'd never been so devastating. "That phone is from my friend. He calls me to check I'm all right."

"What about this?"

She pulled the letter from her pocket, the envelope lost, one page streaming away as she bloodied the other with her grip. Ffion's letter.

"I found it," Amy said, feeling sick. "I found it in the nurses' office…"

"You wrote it!" she screamed, her voice raw. "You drove her to her death!"

"Emma, you're not well."

It was the wrong thing to say, and she knew it immediately. How many times had she riled at those words, the implication that her mind was broken and she was unfixable?

"I can see now," Emma said, tears streaming down her cheeks and mingling with her blood. "You pretended to be my friend! You were getting close so…so you could experiment on me! The doctors, the nurses - they're all working for you, aren't they? I should never have listened, to you, to anyone! But you won't leave me alone, will you? I need to go before you take over!"

She shifted back, her foot touching air as the cliff threatened to crumble beneath her bare skin. Amy took one stuttered step forward, and then halted, caught between two hells. Should she surge forward and make a grab for her, or would her very presence drive her over the edge?

She had to say something, do something. She couldn't let Emma fall. She wanted her to live, needed her to live - for both of them to live, and feel alive.

"I know them," she said, her voice sounding foreign to her, full of tears unshed. "The government, the police. They're after me too, but we can't let them win."

Emma hesitated. "You brought them here," but she sounded uncertain, wavering. "I've seen you, with the police."

"They came because Ffion died. They…They're the good cops. The letter…The letter's from Newport. I couldn't have sent it."

"What about your spy on the phone?" she said, accusing, angry. But if she was angry, she was still fighting - not fleeing towards oblivion.

"He's not a spy," Amy said. "He's my friend. He'd make a really terrible spy."

Emma seemed to choke, but then Amy realised it was a laugh, a small strangled acknowledgement of her poor joke.

"Come inside, Emma," she said, soft, quiet. "If you jump, they win. Come inside and fight with me."

For a terrible moment, Amy thought she was gone, her foot sliding backwards into the air. Then she sprang forward, released, and collided with Amy.

Amy caught her, sinking them both to the ground, gripping her with all her strength.

"You're such an idiot," she railed against her. "Why did you do that?"

"I'm sorry. Please, the spies…"

"We'll tell them all to fuck off," Amy said vehemently.

Abruptly, Emma was pulled away from her. Amy tried to hold on, scrabbling at her blood-stained pyjama top, but a nurse and a police officer were restraining her arms.

"Amy!" she cried, suddenly terrified again.

"It's all right," Amy said, though a nurse was grabbing at her too, trying to drag her up. "They want to help."

"They're hurting me! Don't let them hurt me!"

Miriam gripped at a cut on Amy's arm and she hissed in pain. "What is wrong with you?" she yelled at her. "We'll go inside with you - just let go!"

Her protests fell on the unhearing ears of scared people trying to regain control of a situation so far beyond their understanding as to be absurd. Amy was dragged through the field and onto the road, before being led around to the hospital's main entrance. In front, she could see Emma's shape in the gathering darkness, screaming incoherently.

"You're making her worse!" she shouted.

"You've done enough," came Miriam's retort.

"You've done nothing," Amy spat, furious and sick and helpless again.

She may have kept Emma from the edge tonight, but what could she do now? Against Dr Al-Dosari, the nurses, Emma's own family? What happened to a woman who had lost the best part of her mind in a few days? It was sudden, unexpected - and that would frighten them, as they were frightened now.

As they were brought into the lounge, the other residents watched

183

them, equally filled with fear. Even Ron was quiet, just watching anxiously. Emma was dragged into the clinical room, while Amy was held awkwardly in the lounge, Miriam unsure what to do with her.

"Let go," she said, tugging one of her arms free. "I can't run."

She reluctantly released her and Amy sat on the edge of the sofa, smearing blood on the upholstery as a murky red puddle formed on floor beneath her bare feet. The staff tried in vain to get the other patients to go to bed, to leave the scene, but they lingered like a movie audience waiting for the post-credits bonus scene.

It was Mordecai who came to sit beside her on the sofa, giving her space but also removing her leper status. Eventually, the others sat too, like a vigil for a woman not-dead but very like the banshee screaming in the clinical room.

Banging and shouting erupted in the space outside the ward, muted by the airlock entrance. One of the nurses hurried to find out what was causing the commotion - and returned with the terrified spectre of Jason Carr.

He swept across the room and lifted her off the sofa, into his arms. He enveloped her, holding her upright and bringing warmth and comfort and home with him.

Then he kissed her, sweet beneath the salt of her blood, and she wasn't drowning anymore. Everything would be perfect, if it wasn't so fucking terrible.

"I've got you," he said, and that was all she needed to know.

Chapter 35: The Space Between

Jason had never thought of A&E as a quiet place, a place of safety and security. But now that he was here with Amy, it felt like they were completely untouchable.

He held onto her hand as the doctor stitched up her arms and the nurse carefully bandaged them, after the last slivers of glass had been removed from her flesh. The cut bisecting her left cheek had to wait for the specialists, though it was glass-free. It was currently covered by a large square pad in brilliant white that made even Amy's pale skin appear to have colour.

Somewhere nearby, they could still hear Emma screaming, despite the medication she'd had in Penarth. They'd called a second ambulance for Amy in the end, because Emma needed two people just to keep her safe inside the first. Amy was meant to be with a staff member, but they had no one left to send, so Jason was her only escort - and, he suspected, the only one she would accept.

Amy had told him the story of the cliff top, and he had relayed everything he knew, up to and including the call he'd received from Emma. He felt guilty now for abandoning Corelia and Heddwen outside the hospital, but he'd been desperate. Desperate enough to "borrow" a bike from a teenager. Bryn was trying his best to smooth it over without charges, with Jason's solemn promise that he would reconcile and pay, but he couldn't bring himself to regret it.

She looked worse than he had imagined, though the blood and the bandages weren't helping his impression. She'd lost all the weight she'd gained after a year spent with him, perhaps more. Her nails were bitten to the quick and the circles beneath her eyes were dark purple smudges that contrasted with the muddy green-brown of her eyes under the hospital's harsh lights.

Jason rubbed at his lips, self-conscious. The state of her hadn't stopped him acting on impulse, seizing the moment. Why the fuck had he done that? Why had he tipped the balance on their friendship when her mind was fried and he was aching from her absence? She deserved better than that - more thought, consideration. More time.

He didn't want her to go back to Penarth, but it wasn't his call. He'd only got into the ward by wielding the word "carer" and probably looking like some kind of bruiser who wouldn't take no for an answer. The shaved head and tattoos tended to work in his favour when there was a locked door to be opened.

When Amy dozed off with painkillers thrumming through her bloodstream, Jason carefully untangled his fingers from hers and laid her hand gently on the blanket. He crept out of the cubicle, finding Bryn and Owain lurking together, pointedly not speaking to each other.

Technically, there was no more need for police involvement in this incident, but Jason had called Bryn because he was in need of someone, anyone, who could help make sense of this mess. Bryn had made it official police business only because Cliff House seemed particularly cursed and apparently this could be a "safeguarding investigation" or some other problem with negligence. Jason had thoughts of his own on that score.

He approached the silent pair and made a point of turning to Owain first. "How's Corelia?"

Owain blinked at him, shifting from foot to foot as if he was preparing to scarper. "Moved hospital - Heddwen's gone with her."

Jason nodded. It was the right step to take. "Did anyone get a good look at him?"

"Nurses say he was wearing a bike helmet - southern English accent, just under six foot, white. Heddwen's going to sketch what she saw anyway, see if we can work with just the eyes."

"Good work," Bryn said.

Owain looked at him, stunned to silence, like a wayward son who had ambled home only to find his father proud.

"How's Amy?" Bryn asked.

"Sleeping. Is she going back there?"

Bryn's face was thunder, barely contained. "We're waiting to hear from Frieda Haas."

Jason looked between Bryn and Owain, but the older cop wasn't conscious of his remark. It wasn't Jason's place to tell him either, and Owain's silently pleading eyes said it all.

186

"I think she wants to go back there." He hated the words, wanted to take them back immediately, but it was the truth. Amy had been firm on that point, and she was still the boss. Jason liked it that way, even if it meant she wanted to charge into danger in exactly the same idiotic way he did.

"Is she demented?" The words were practically shouted but, at a quelling look from the nearest nurse, Bryn reined in his temper. "Why on Earth would she go back to that cesspit?"

"She doesn't want to leave Emma alone."

"She can't take responsibility for the girl - she can barely look after herself!"

"Never stopped her before." Jason was acutely aware of how much Amy worried about him, how she prized his safety over her own. It was terrifying, but also comforting. He liked to think of himself as a free man, but it was dawning on him that he'd chosen to tie himself down and he almost liked it.

"It's not up to her anyway. It's for Frieda and the powers to decide. I'm sure they'll have concerns about the security of the place. I'll talk to her." Bryn moved quickly, sneaking into Amy's cubicle before a nurse could spot him.

Jason didn't look at Owain, didn't know what to say now he'd been left alone with him. Part of him itched to talk about the case, the CCTV footage, but that would reveal he'd obtained it illegally. Most of him wanted to rail against Owain for screwing over his sister. Not in A&E, though, surrounded by people fighting for their lives or moaning with pain.

In the end, he had only one thing to say. "Take care with her, yeah? She will ditch you in a heartbeat to get what she wants."

To Jason's surprise, Owain laughed, a tired sound devoid of mirth. "I know that. She thinks she's won me over to the cause." He scrubbed at his face with his hand. "If I have to appease her to keep her away, then that's what I'm going to do."

The manipulator was being manipulated. Jason wasn't sure if he should congratulate Owain, or commiserate with him that this was his only option. "You should tell Cerys."

"She's better off where she is, hating me. Frieda can't get to her then."

Jason wanted to argue his sister's corner, tell Owain that she would kick his arse if she knew he was trying to protect her like this. But he wanted the NCA investigator sniffing around his sister and his friends even less than Owain did. He wasn't even sure if this broken, distant creature was capable of loving her anymore.

"Good luck with it then," he said, finally.

Owain nodded, and they parted in the middle of A&E, Jason's instincts telling him they'd never meet like this again.

Chapter 36: A Matter of Trust

Despite the night she'd had and rousing her from sleep, Bryn found Amy's mind surprisingly ordered.

"The letter is gone?"

She nodded miserably. "It went over the cliff edge. Emma had the whole thing twisted up in her mind. She took the letter, and the phone. There's no accomplice in the hospital."

"Catriona is analysing Tony Rogers' research. He might've recorded something useful."

"I don't trust him."

Bryn privately agreed, but if she had to go back to the hospital, he didn't want to upset her further - even though he had to stir up her anxieties for her own good. "Did they tell you about the video?"

"Someone's watching me. Though Jason said the video started before Ffion's death. I wasn't going outside then. He must've been watching for something else."

Bryn decided not to ask how Jason knew this. "Watching for Ffion?"

Amy winced, the tape on her face blunting the motion. "I don't remember her very well, but I don't think she went outside much. Maybe he was working out how to get in."

"There's no evidence of illegal entry."

"It's not difficult to reach those rooms. Emma and I ran through a hedge and got to the cliff top. If her window was open, someone could've given her something."

Bryn was sceptical. They were entering the territory of blow darts through the window, and he wasn't sure the evidence was leading that way. Not that they had a lot of evidence to go on. "Have you seen anyone?"

Amy smiled, but it didn't reach her eyes. "I only saw Death."

Bryn chose not to go down that road. "You got anything else?"

"Frieda Haas offered me a job."

His face must have been a picture, confirmed by Amy laughing at him.

"That's not funny, Amy."

"It's true. She wants me to work for the National Crime Agency's Cyber Crime division. It takes a hacker to catch a hacker."

"In exchange for?"

"I avoid prison, and Jason and the rest duck the charges. I still have to give up all my money and my house."

And the rest. Frieda had threatened Amy with his job, and Owain's, and Cerys'. "Are you going to take it?"

"I need to get better," she said, staring at the white bandages on her arms. "I can't take care of Jason like this."

"What about you?"

She looked at him, with a small hint of a smile. "I couldn't hide away forever. It was always going to catch up with me. I hate Frieda - I really hate Frieda - but I can't let Jason go back to prison. It would kill me."

Bryn knew this wasn't hyperbole from Amy - she couldn't survive with Jason in prison, and Bryn wouldn't let that happen. He was helpless to support her, but Frieda, orchestrator of this misery, could offer her an out. Would she be happy working for Frieda? No, but she would be alive. Sometimes, that was enough.

He left her, inviting Jason back into the room, and moving through the hospital. He wanted to scold Corelia and Heddwen for getting involved in this mess, but they were holed up in Bristol, guarded by local police until Cardiff had got their act together.

Instead, his feet carried him to the Critical Care Unit, where he was admitted without question despite the late hour. The slightly harassed junior doctor met him halfway across the ward.

"She's still sleeping most of the time, but I think she'll soon be ready to step down to the neurology ward. She definitely can't be interviewed until after the psychologist has cleared it."

She was gone before Bryn could question her further. Had she been talking about the right patient? The last time he'd seen Indira, she'd been on a ventilator, awaiting surgery, her brain too swollen to allow her skull to continue containing it.

He approached her bedside with trepidation, anticipation. Her head was carefully bandaged, but she was breathing by herself, even though she was still surrounded by lines and monitors. She looked peaceful, undisturbed by pain or the weight of the investigation continuing without her. Bryn envied her rest, but not that it had come at such a price.

Dragging his eyes away from the steadily bleeping screen, he was surprised to see her looking at him, the corner of her mouth turned up. She mouthed "hi" and he smiled, ignoring the suspicious wetness of his eyes.

"Just seeing when you'll be reporting to the lab," he said.

He expected a smile, maybe even a laugh, but instead she frowned, wrinkling the bandage across her forehead. Shit, Hesketh, that was a stupid move - she'd been assaulted in the lab. Why the hell had he reminded her of that?

"Blood pressure," she said, the words sounding odd and slurred, completely unlike her.

Bryn looked back to the monitors, but nothing was alarming. "Your blood pressure is fine. Forget I said it - go back to sleep."

Now she was laughing at him, her eyes dancing with it. "Not mine. Hers. Blood pressure."

She was talking about the body, about Ffion Ellis. "What about her blood pressure?"

"The meds," she said, with that thick, laboured voice. "Check the meds."

"I hope you're not making poor Indy work, Detective." The nurse swept to her charge's side like an avenging angel. "She needs rest if she's going to keep her date with the speech and language therapist tomorrow."

But Bryn had enough, more than enough. It had slipped his mind, the outsourced "post-mortem" - gleaning what information they could from Indira's words and the doctors' notes. It had been less than a week and Rob had a full-time job to perform as well as helping Bryn out, but now Indira had told him exactly where to start.

Of course, her brain had been scrambled and her skull opened up, but Bryn trusted Indira Bharani in Critical Care over any other person in that lab.

"Thank you," he told her, touching her fingers lightly with his. "I will find him."

The grip on his fingers told him she trusted him too, that she knew he would do right by her and this case. That it wouldn't all be in vain. He wished he had her faith.

Chapter 37: None So Blind

It took only the morning light, a run of stitches to her cheek, and one phone call to bring them back to their temporary home, their prison. They travelled together, in silence, Emma's whole body dulled with sedation and Amy's anxiety spiking just looking at her.

Emma couldn't go back to her room, but as Tony had discharged himself, they had a little more space. Carwyn, however, refused to move, upturning his commode over the healthcare assistant's new shoes.

Dr Al-Dosari reluctantly opened the female corridor again, returning Amy and Emma to their old rooms. Ffion's room was still cordoned off by yellow police tape, and Amy's heart leapt with the opportunity. Maybe she could find something the police had missed?

First she had to endure Lois' fussing. Emma, by contrast, received a degree of caution - they had never expected such actions from her, and now regarded her warily. She therefore stayed in her room, comforted only by tea and toast.

Amy tried to talk to her once or twice, but Emma still remained suspicious of her. She seemed to reluctantly accept that Amy wasn't leading a team of spies and yet they were nowhere close to the easy friendship they had enjoyed before Ffion's death. Amy hoped it would pass, now the staff saw the full extent of Emma's illness. Surely now they could treat it with something besides knocking her out, waiting and hoping for a miracle?

With Carwyn in a foul mood and Tony gone, Amy's choices for company were reduced to nursing staff, Mordecai and Ron. As Mordecai never emerged before midday, Amy wandered over to Ron in the garden, wondering where his head would be today. He seemed to have turned a corner, his mute rage against himself replaced with a constant flow of confession - he was never touching steroids again, he had been frightened for Amy and Emma, he hoped her wounds didn't hurt her too much, she was the most beautiful creature he'd ever seen…

Amy quickly removed herself from the conversation before it could escalate further and returned to the lounge. She flicked on the television, for lack of anything better to do, and the news appeared. It was unlike the nurses to allow this, as the channels were usually kept to music videos and innocuous daytime television. She settled down to watch, letting the problems of the wider world wash over her, distracting her from the itch of healing skin and her own impotent role in this mystery.

At least she had seen Jason. She had more than seen him - and she felt her cheeks heating at the memory. The rest of the evening may have blurred with adrenaline, but not that moment - he had kissed her, desperately kissed her, and she had responded.

How did he feel about it now? Was it some stupid reaction, in the moment? Did he now regret it? Or had it been brewing inside him for months, as it had been for her? Too many questions and no way to obtain answers. She wished she hadn't slept through most of their time together yesterday, or had at least been brave enough to mention it. Though she could never chance the rejection, wanted to hold on to her time with him while she could. She was a coward.

Just before lunch, Mordecai stumbled out into the lounge and collapsed on the other sofa. He smelled strongly of alcohol, but he also looked pale and sweaty, like a man under fever.

"Are you all right?" she ventured.

"It's all gone," he said bleakly.

"What's gone?" she asked, but she already knew. The alcohol wasn't fresh on his lips, but that old smell of hangover, one that Jason had frequently worn whenever Dylan was involved in the drinking.

He didn't reply, his eyes closing as his body went limp on the sofa. Then his head bashed down hard on the sofa's arm, his legs and arms jerking like a marionette, careering him off the sofa and onto the floor.

Amy screamed and jumped back, watching him with a helpless fascination. This was what they meant about watching a car crash, a train wreck, caught up in a tsunami on the television. She could do nothing, and she couldn't look away.

Lois pushed her aside, begged her to go back to her room, as the staff all leapt to action and the younger doctor tried to hold him together.

"Did he take his medication?" he called, and the nurses cried yes, uncomprehending of the scene before them.

"He was drunk last night," Amy said, and then repeated it again, louder and louder, until they heard her.

"How could he be drunk?" Lois demanded of her.

"He's been drunk for days," she said.

They weren't listening, too wrapped up in Mordecai fitting on the floor.

Amy would not be disbelieved again. Moving at speed, she headed for the male corridor, past Carwyn's door and into Mordecai's unlocked room.

It smelled of stale sweat and sour vomit, and she tried not to gag. The window was open, but the curtains were drawn, leaving the room in inky darkness. She avoided the obstacles of unidentified fluids and discarded clothes, casting open the curtains to conduct her search.

She started with the best hiding place she had found, and immediately hit gold. Stuffed inside the plant pot was a series of old socks tied together to form a rope. A plastic hanger was leaning up against the window pane. Had he meant to hang himself? Where would he put the hanger? The rooms were designed to remove all opportunities, and surely the plastic would buckle and break before he succeeded.

She turned to the open window to escape the smell and instead found her answers. Below the window ledge, a row of empty bottles sat on the grass, each with a twist of wire around the neck to allow them to be hooked. Amy fished for one out the window and caught it on the third attempt, carefully bringing it up and into the bedroom.

It was an empty bottle of cheap vodka, flavoured with something artificially sweet - a berry of some kind, she thought. Above the peeling label, a message was scribbled in marker - "For your help, T".

Clink. Clank. The truth all came together in an instant. The dark figure outside the window late at night, the whispers in the dark, the clanking of chains. Except not chains but bottles. Bottles of alcohol to fuel a desperate man's confessions - and find a story.

Amy gripped the bottle so hard she thought it would splinter, and then marched out of the room and down the corridor, brandishing it before her like a talisman.

"It was Tony!" she shouted, momentarily oblivious to the paramedics who had arrived and were loading Mordecai onto the stretcher.

Lois took the bottle from her hand and stared at it. "Where did you find that?"

"It was outside Mordecai's window. Tony gave them to him! He kept him drunk for information. Now do you understand?"

But Amy could see that she didn't, didn't want to understand or see or realise what had been going on right under their noses. That Emma's threatened jump and Mordecai's seizure were within their control, avoidable - if only they had paid attention.

Amy felt sick with their ignorance, and her own. She hadn't trusted Tony, but she had thought she had control over him. Tempting him with her story, using his research, shopping him to Bryn. He had used her, and Mordecai, and maybe even Ffion in his thirst for information, for a story.

She had failed to see him for what he was. What else had he kept hidden from her? What further prices were left to pay?

Chapter 38: Follow the Rabbit

Going home to Cerys and Gwen had been difficult. He'd wanted to stay with Amy, but couldn't, and now he would have to explain himself to his worried family.

After two cups of tea and a third repeat of the night's events - excluding any mention of Owain - his mam had insisted he go to bed, and his sister had reluctantly let him go. But he couldn't sleep, the streetlights on the ceiling his companions in insomnia. Jason prided himself on sleeping through anything, but his head was too full of Amy, abandoning her, and his conscience wouldn't let him alone.

Rising in the morning after only an hour or two of dozing, he showered, redressed his leg, and threw on the freshly-laundered clothes his mother had kept for him. They were a year or so old now, his more recent wardrobe locked into Amy's former flat, but they were comfortable and familiar, and he needed that.

When he tried to call Cliff House, he was stonewalled by the receptionist and then by the nurse. She wouldn't confirm or deny that Amy was there, and hung up on him. Frieda still had an iron grip on proceedings. His communication effectively cut off, he could do nothing but stew - and bother Corelia.

"The credit card is a pre-pay - they're not too common over here. With some of Amy's more…sophisticated tools, I discovered it was bought at LAX."

Jason took another drag of his illicit cigarette, outside his mother's kitchen window. "At what? Is that like…a hacking shop?"

Corelia laughed at him. "It's an airport - Los Angeles International. And it was purchased about six months ago, with five hundred dollars on it."

That made no sense at all. "How did the killer get a credit card from America?"

"It was probably sold on with some cash remaining on it. Airports are fairly anonymous places. It's good business."

"So the card tells us nothing." Jason was disappointed. He'd thought the number plate would lead somewhere useful.

"The username is more promising," she said. "I've found a couple of close variations of it - shaman1969 and shamtheman69. No email or blogs, but a few interesting posts on drug forums in the past few weeks. Lots about mushrooms, peyote, morning glory seeds. I've dug a little deeper, and they all seem to be tripping plants."

Jason had done mushrooms once - and never again. He never wanted to play with fire, or his father's ghost, and he had come-to crying in Lewis' lap while his best friend panicked over him. "Ffion had hallucinations."

"She was also in a mental hospital. Anyway, gotta go - the OT here is a mega bitch and wants me to show off some kitchen skills. Later!"

Jason scowled at the phone and shoved it in his pocket. Amy was also in a mental hospital and she didn't hallucinate. While he didn't know much about Ffion Ellis, her keeper at home said she had depression. Did that involve hearing and seeing shit that wasn't there? What would taking an hallucinogenic drug do to you if you already had hallucinations?

Jason was about to text his findings to Bryn, such as they were, when he decided to deliver them in person instead. He started walking towards Cardiff Police station, and lit another cigarette. He'd quit when Amy was home, he told himself. He'd quit when he felt useful again, and whole.

The streets were still slick from last night's rain, with the sky threatening a further downpour whenever it so chose. He was used to people crossing the street when he walked towards them, but he was conscious of it today - how he looked, how he carried himself. Like a walking threat.

Amy never saw him like that. From the first moment she'd let him into her flat, she'd treated him like a real person. Well, at first, she'd treated him like a super maid, but she'd then let him into her little nerdy world and her entire life. He'd become part of it and living without it now was driving him crazy.

The police station was busy, as usual, but they all knew him there. He was escorted towards the detectives' office almost immediately, though he could've found his way there with his eyes closed.

He bumped into Catriona in the corridor, who looked at him suspiciously. "Why are you here?"

"Helping the police with their enquiries," he said, with more cheek than rancour. He had warmed to Catriona, even if she was part of Owain's betrayal with the Cyber Crime Unit, but he was pretty certain she hated him.

"Have you seen Owain?" she asked.

"Last night," he said. "At the hospital. Why?"

Her face was suddenly stormy. "Then where the fuck is he now?"

She'd gone before he could say anything further. Who was he to get in the way of the internal politics of the police department?

As he thanked his escorting uniform and approached Bryn's desk, he could hear that the phone was on speaker as Bryn took down some notes.

"Two weeks? We can't get it back any quicker than that?"

"That's fast, Detective," Rob Pritchard's voice said through the phone's shoddy speaker. "I've prioritised the samples, though I make no guarantees. They were in the hospital, after all, and not our own laboratory's storage."

Bryn acknowledged Jason with a nod, and kept talking. "What about her medications? Anything about blood pressure there?"

"She was on a couple of antihypertensives - we'd need to know from the hospital records whether she was taking them. Antipsychotics tend to cause hypotension rather than hypertension, though there is neuroleptic malignant syndrome to consider."

"Speak English."

"A bizarre effect of antipsychotics. Though the biochemistry tells against us here - I would've expected her CK to be much higher."

It was clear that this was as much gibberish to Bryn as it was to Jason. "Anything else?"

"Phenelzine is an interesting antidepressant. Under the right circumstances, it might cause a malignant hypertension."

"What kind of circumstances?"

"Mostly dietary. The wrong kind of cheese or wine or Marmite. The staff should've placed the patient on a special diet. Alas, no stomach contents to prove it, one way or another."

"What about drugs?" Jason said suddenly. "Like magic mushrooms?"

Rob's voice turned irate. "Is that Jason Carr? I thought he was back in prison!"

"Drugs, Rob. Any drugs?"

"I'd have to check, but some drugs do interact with antidepressants and antipsychotics. I would need to know which mushroom exactly. Though why a lady of sixty-eight would be indulging in psilocybin, I have no idea."

"Leave that part to us," Bryn said. "Thank you, Rob."

Hanging up on the medical examiner, Bryn shot Jason a "spill now" look. Always happy to oblige, Jason sat backwards on the nearest office chair and stole a biscuit from the half-empty packet on the detective's desk.

"Corelia says the credit card was a pre-pay, bought in LA. The username is linked to all these drug forums. Mushrooms and other natural highs, she says."

"Assuming Ffion Ellis wasn't a secret user, that gives us a clear link to poisoning, and supports Amy's idea that this guy has an accomplice on the inside."

"Amy needs to be moved," Jason snapped, loud enough to quiet the entire office.

"One step at a time," Bryn said. "We have no evidence yet."

"What, we're going to wait until she's dead?"

"Calm down, boy. She's not dead - and not likely to be. They're keeping a close eye on her. Frieda's made sure of that."

"I hate her," Jason muttered darkly.

"Right now, she's protecting Amy because she plans to use her. We need to rely on that goodwill for the moment."

"Did you find anything in the van?"

"Dead end - everything useful burnt away. There was a quad bike in the back, but it was unregistered and barely recognisable."

Jason scowled at the lack of evidence and shifted his aching leg, which only made it hurt more.

"You need to go home and rest - do I even want to know?"

"Car racketeers own bitey dogs."

"Go home," Bryn said, adopting his parental voice.

It was the last thing Jason wanted to do, but did he really have a choice? He couldn't help Amy if he wasn't fighting fit and they'd run out of roads to run down.

"You'll let me know - "

"Of course."

Bryn would tell him, rightly or wrongly, because he knew Jason needed to know. Amy's safety was his whole world and he wouldn't let her down again.

Chapter 39: Trade in Lunacy

Unable to sleep, Amy turned on the television and saw her own face staring back at her.

The early morning news reports were discussing the Saturday papers, and prime amongst them was Tony's exposé. He hadn't skimped on the details, with all the latest juicy titbits - including Emma's suicide attempt.

"What are you - oh my God!"

Miriam tried to turn off the television, but it couldn't be unseen. The world would not be kept out any longer.

From seven o'clock, they started to arrive. Strange cars and news vans, all gathering at this small mental health unit in Penarth, waiting for the asylum to throw open its doors. Amy watched discreetly from behind a curtain in the dining room, and stopped Ron entering the garden.

"Oh, they can't see me," he said, in a loud stage whisper. "I'm invisible today."

The nurses opened the doors to allow the cigarette smoke out, breaking the letter of the law but keeping their last few patients protected from the prying eye of the media. They took their pictures anyway, calling for Amy and Emma and Carwyn to show themselves.

When Darren came on the day shift, he had a copy of the offending newspaper in hand, which he oh-so-casually abandoned on the table in the lounge. Amy's hold over him was paying dividends.

She pored over the article, wincing at the sensationalist language and the sketchy but cutting summary of her own crimes: "hacked secure systems to steal millions of pounds and pervert the course of justice". She disputed the last count on moral grounds, but Frieda would probably lay far more at her door.

Carwyn came off worst of all, with Emma and Mordecai listed only as examples of supposed mismanagement. Amy couldn't forgive Tony for his deliberate poisoning of the young singer, driving him back to his addiction and then to secret, painful withdrawal. She also couldn't forgive the staff for failing to notice.

Amy returned to her room, away from the vast walls of glass that made the hospital literally transparent to the gawkers outside. Darren called her for lunch about midday, but she was lost in herself, in the article. At her whole life reduced to those sparse lines of crime.

Rap-rap-rap!

Amy nearly jumped out of her skin, leaping from the bed and crying out. She stared at the closed curtains - who was it? Had Tony's accomplice returned? Or the man himself?

"Emma? Come on, Emma - just talk to me!"

Amy threw open the curtain. A man with a camera started clicking, and she dropped it back. She hit the nurse alarm, more angry than afraid, and peered through the curtains as a couple of plain clothes officers escorted the photographer off-site. Amy assumed they belonged to Frieda and was silently grateful for their presence.

As the journalists increased in noise and number, Amy bit the bullet and went to check on Emma. She had no idea what kind of reception she would receive, but the muted glare from Jemima the healthcare assistant, sitting in her bedroom, didn't fill her with confidence.

Emma was lying on her bed, curled up facing the wall. Half-eaten toast and cold tea sat on the bedside table. Amy gingerly sat on the corner of Emma's bed and waited.

"They haven't gone away."

Her voice was quiet, almost too quiet to hear, but Amy felt every word.

"What did the doctor say?"

A small huff of laughter. "More pills. It's always more pills."

Amy knew that feeling well. "Did they help?"

"They just made me sleepy. But I can't sleep."

This new, fluent Emma worried Amy more than the previous hesitant one had. It was as if something inside her had broken and all the bad stuff was leaking out into the open. Amy wanted to shutter it up - but was that selfish of her? Maybe Emma needed to share all this darkness. Amy would have to suffer to hear it.

"Do you still want to jump?"

The words were out before she'd fully thought them through. Jemima looked shocked, but Amy was tired of moderating her feelings for those around her. Hiding had got her precisely nowhere, and look what it had done to Emma.

"Yes." Quiet, so quiet. "It won't work, though."

"No," Amy agreed. "You can't run away from your own head."

The article was unfortunate.

Journalists meant attention, and attention meant scrutiny. The police would work harder now, dig deeper. He couldn't afford for them to get too close.

Leaving the camera behind had been a devastating blow. He'd considered another break-in, but they'd probably downloaded the video straightaway. The bastard nerds had crippled the police computers instead of giving him a way in and he didn't dare chase down that man again, the one he'd followed to the hospital. So he was reduced to fretting in his studio.

What could he do? He'd come so close to pulling the whole thing off perfectly, and now he'd shot himself in the foot. He should've been more careful, and he should've kept a closer eye on the hospital. He'd always been suspicious of that bloke and his friend, making their dodgy exchanges in the garden. What else did he know? What could he have seen, observed, written down? Was that other bloke also in on it all?

He'd come so very close, but he couldn't use the same tricks again. He had to think of something new, something to get him out of this bind. His other project, his baby, wasn't getting the appreciation it deserved. He was on the verge of being labelled a failure. He could not afford to fail.

What options did he have left? He'd lost control of the situation again and he saw no way to regain it. Unless...unless he could use these fuck-ups to his advantage.

The hospital wasn't safe - that much was clear. The police, the people who regulated such things, might want to shut it down. What would happen then to the patients, the staff, the evidence? It would all disappear, just like that.

Could he give that process a shove? What if he reported the hospital as unsafe, or shopped that doctor for...what was it? Malpractice. Yeah, that was what it was all right. He had a legitimate reason to complain, and his evidence was plastered all over the newspapers. The media always won.

He was used to taking a bad situation and making it golden. He had come good again and again, and that was why he was confident this plan had to work. When you got rid of the dross, what remained could shine - and he was going to shine so fucking bright.

He wrote a few emails, sent a feedback form, tipped off a few journalist contacts with "exclusive" details, and then brewed up peyote tea to bring peace to his afternoon. It was exactly the trip he needed to dissipate the stress.

Tomorrow, he'd launch his offensive, and then Monday, he'd strike the final blow. He wouldn't just bring down one person - he'd destroy an entire hospital. Those were the kind of leadership and management skills one needed in life, Mama.

Thank fuck, they would all finally see - and accept him. She could fuck off, really, because no one wanted her.

This journalist had triggered his master plan. It was all coming together just as he wanted.

Chapter 40: To Whom It May Concern

Jason's resolution to sit home and wait lasted until Cerys emerged from her slumber at midday, eyes shining with excitement.

"I have an idea - what if that letter was a reply?"

It took him a moment to make sense of those words, completely out of nowhere, as his sister hung in the kitchen doorway.

"A reply?" he repeated stupidly.

"The threatening letter, the one that blew over the cliff. What if it was a reply to something Ffion sent?

"Why would she write to someone who wanted to kill her?"

"She wrote to that boy's father, remember? Rambling guilty letters. From the statement Bryn took from Amy, she said it felt like the writer knew her - personally."

"Did Corelia tell you that?" There was no way a probationary constable was meant to be leafing through the evidence in a hot murder case, and no legitimate way for Cerys to see them with the police servers still down.

Cerys tossed her head, which only slightly quivered the blonde tufts of gelled hair arranged there. "If she wrote letters before she went to hospital, maybe there's evidence at her place."

"The SOCOs already looked it over."

"Maybe they missed something. What - you giving up?"

That was all it took for him to climb onto the back of his own bike, leg still throbbing, as Cerys drove them both over to Ffion's accommodation. Mared the manager was perfectly civil, picking their brains about whether they'd ever get the body back and if it would be a funeral or a memorial.

"Her daughter's half-crazed with it - ringing all the time, she is. I hardly know what to tell her. Of course, she can't come down. She did so well for herself, in the City. They can't just up and leave those kind of jobs, you know."

Jason and Cerys nodded along, with "hmm" and "ahh" in the right places. Someone had left a bunch of flowers propped up against the frame of Ffion's door, which were now wilted. Mared dutifully unlocked the door and let them inside.

"Still can't find those apples," she said wistfully, and left them alone.

Jason remembered the smell from last time, but it had intensified. He walked around the room, sniffing like a bloodhound, while Cerys started searching under the bed and in all of the drawers. He opened the window to let out most of the stench, and then resumed his search. This was one thing Amy couldn't do with all the computer power in the world. When she developed smellovision, he was fucked.

His nose brought him back to the overflowing bookcase. The edge nearest the door showed that it was missing its backing, though it was flush against the wall. Pulling out the largest, heaviest books from the bottom, Jason discovered a row of apples, in varying states of decay. But nothing else was hidden in that space.

He turned to the books, despite Mared's previous assertions that Ffion had never read them. One was bookmarked over a dozen times, with little scraps of paper - "The Spiritualist's Guide to Demonology", with a terrifying creature lurking on the front. Opening the book was like a window into Ffion's mind - she had marked passages in red pen, and littered the margins with notes: *They're coming for me. No escape. Warn him.*

'Warn him'? Who exactly needed warning? Was it Cezary Kowalski, who had ignored her letters despite his grief? Or was it the sender of the letter from Newport, one so full of bile that it might as well have come from a demon?

The next-most worn book was a tome on "The History of Sailing", with a magnificent oil painting on the front. Jason opened it up - and found it hollowed out, concealing multiple letters, writing paper and pens.

"Got it," he said, laying out the contents on the floor.

Cerys threw him some gloves from her pocket and together they went through the letters. All from Newport, and all filled with vitriol and hatred. Unsurprisingly, there was no return address, and the letters ran along the same poorly-spelled themes - how much he hated her, her worthlessness, her various crimes.

"Listen to this - 'Why don't you give up and die? You can't fix all you fucked up, bitch.'"

Jason peered over Cerys' shoulder, confirming she'd been generous with the grammar and surprised she'd made sense of the words at all. "It's definitely personal. See here? 'I hate you and the - '" Jason squinted at the page. "What does that say?"

"I think it's meant to be 'hellspawn'."

"Right. ' - you and the hellspawn always torturing me without a trial or nothing. Fucking stop! I won't ever love you.'"

"Sounds like the writer's haunted by the same demons."

"Maybe this is someone she knew from hospital in the past. Mared said she'd been in and out of those places."

Jason looked through the sheets of writing paper, hoping for something else that might lead them to the mystery letter writer. Finding nothing, he gave the book itself a once-over. It appeared to be missing the first few pages entirely, before someone - presumably Ffion - had taken a knife to it and hacked a large rectangle in the centre to store her letters.

He almost missed the tiny black marks under the letters of the remaining text, running either side of the hollow. Fuck, she'd been paranoid. Copying out the letters, he realised that the left-hand side spelled out "Melissa" and then an address in London. Presumably her daughter.

The other side spelled out the name "Aaron" and another address, ending in N-E-W-P-O -

"Got him!" he said, waving the address in Cerys' face. "She wrote his address down in the book. She was writing to him."

He stood up, raring to go and hunt down this bastard, but Cerys hesitated.

"We need to do this properly," she said. "He's killed a woman and stolen a body. We can't just run right in there."

Jason looked at her as if she'd lost her head. "We've always run right in there."

"Look how that's working out for us. No, we need to do this properly. We need to give it to Bryn, get a warrant."

Jason blew air through his lips. "When did you turn into a copper, eh?"

"Well, my big brother was such a good role model…" Cerys removed a large evidence bag from her satchel and carefully placed the book and its contents inside. "We did good today."

Jason felt it, he did, but he also itched to act. Playing by the rules took too much time, time that kept Amy in danger and left him feeling next to useless. But if they were to catch this Aaron, they had to do it right. If that meant he had to play patience, that's what he would do.

"Let's ring up the old bill then," he said. "It's time to go hunting."

Chapter 41: Exodus

Sunday was washed away in a deluge, the rain beating on the windows well before dawn and turning the garden into a swamp.

The rain had the added benefit of flushing out the journalists, who were only prepared to suffer for their art until their socks were soaked. One by one, they trudged back to their cars and vowed to return when the weather cleared up. Amy was glad to see the back of them.

She'd stayed up late on Saturday night, talking with Emma about everything and nothing, the reality and the fantasy of their enemies and how this place was among them. The accompanying nurse huffed at them, but they didn't care. They lulled themselves to sleep with hot chocolate and a feeling of satisfaction, of true communication.

As Amy munched distractedly on a piece of toast, she saw a man in a suit emerge from the bedroom corridor. From the top of the plastic bag in his hand, Amy recognised the bright purple and black fringe of one of Mordecai's coats.

She crossed the lounge to intercept him, ignoring the way he recoiled at her approach. "How is he?" she asked.

"Alive," the man sniffed. "He'll be better at a more, ah, exclusive centre."

Amy smiled, ignoring the slight. "You should sue," she said sagely. "I'd start with Tony Rogers, the journalist, and then the hospital."

"Thanks for the advice," he said, the words icy sarcasm.

Amy was beyond being wounded with words, and she watched him go without much ill-feeling. She'd been hurt worse by her own kin.

And then there were three.

She had just finished her second cup of tea when a crew of paramedics arrived. She watched them stop for a biscuit and a cuppa with the nursing staff, before Jemima fetched Ron in from the garden.

"Into the shower with you!" she said. "You can't travel like this!"

"Am I going somewhere?" he asked. "Will it be nice? Will it be raining there?"

"It's a hospital in London. I'm sure you'll like it."

Amy's heart sank a little further. The hospital's reputation had obviously taken a blow, and now everyone was being removed. She would have to get used to a different hospital, different staff, different treatment plans. She would be far away from Jason, from everyone - and from this mystery.

Before she was moved, she had to gather the last pieces of evidence from this place. Returning to her room, she attracted no undue attention - and then she walked past Emma's door to where Ffion had stayed, slipping through the criss-cross of police tape.

The room was a mixture of chaos and sterility. Anything that could be bagged had been removed, but the marks of Ffion's last hours remained. The blood stain on the floor, the rake of nails across the wall, the clumps of hair torn out at the roots.

Amy went to her favourite hiding place first - the base of the plant pot. But if anything had been left there, it had already been found. Her thought was for more letters. Where would someone hide letters?

She opened the pillow case, untucked the sheets and checked the bedframe, but she didn't find anything except broken fingernails and the odour of unwashed feet. She tried the bathroom next, attempting to open up the toilet cistern like in the movies - but it was sealed tight. All the toiletries had clearly been bagged and tagged, so the bathroom was a bust. Amy even started tapping on tiles before she realised she was losing it.

As she was leaving, she caught sight of herself in the mirror. She was pale again, ghostly, the black stitches on her cheek stark against her skin. Yet she looked determined, bold, filled with something strong and decided. She wasn't the frightened child she had been when she first came here. She was Amy Lane again.

Back in the bedroom, Amy scanned every inch of the room for some clue as to where Ffion might have hidden things. Because she had undoubtedly hidden things. You didn't survive in a place like this without finding some form of privacy.

It was the reflection that gave it away. The banal Impressionist print on the wall reflected its murky colours towards the ceiling, the light hitting the bottom just-so and yet neglecting the top. Carefully, Amy lifted the painting away from the wall, the anti-hanging tag coming away easily and a small cloth bag falling to the floor.

To Amy's disappointment, it definitely wasn't big enough for a letter. However, when she carefully shook out the contents of the bag on the floor, she was puzzled by Ffion's treasures - a key ring from Llanfair PG, a frayed friendship bracelet in blue, green and red wool, and a handful of naked chocolates, whitened from exposure.

Amy replaced the items in the bag, disappointed, and returned the picture to the wall. She stuffed the bag in her hoodie pocket - it might tell Bryn something that she couldn't decipher.

Checking that everything was the same as when she'd arrived, Amy navigated her way through the police tape and back towards her room. As she neared the end of the corridor, the air was filled with shouting - and her name.

She ran out into the lounge, where Emma was screaming, two nurses trying to restrain her. By the door, a severe woman with a black bun too jet to be natural couldn't bear to look, the picture of discomfort. Beside her stood a man with bleached blond hair and a tan.

Amy instantly pegged the man as Emma's brother, and she could see some family resemblance if she looked hard. But where Emma was curved, her brother was angular, and where she was plain and unassuming in dress, he wore a brightly-coloured woven belt fringed with beads, and a loose cotton shirt, despite it being November. The woman looked nothing like them, and was perhaps not even old enough to be their mother.

When Emma saw Amy, she stopped shouting and instead cried, desperately trying to break free of the nurses' hold. "They want to take me away!"

Amy rushed straight in, despite the nurses' warnings, and embraced Emma. She held her close and, finally, the nurses released her so they could hold each other. Mourn their time together.

"It'll be okay," Amy told her. "You'll be better away from here."

"I'm not ready to go home. I'm not well."

Amy looked dubiously at Emma's brother and probable mother. "They'll look after you."

"Will you call me?"

Amy didn't know how to tell her that she couldn't call, or write - that she would probably never see her again. She didn't have the words for so much pain.

"You'll be okay," she said, instead.

"Max, we need to go. I have an appointment."

"Do you have no control in this place? I want that woman off my sister."

Amy looked at both nurses with a warning glare. "Emma, you need to stand up. It's time to go home. You can write to me when you get there. You can write every day."

With Amy's slender frame under both arms, Emma managed to get to her feet, sniffing loudly. She bent down to the bag by her feet, a tatty patchwork affair that heavily featured owls. She removed a jar of the artisan peanut butter that she loved and pressed it into Amy's hands.

"Emma, I bought that for you!"

She ignored her brother, meeting Amy's eyes. "Don't eat it all at once."

"I won't," Amy promised, as solemn as a vow.

"Bye, Amy," she said.

"Amy? This is that Amy girl?" Emma's mother was now looking at them both with a piercing glare. She took hold of Emma's arm and pulled her back, towards the door. "We're going home, Emma. We have work to do if you're going to get on, hmm?"

Max shook his head at her, his big brown eyes radiating the false charity of his heart. "I feel sorry for you," he told her. "You want to be with someone like my sister, to feel good about yourself. She doesn't need or want you. Don't contact her."

Amy glowered at him but said nothing.

He gestured to the nurses. "You want to restrain her - she's the dangerous one! Who drove my sister to the edge?"

"Come on, Maxi - don't make a scene. We've had enough of that."

Cowed, he retreated beside his mother.

Amy held up her hand to wave, but they were gone, the door closed on another chapter of her life. Yet another thing she could not get back.

Chapter 42: Celestial Navigation

Bryn could've done without Jason and Cerys Carr haunting his office on a Sunday, but it turned out he didn't have much of a choice.

When the siblings turned up on Saturday evening, pleased as punch and like something straight out of the Famous Five, he knew they were onto something. Unfortunately, they needed probable cause for a warrant. He could chance it and knock on the door but, if this guy was the killer, he would clean out and scarper before they returned with the right paperwork.

No, he needed to do this properly if they had any chance of making this crime stick. But they had sweet FA connecting him to the death of Ffion Ellis. For some reason, Jason and Cerys thought that sitting in his office and nagging him would just make the evidence turn up. Perhaps Jason was now too used to Amy's magic.

"Can't you just bring him in for questioning?" Jason asked.

"He can refuse. All we know is that Ffion has his address and he lives in Newport, from where the letters were sent. It's not enough to hold him."

"Got the report on Ffion's book here," Cerys said, from a computer terminal by the coffee pot. Owain had restored the server to partial operation, but it was slower than a speeding snail. "They found a third address along the bottom, which belongs to Kowalski. The last letter she wrote imprinted on the next sheet down, but it was another rant to him about his son and demons. Nothing new there."

"Let's see the transcript anyway." If they were going to clutch at straws, they might as well have all of them in hand.

The printer spat it out and Jason picked it up, lips moving soundlessly as he tried to decipher the scrawl.

"Is this a private party or can anyone join?"

Catriona was dressed down for the weekend, in an oversized knitted jumper and jeans. She cradled her laptop with one arm like an infant child, looking uneasily at Jason. Expecting to be kicked out of a police office because an ex-con was sitting in the room.

"Pull up a chair," Jason said. "You got something?"

"I just finished with the video. He really fixated on you, Jason, and the hospital, but less on the rest of the investigation. You see anyone strange hanging around?"

Jason shook his head.

"The footage of the van burning is pretty shoddy - the flames and the explosion white-out the image. I can't get a clear shot of him anywhere. Good news is that he filmed the body dump."

Bryn stared at her for a moment. "He filmed it? All of it?"

"Enough for me to guesstimate a location."

She set her laptop on the corner of his desk, but he shoved the keyboard and clutter out of the way to make room. The screen showed a topographical map of South Wales, but Catriona brought up a tab with the video inside it.

"Here's the first bit - you'll soon get the idea."

He had his back to the camera, a bright light shining on the bare earth and casting his face in shadow. Slowly, he started to dig, each shovelful seeming to take an age. This continued for a minute or two before Catriona stopped the tape.

"He digs for a bit, rests, digs some more, and then repeats the next day. Three days in total. Luckily for us, it didn't rain on the Monday."

She fast-forwarded the clip. Brilliant starlight shone down on his efforts, competing with the high-powered lamp he'd set up, showing the digging man waist-deep in the pit.

"He went for the production value of the stars. Rookie mistake."

Catriona brought up the map again. She toggled something on the sidebar and the view rotated, so that they were instead looking up at a massive starfield.

Bryn was in awe. "You can locate the body from the stars."

She was grinning, caught up in the joy of the find. She reminded him of Amy then, that keen mind leaping to exploit all possibilities and looking for approval. "I had to do a lot of the matching by hand, but I've narrowed it down to about a mile square in the middle of the Brecon Beacons. Shouldn't be difficult to find - and the nearby campsites might've hosted our one-man digging show."

Bryn stood up. Jason was shrugging on his jacket and Cerys gathered up her bag. He was never shaking off these two, but at least it kept them out of trouble.

"As long as you take a turn with the spade."

As the day wore on, the hospital started to shut down. The staff dwindled down to just one nurse overnight. The kitchen was shut up, the fridge loaded with sandwiches and salads until they could work out what to do tomorrow. How to handle their one remaining patient.

Amy resisted Lois' attempts to talk to her that evening, choosing instead to eat Emma's peanut butter on toast in her room. The silence of the ward was oppressive, unnatural. As the sun set, she wanted nothing more than to escape, to run free, to shake off the shadows. Yet with the darkness came the sadness, the deep gnawing sadness that she thought she had moved beyond. It had been lurking there all the time, deceiving her into daring to hope.

Amy took her one pilfered cigarette and walked down the corridor, across the lounge and through the closed dining room into the garden beyond. It wasn't silent out here, the cawing of the gulls and the wash of the sea against the rocks reminded her she was grounded, that she wasn't truly alone.

She had never felt so alone.

With shaking fingers, she placed the cigarette on the wall-mounted lighter and forced it to smoulder. Against her lips, it tasted like sour ash, but it brought warmth to her lungs and a rolling to her stomach. A false sense of security, knocking the edges off her anxiety.

How long did Frieda intend to keep her here? Had she seized on this opportunity to break her, to force her hand into accepting the offer? Was this why she had harried Corelia, but given Jason total freedom? The stick and the carrot.

Amy wanted to throw it back in her face and rebel, but the last operating strands of her rational mind insisted she think it over. Working for the National Crime Agency. Hunting down her fellows, testing their cyber security, the usual mundane shit. Though it occurred to her this was the only way she'd get back her computer, any computer, and the only way to buy her freedom. To return home with Jason.

Amy took another drag of the cigarette and walked further out into the garden. A cloud shifted across the sky, revealing a smattering of stars, before another took its place. She was cold in just her hoodie, but she didn't want to leave this space. How strange that she should find comfort outside, when it had only held terror before.

Clink. Clank. Clink. Clank.

The gate to the car park was closed, but he was watching her over the bars. He was a smudge, barely there, but she could feel his gaze on her. She wanted to shout, to scream, for help to come, for anyone to hear - but her breath caught in her throat. She was alone.

He pushed open the gate like it had never been there at all and took a step forward. She couldn't move, rooted to the ground, all the old doubts creeping up her throat and threatening to strangle her. Could the fence hold against a bullet? Did he even need to shoot her? Had he already poisoned her and these were her dying gasps in the garden? Had he come just to watch?

Clink. Clank. Clink. Clank.

His rattling steps were worse than any gun, speeding towards her as if he could walk on water, his face always in shadow and his clothes blacker than the night. There were no stars, no moon - she was alone in the pitch black with him, and she couldn't force her legs to carry her away.

Clink. Clank. Clink. Clank.

He reached for the fence between them - and it rippled. The molten plastic puddled around his feet, and he was still coming, he was reaching for her. She was choking, she was dying -

Someone grabbed her from behind.

Amy screamed.

"Amy? Amy, what's wrong?"

It was Sandy, her Scotch tones soothing as she held her arm. Amy looked at her, relief mixed with paralysing fear, and then she looked back.

He was gone. The fence was intact. She realised in horror that he had never been there at all, that her mind had betrayed her, and she had truly been alone in the dark.

"I thought I saw someone," she said.

Sandy rubbed her arm. "All those newspaper men have gone home, love. Come inside now and have a cup of tea."

Amy allowed herself to be led, but with one eye on the fence. He had seemed so real, so vivid. The colours of the night were still swimming before her eyes, like oil on water, a kaleidoscope of blackness. What the hell was going on?

Were Emma's demons coming for her too? And Ffion's? If she allowed herself to be rational - an easier task with one hand around a mug and the other clasped in Sandy's - she could start to see a pattern emerge. The nightmares, the agitation, the fear, the hallucinations - they were all similar. Amy had experienced nightmares here, beyond her usual paroxysms of despair, but she had dismissed them as part of her illness. What if it was more than that?

What did Emma, Amy and Ffion have in common? This hospital, sure, but what inside it? Was there literally something in the water?

Amy peered at her mug of tea as if it had bitten her. Was she slowly poisoning herself? They had been acting like the killer had targeted Ffion Ellis, but what if that wasn't it at all? Maybe he had a vendetta against all of them, or what they represented. Maybe he wanted to wipe them all out.

Except there was only her left.

"I'm going to bed now," she said, leaving her tea untouched.

She needed to find a way to contact Bryn tomorrow, share her theory. Until then, she could limit her exposure - she wouldn't drink anything, eat anything or touch anything that she could avoid.

The poison was somewhere in this hospital, and she would rather starve than fail now. They were so close - as long as the killer didn't get to her before she could find him.

Chapter 43: Here Lies Justice

Catriona's calculations brought them right under the shadow of Pen Y Fan, the tallest peak in the Brecon Beacons and therefore one of nature's tourist traps.

The local campsites were numerous - from the five-star "glamping" enclosures to a farmer's field with a cold tap, the national park and its surrounds catered to every budget. After spending one lonely and desperate spring night out in the Welsh countryside, Jason could no longer see the appeal.

Catriona had divided the detectives and uniforms into small hunting parties, each canvassing a specific area of her star-crossed map. Obviously, she'd chosen the most likely spot for herself and so Jason, Cerys and Bryn had been determined to accompany her. As their thin procession made its way across the park, Jason buried his hands deeper into his coat pockets, trying not to trip over the heather and regretting his insistence on joining them.

"I don't think campsite door-knocking will get us anywhere." Catriona trudged through the shrubs in her Wellingtons as easily as if it were her living room, the moonlight streaking through the cloud to light their way. "My bet is that he went wild."

"You mean, like, up a tree?" Cerys asked.

Jason shuddered. Another experience he couldn't recommend. Tree houses may be a great kids' game, but a grown man could not spend any amount of time up one without seizing up and falling out.

"It's when you take your tent off the beaten track and pitch it anywhere." Catriona seemed both knowledgeable on the subject and intent on the specific path they were taking. "It makes you much harder to find."

"Are we at the perimeter yet?" Bryn huffed and puffed along behind, reminding them he had a few decades on them.

"Passed it five minutes ago." Catriona gestured to either side of her. "But we've got tracks."

Now that Jason looked properly he noticed the bent and broken gorse in parallel lines, with their snaking procession bang in the middle.

"He didn't take the easy route," Cerys said, stepping over a small boulder in their path.

"My guess is that he's not used to the terrain. He knows enough to camp wild, but not enough to avoid the rough patches."

"Do you come out here often?" Jason asked, only realising when Cerys giggled that he'd used a corny pick-up line.

Catriona stopped and stared at him. She must've read a degree of innocence in his expression because she soon carried on walking. "Every other weekend or so. My father likes to be outside."

Her tone told him not to pursue it further, and they continued for another few minutes in silence, the peak of Pen Y Fan frowning down at them. Abruptly, Catriona stopped and kicked at the nearest heather - which obediently fell over, roots exposed.

"Here," she said and unslung the holdall from her back, the one she'd insisted on carrying despite Jason's numerous offers.

"You got a couple of spades in there?"

"We leave the digging to the professionals. We're just setting up the cordon and radioing it in."

Bryn obediently called in their location, as Jason and Cerys helped Catriona mark out the probable burial site. The SOCOs arrived within half an hour, setting up their floodlights and forensic tent, before disappearing inside.

Jason really hated waiting. He particularly hated waiting outside in November, with only his kid sister and two taciturn detectives for company. Sure, Bryn could be good for a laugh, but he was equally grumpy from their night's walking.

Catriona was restless, flitting around the cordon anxiously. "Something's not right," she mumbled to herself.

Seemingly the only one to hear her, Jason came alongside her. "What is it?"

She gestured around their location. "Where's the campsite? Surely the camera tripod would've left a mark? The van stood still here a while, sure, but how long? We had bad rain last weekend - why didn't it sink deep into the mud?"

One of the SOCOs came out of the tent and held up half an antler.

"Unless you're after a deer stalker…"

Catriona kicked the cordon post. "Fuck it!"

The radio crackled to life. The door-knockers had found a campsite that had leased a caravan to a "weird bloke" who had parked his van outside for two days, and set off on a pushbike every night at dusk.

Marking the campsite on the map, it was outside the western border of Catriona's map. Technically, the whole area was within cycling distance, but it made sense to start nearest the site.

One of the other teams was closer, even though they'd been stood down, so Catriona reluctantly let go of her chance of discovery. Instead, they huddled in the back of the SOCO van and drank tea from a flask until they knew the score.

"Too old for this," Bryn muttered, creaking as he stretched out his knees.

Jason thought of Amy, snug in her hospital on the hill, probably enjoying some medicated sleep. His body ached to be home, sitting on the sofa with her, one of the Alien films playing in the background as they drank their red wine down. It was hard to believe that vision of home was gone. If Amy did get out - no, when she got out - where would they go?

Even with what Amy had been paying him, he didn't have enough money to get a place. That income was also kaput, because Amy would surely lose all she had to Frieda and her lot. He could get a job cleaning, but that paid pennies and what would Amy do without him? What would she do with her time, with no computer access? He couldn't imagine her with an ordinary job, flipping burgers or waiting tables.

Would it be enough to be back together? Or would the loss of what had brought them into this partnership be too much for them to weather?

"You've got a face on you like you swallowed a lemon."

His sister - always with the compliments. "Just thinking."

"It's bad for you," she said, breezily. "Stop it right now."

That's how she was getting by - not thinking. Because if she stopped and thought, she'd see that her ex-boyfriend had rebounded into deep trouble and she was alone with only the police force for company. Jason had used that particular technique to good effect over the years and recognised it well. Reality always caught up with you though, whether it was inside a prison cell or coming out the other side with nothing.

Right now, this felt like those days after jail. No concept of the future other than it had to be better than this. No hope, but desperately scrabbling to find something like it. Treading water to stop himself drowning, wondering if it would be better to just let himself sink.

Amy had saved him from that. How was he going to repay the favour?

The radio burst to life in Catriona's hands: they'd found a likely dump site and were requesting SOCO assistance.

"Time to go, old man," Jason teased, levering Bryn up off the floor of the van.

"Less of that, boy."

He needed a plan, that was the problem. He'd never been the one with the plan - that was always his mate Lewis when they were boys, and then Amy. But if his miscreant sister could become a police officer, he could find the balls to get their lives back on track.

Cerys was playing with her phone, something nervous in the way she turned it over and over in her hands. Had Owain been messaging her? Could the bloke not decide whether he wanted her close or as far away from him as possible?

Jason nudged her shoulder, wordlessly asking her what was wrong. She shook her head, trying to brush him off, but he was her big brother - he knew when she was hiding something from him.

She grimaced. "Message from Corelia."

Holding out her phone to him, she invited him to look at the text. It read:

Something off with Amy. Will monitor and call if urgent. C#

Jason wanted to run down there, right there and then, but he restrained himself. They weren't going to let him in, not in the middle of the night. "Nothing else?"

"She'll call if something happens," Cerys said.

"That's not fucking - " Again, he reined in his temper and took a breath. "All right. We'll wait."

They needed to find this woman and find out who killed her. It was what united Amy and him, what continued to unite them, and until a plan formed in his head, this was the best way to keep them together. To keep Amy safe.

Jason would do anything to ensure that.

Chapter 44: Chess Master

Amy woke to the same silent world in which she had gone to bed, though the nightmares had chased her down and made her quake with terror. At least the morning brought clarity - she was certain now these horrors were artificial. She only needed to prove it.

She approached the nurses' office, emboldened by fear, and asked to use the phone.

"You know you can't, Amy." Lois looked genuinely sad to say it, but the rules were the rules.

"Then can you please call Detective Bryn Hesketh and ask him to visit me? It's important."

Lois' expression turned to pity. "I heard you had a bad night."

"Please call him," she repeated. "It's about Ffion."

"Why don't you have some breakfast?"

"I'm not hungry," she lied, her stomach growling with it. Her mouth felt tacky and she longed for water, but if she was right about the poison, she had to stay away from all food and drink until Bryn came. Her own personal discomfort was worth it to get to the truth.

She returned to her room and idly sorted through her belongings. She couldn't have any plastic bags to pack - too risky - but she could make sure her things were in order. Bryn would get her out, she knew it. She even showered and washed her hair, putting on fresh clothes to make the best impression she could. She had to look sane for this.

Lois put her head round the door just before ten o'clock. "Amy, you have a visitor."

She practically ran through the door, pushing past Lois and out into the lounge. The Conference Room door was ajar, so she made her way inside, ready to drag Bryn to her room for the evidence briefing.

Except Bryn wasn't there.

Her mother sat bolt upright on her chair, staring into space. Her father paced in front of the window. Neither looked at her as she came into the room. Lizzie was nowhere to be seen.

Amy took a deep breath, and another. She closed the door and took the closest chair. If she was entering the lion's den, she wanted a clear escape route when the growling started.

Then she waited. If they wanted to see her, they could deign to speak to her. She wished in that moment that she had a cup of tea and a thick slice of toast, both fuel and props to hide behind.

"Well?" her father said, impatient as always. "What do you have to say for yourself?"

Amy did not look at him, tried to keep her face neutral. To give nothing away. She was surprised at how quickly the old habits returned, how her survival instinct kicked in. But she was not a helpless child anymore.

She groped around in her mind for any idea of how to act differently, be different. Her sister had always adopted the same submissive role, but what about Cerys? Jason? Not that Gwen would ever be the kind of shit that Amy's parents were.

What would Jason do? He would stand up for himself. Defend his position. He would make himself clear, and heard. He would apologise only if he believed he was in the wrong.

Amy would not apologise now. Not for anything.

"Why are you here?" she asked.

Her question clearly surprised him. He had anticipated the upper hand - a monologue punctuated with simpering and concession, not a challenge straight out of the gate. "We want to talk to our daughter. You owe us that much."

"I owe you nothing." Her voice was cool and calm. She had always kept her temper better than Jason.

She could see that her father was struggling to keep control of his. "You will respect me, Amy. I am your father."

"I respect those who respect me."

Her mother finally looked at her then, affecting her actress' tears. "We did everything for you. Everything."

She almost laughed then. "You tried to fix me with pills and, when that didn't work, you left. Tell me, Mummy - was that all you could do?"

"So you broke the law," her father preached from the pulpit of his own ego. "You stole from your parents."

"We survived. Did you know Gran had dementia? Her brain rotted from the inside. You didn't come home for her funeral."

The anger melted away to be replaced by something that looked like shame. It sat poorly on his features, as if he didn't quite know how to wear it. It didn't last, the anger soon returning, the swell of fury that she remembered well, and his habitual disdain with it.

"It is your grandmother that we wish to speak of. I am letting you know, out of courtesy, that we intend to challenge the will."

Amy blinked at him. "What will?"

He laughed, a false sound designed for the boardroom. "Don't play innocent, Amy."

She didn't rise to his bait. "I have no idea what you're talking about."

"You influenced her!" he accused. "You took a sick old woman and used her for your own ends. Stealing from your parents wasn't enough - oh no! You had to steal from her too!"

Amy tried to make sense of the truth behind his accusations. "Are you saying Gran made a will?"

Her mother started to look uncertain, but her father was unmoved.

"Don't play coy. We know that is a lie too. Taking up with a convicted criminal!"

Amy almost wished she had started an affair with Jason, just to have the satisfaction of flaunting it in their faces. Though he was more important than that. He deserved better than to be used as a weapon.

"You are challenging her will," she said slowly, trying to find her way, "because you don't like the contents. That means she left you nothing. Instead she…gave her money to me and Lizzie."

"'Lizzie and I,'" her mother corrected, which even Amy knew was wrong.

The reddening of her father's face confirmed the truth of her statement. If her grandmother had made a last-minute will change, her infirmity of mind could well give him grounds to challenge it. Normally, Amy wouldn't care about her grandmother's tiny estate - but she had nothing. This could be her lifeline.

"When was the will made?" she asked.

Something twisted in his face - was it doubt? No, never from such a man. Was it a tell? Had she caught him out? Her mind struggled to keep up with the games in the room. Why had they come here? Had he hoped to provoke an apology, a confession? That would be like the

Amy he'd once known. Armed with that, he could skip back to his lawyers with the "evidence" and his challenge would be sealed.

She had not behaved as expected. She had fought him - and now discovered a chink in his armour.

"You don't have to tell me," she said. "My lawyer will find out easily enough."

"What lawyer? You can't afford a lawyer."

Which was probably true now, but Joseph Treves would still help her. He was a good soul and she had trusted him with the worst of her crimes. He would find someone who specialised in testamentary law and he would lead the fight himself. Despite everything, Amy still had good people she could rely upon.

She did not respond to her father, merely smiling at him. Let him think what he wanted. She would still be able to see the will, regardless.

He couldn't stand the smile. He had to play his hand, if only to wipe it from her face. "Our lawyers say we definitely have a case. And how will you defend yourself in prison?"

Time to play one of her cards. "I'm not going to prison. I'm going to receive a full pardon and a new job." She watched the colour drain from his face with glee. "I'm too much of an asset to be locked away."

"You're lying - you're a born liar! You will spend the rest of your life locked away. That Haas woman told us!"

Now there was a woman who deserved to be called a liar. Amy could see her father realising that. It was the best therapy she had ever received, watching her tormentor slowly crushed under the weight of his own actions. He'd thought he would finally bring his youngest daughter to heel, and instead she was eluding him - defeating him, even.

"I'm not going to prison," she repeated. "I am going to keep my grandmother's money. You can't hurt me any more."

He strode across the room towards her. She stood instinctively, ready to run if she needed to. She would not cower. Never again.

His jacked flapped open, a thick envelope visible in the inside pocket. What were the chances he was carrying it around with him, this will? Could she lift it without him striking her? Would it be worth it?

He confirmed her suspicions by pulling out the envelope and waving it at her. "You will never see a penny of it. You won't get her money or my money - none of it!"

"I want nothing to do with you."

He couldn't accept that, couldn't believe it. "You are my daughter and you will do as you are told!"

She snatched the envelope from his hands and ripped out the sheets. He was too shocked to stop her, but she only got as far as the date before he reclaimed it. His arms shot out and pushed her against the wall, holding her there with her toes off the ground, but she was laughing, laughing harder than she had in weeks.

"Stop it! Stop laughing!"

"I was twelve," she gasped, practically shaking with the force of her mirth. "She wrote it when I was twelve."

No court in the world would believe that a twelve-year-old girl had corrupted her grandmother into changing her will. He had shown his hand, and it was all bluff.

He pushed her harder into the wall, stopping her laughter by stealing her breath. Her mother did nothing, like she always had, too afraid of those same hands. Always so afraid, bound to the rules in case they could save her.

She felt the door open and suddenly the pressure was gone, her father flying backwards and hurtling over the chair she had been sitting on. A strong arm caught her before she fell and she recognised the grip, the warmth and the comfort of it, the scent of him and the power. The power that had floored her father with one punch.

"Touch her again and I'll kill you," Jason said.

Chapter 45: Biohazarding

If Bryn hadn't arrived at that precise moment, Jason would've been back in jail.

He was shaking with anger, and the only thing staying his arm was Amy hanging off it. Her father, like all bullies, wouldn't come at someone stronger than him. He didn't even try to report Jason to the solid detective in the doorway, correctly assuming that he would land himself in more trouble if he tried to tell his version of events.

They left without further fuss and Bryn firmly told the nursing staff that Amy's family were not to visit her again or he would raise another safeguarding procedure to protect her - did the hospital want that added to their list of woes? They did not, it seemed, and left Amy alone with Jason without comment.

While Bryn called in the incident, Jason sat Amy on the sofa in the living room and knelt down in front of her, trying to check her over despite her reluctance to admit anything was wrong. He tried to offer her a cup of tea, sure that would work where everything else failed.

She pushed it away. "Poison."

Jason thought Amy had finally lost it. Is this what Corelia had meant about something being off with her? "It's tea."

"I've had the same thing that got Ffion and Emma. I'm sure it's here."

"Start from the beginning."

"Do you have any chocolate?" she asked.

He had half a bar in his pocket, and the dregs of a bottle of Coke. She consumed them both eagerly, before dumping the rubbish on the nearest table.

"I saw a man last night, coming at me in the garden."

Jason tensed. "It was him?"

"No. It was in my head, but it felt real. I thought I was going to die."

This is definitely what had sounded Corelia's alarm bells. "You've been under a lot of stress - "

"It was more than that. I had the nightmares too, the ones about

233

being hunted, and all the colours were wrong. It wasn't stress. I know what stress feels like."

Jason had to concede that point. "Then what was it?"

"I think we're all being poisoned. Something in this hospital is driving us mad. Maybe it builds up over time. That could be why Ffion was first."

"We were looking in the wrong place." It seemed so obvious now, why they were hitting dead end after dead end looking into Ffion's life. "We thought Ffion was the target, so we went around the houses looking for who might want to kill her."

"I think it's more against the unit than us. That makes it harder to find the perpetrator."

"What could it be in?"

"The water. The bread. Maybe something more specific than that. I need Bryn to test some samples."

It was both a wild theory and one that made a whole lot of sense. "We can test the body and narrow it down."

Amy looked straight at him. "You found her?"

"Last night. They've put her under twenty-four-hour armed guard." Jason had found it bizarre to be escorted by so many cops with guns and know they weren't there for him.

"I don't want the samples to disappear." She placed her hand on his arm, holding it there as she looked earnestly into his eyes. "Can you talk to him?"

"Don't know why you think he'll listen to me over you."

"I'm crazy, remember? Nobody listens to me."

"I'll always listen."

She smiled then, a genuine smile that warmed her eyes and set the green flecks dancing. Despite the stitches, despite everything, she was beautiful. "I know."

She took a small bag out of her hoodie pocket and pushed it into her hands. "I found this in Ffion's room. Bryn has to test this. Tell him."

Jason found Bryn in the deserted café area outside the ward doors. The place was creepy when no one was about, holding its breath in anticipation of a prison break or worse.

"Is she all right?"

"No thanks to that bastard. She has this theory - and I want you to hear it out before you label it as nuts."

Bryn listened as Jason repeated Amy's unscientific findings and experiences on the ward, but he soon started nodding along. "If we think this man's into drugs, then it makes sense. Though from what the lab boys have said, these types of drugs are more up-and-down than building up. They're not addictive or anything like that."

"One thing poisoning them all at once, not a little bit at a time?"

"The scattergun approach explains why we've not had much luck with Ffion's connections. Though we've now confirmed the location of this Aaron - he's moved a few doors down. The judge is considering a warrant for this afternoon."

"Is there a test for these mushrooms or whatever? Can we get forensics down here to have a look?"

"They're turning over the woman's stomach contents this morning." That was something Jason hadn't needed to know. "We can then work backwards from what she last ate. They told me it might take a couple of weeks to find out exactly what's in it, even knowing where to start looking."

"Adding samples of whatever will just delay things." A plan was forming in his mind. It wasn't exactly the best idea he'd ever had but he had to do something to make himself useful. "Do you think you could wrangle me staying here for the day?"

Bryn looked at him suspiciously. "Why? What are you up to?"

"I could narrow down the samples."

"Are you suggesting that you're going to eat the evidence and see what happens?"

"You got a better idea?"

Bryn scrubbed at his face with his hand. "You kids are going to be the death of me."

Jason beamed at him. "I'll be careful. I've got Amy to think of."

"Don't let her eat anything…"

Jason shot him a withering look. "I'll get her food out of the vending machines. Nothing's going to happen to her while I'm here."

"I don't doubt it. Good luck."

Jason held out the bag Amy had entrusted him with. "But you have to test these. I promised Amy."

Bryn reluctantly took it and Jason waved him off, before returning to the ward laden with more snacks and drinks for his boss. He dumped them by her side on the sofa, watching her eyes light up at the feast. His Amy was still in there, despite everything.

"So, what's good to eat around here?"

Chapter 46: Generation X

The home of Aaron Shaw made Amy's run-down house look like a palace. Before Jason had got to it anyway. Bryn had seen the boy work wonders in his time with that girl.

It was located in the middle of Newport's Bettws housing estate, a council build from the '60s which had been half-gobbled by the Right to Buy scheme and yet retained the same community. While other flats had tried to brighten the samey-sameness of their world with flowers or had evidence of their kids' toys outside, this flat was marked by fag ends and dog muck on the doorstep.

Cerys knocked on the door, two uniforms at her back. Bryn stood to one side, waiting for the inevitable barking dog to start up. Instead a baby cried through the door, causing all the coppers present to look at each other in confusion.

The woman who opened the door was in her early twenties, while a two-year-old child of indeterminate gender clung to her knees. "Can I help you?"

"Does Aaron Shaw live here?" Cerys asked. They could just barge in, of course, but it was nicer to be invited. Less chance of a stake through the heart.

The woman suddenly looked tired, worn beyond her years. "He's walking the dog. What's this about?"

"We have a warrant to search the flat," Cerys said, handing her the paper. "If you'll let us get started, I'll explain it to you."

"There aren't any drugs here. He said he'd got rid of them all before we moved in."

"It's not about drugs," Cerys said. "Can we come in?"

"You're going to anyway, aren't you?" She stepped aside, taking the toddler with her. The child silently watched the procession, overawed by their presence.

Bryn was surprised at how clean it was inside, uncluttered and well-kept. True, the carpets were worn and the walls marked, but someone had done the best job they could. The uniforms started the search, while Cerys guided the woman into the spotless kitchen and Bryn followed.

"You'll be expecting tea and all, I reckon. Well, there's nothing here. I cleaned it all out. I made sure."

Something about her made Bryn think she was a little too eager to protest Aaron's innocence. "But you had your doubts."

She filled the kettle from the tap, avoiding their eyes. "He'd been upset lately, that's all. No crime in that, is there?"

"Does the name Ffion Ellis mean anything to you?" Bryn asked.

The kettle shook in her hand and she replaced it, not looking at them. "Why?"

"She's dead. We believe Mr Shaw sent her letters."

She laughed. The child on the floor clapped their hands. "You've got that all wrong. It was her that was writing him letters. So many bloody letters. It always upsets him. She only does it when she's ill, see. Then he drinks to make it all go away. I fucking hate that woman. Why can't she just leave Dad alone?" Only then did the first part of his words register. "Wait…she's dead? When was that?"

"Two weeks ago."

She clapped her hand to her mouth. "She was the one on the news, wasn't she? The one that died in the mental hospital and then went missing. Da didn't have anything to do with that! He's been here, the whole time. He never goes anywhere now, except to take the dog round the block. It wasn't him!"

"Did he write her letters?" Cerys stuck to the point.

The kettle boiled. She used it as an excuse to delay her answer, her actions stiff and deliberate, as if she was struggling to remember the steps. "Why didn't anyone tell us?" Her voice shook with emotion. "Someone should've called, shouldn't they?"

"You're her granddaughter," Cerys said.

Once she'd said it, Bryn could see some resemblance. The same mouth and nose, perhaps. What else had she inherited from that unhappy woman?

"The rotten branch of the family tree," she said bitterly. "Even though he insisted on giving me the bitch's name. He was taken away from her when he was just a kid and she never paid any attention to him - until the bloody demons came for her again."

"He was adopted?" Cerys asked.

"Sent to an orphanage. This was when she was younger, before her marriage and that perfect daughter. She was sick even then but no one realised until later. No one cared what it did it to him."

Another child, one removed from her custody in her early life. The daughter and carers had mentioned nothing about him - if they'd even known he existed. All those careful background checks, and yet they'd missed this.

"Do you know if he kept her letters?" Bryn asked.

Ffion's mouth twisted. "Every last one. He even ate the bloody sweets she sent him."

"Sweets?" Bryn remembered Amy's insistence that he at least take the chocolate for testing. "When he was upset...was that after the sweets arrived?"

"You think his mam was sending him drugs? There's no way. That's why she wanted nothing to do with him, the drugs. Why my mam wouldn't talk to him neither."

"Think, Ffion," Cerys urged. "Was it about two weeks ago?"

She looked at them, horrified. "About that," she said, finally.

"We need to see those letters," Bryn said.

"Fi! Why you left this door open?" The bellow from the front door was accompanied by the warning growl of a dog.

"Let me handle this - please," Ffion begged, before heading for the kitchen door.

But one of the uniforms had broached the corridor before she could act.

"What the fuck are you doing in my house?"

"Not in front of Katie, Da - please!"

"You let these scum into my house, didn't you?"

"It's about your mam."

Bryn followed Ffion into the corridor and took a good look at Aaron Shaw. He appeared older than his fifty-one years, grey and balding, overweight and nicotine-stained. His dog was a scruffy terrier, with a bark much bigger than its bite, but he held the lead in a vice-like grip.

"I don't want to talk about her," Aaron said, his voice trembling.

"Da...Da, she's dead. The police have come to tell us."

It wasn't quite the truth, but it was better than seeing him run. Aaron listed against the wall, breathing hard, and trying to blink away his emotions. The dog whined and pawed at his shin, but he wasn't able to focus on anything but what was happening inside his own head.

"Come and sit down," Ffion said. "I'll make the tea. You just sit down now."

He sat in the armchair, a horrible old thing that belonged down the tip. Bryn sat opposite him, just watching, as the man caught his breath and slurped at his tea.

"Ffion said you had letters from your mam, before she died," Cerys said, as gently as she could.

"Just nonsense," he said. "Rambling on and on. Like she always did when she was touched. I paid them no mind."

"Did you ever reply?" she said.

He looked at her, opened his mouth to deny it, and then subsided. "So what if I did? She never read them."

"I've read them, Mr Shaw."

He flinched at that, huddling behind his tea and his dog. "I was angry. That was all. Just angry."

"She sent you some sweets. When was that?"

He waved his hand dismissively. "Don't know - who cares? She said they were a peace offering, 'cause she wasn't long for this world. Same old nonsense about demons."

"Did you eat them?"

His whole face twisted. "Something wasn't right with them. I had one, but it was…it was like the old days."

"Your daughter said you used to have…a problem."

He laughed at Cerys' careful words. "I had half the dealers in this town on my back. It was just like dropping acid, this chocolate. Bright colours and swirls and all the fucking demons of the world. It was like her letter come alive. I binned the rest."

His account matched Amy's exactly. They had a connection, but not causation. Maybe Aaron had sent her the chocolates and tried them out before he popped them in the post? Perhaps he hoped that playing the victim would lead them up the garden path.

Yet looking at this sad, pathetic man trying not to cry into his tea, Bryn couldn't believe it of him. Something else was going on here.

"I'll need all the letters she sent you."

Aaron looked up at that. "Can I…can I have them back after?"

Bryn's heart ached for him, this man so desperate for a relationship with his mother that he would treasure her letters filled with demons and warnings and agony. "I'll do my best."

They left him sitting on the sofa with his daughter and her child, lamenting their family matriarch who continued to bring them nothing but pain.

"What now?" Cerys asked.

"We test the chocolates Amy found in Ffion's room - fast track them if we can. Then we can stop your brother eating everything at the mental hospital."

Cerys looked appalled. "He's trying to find the drug? Is he totally fucking mad?"

"Probably."

"No, you don't get it." She seized his arm, scaring him with the look on his face. "He had this one trip. He remembers none of it, but he tried to gut his best friend, smashed up one of their dens. Lewis told him never to take that shit again."

Bryn blanched. "Buckle up," he said. "Let's save that boy from himself."

Chapter 47: The Mad Hatter's Tea Party

Success was about conviction and confidence. Conviction and confidence. He repeated it several times to make sure, but it sat perfectly on his tongue.

He had been set on his goal from the beginning - recognition, power, dominance. As was his birthright. He was not a murderer. He was not driven to use such crude tools. The old woman's fate had been unfortunate, but she was collateral damage in a greater scheme. No one would miss her, not really. No one missed the damaged.

If one were going to bring about a death - he would not stoop to call it murder, because his hands were clean as the driven - but if one were, the most effective way would be to cause an accident or a tragedy. An accident might be the brake failure of a car, for example, or a misunderstanding at a level crossing. These things happened.

A tragedy, well...only in the eyes of the weak could it be called a tragedy. He preferred the term "natural selection". Those fit for life would live, and those unfit would die unmourned. That included those who raised a blade to their own throat, or pulled the trigger when the muzzle sat against the temple. He was merely aiding natural selection.

He had come so close. If that girl hadn't interfered, it would've been fucking perfect. Now, at least, she had form. She had been labelled suicidal. If she died by her own hand, no one could say it wasn't predictable. Expected. No one would even consider she had been led to it.

Before, his methods had required caution. She was constantly watched, monitored. Now he was free to act, to do what needed to be done. As swiftly and painlessly as possible. He had no wish for her to suffer. He just wanted her gone.

He stood in the kitchen and he made up the tray - sweet shortbread biscuits, a pot of fine Earl Grey for two, and one mug with a teabag he had prepared especially. He had even tied a little purple ribbon on it, one that matched the work of his favourite organic, vegan shop. For authenticity.

They sat together in the drawing room - what their mother affected to call the room looking out over the ocean - saying nothing, doing nothing. He set down the tray with a small flourish, leaving the tea to brew before setting the mug down in front of her.

"What is it?" she said.

"The doctor said you mustn't have caffeine." His mother had always been his best ally in this game and she played her part to perfection.

"It's 'erbal," he said, pronouncing it in the American fashion. "You'll like it."

She sipped at it warily, but the addition of passion flower and rose petals masked the bitterness beneath. He watched her drink it down, the smile spreading over his face.

"You're happy today," she said.

"I'm just glad you're home."

After the second cup of tea, Jason still felt fine and so Amy made herself a cup. The caffeine withdrawal headache outweighed the fear of hallucinations at this stage.

He'd sampled the bread, the biscuits, the coffee, the tea and the milk - and nothing. They'd waited half an hour each time and now it was getting dark outside, the nurses tutting at them every now and then in the hope that Jason would leave. Amy was never letting him go again.

"What else did you eat yesterday?" he asked.

Amy wracked her brains for the answer. "I think I had some cheese. There was a hot meal at lunch, but we can't replicate that."

Jason dutifully chewed on an individual chunk of cheese that proclaimed it was cheddar, but actually resembled greasy rubber. "What about dinner?"

"They offered me a sandwich, but I had toast."

"With butter?"

"No, with the cheese." But that wasn't right. She hadn't wanted their imitation cheese or rancid margarine last night. What had she eaten?

She looked around the kitchen for inspiration. Was it jam? No, there was only marmalade left and Amy despised the stuff, the artificial sweetness of it. Nothing like a delicious smooth…

"Peanut butter!" she cried and left Jason in the dining room, pelting along the bedroom corridor and retrieving the precious jar from her room.

Only as she returned up the corridor did she feel the weight of it, the certainty pulling her down with every step. Because if the peanut butter was to blame, then there was one obvious person at which to point the finger.

"Emma gave this to me," she said, setting it on the table between them. "Her brother brought it for her."

Jason looked at it sceptically. "Did Ffion eat any of it?"

Amy deflated. "I don't think so."

He pushed it to one side. "We'll do it next anyway."

Amy didn't sit down, taking the jar back into her hands. "What if this is it? What if this is the key? Emma is at home with her brother right now."

Jason took it out of her hands. "Then I'll eat it right now."

He unscrewed the lid and stuck a tablespoon in it.

"Are you sure - ?"

It was already in his mouth. "Bitter, for peanut butter," he said, swallowing it down.

She watched him carefully. "How long will it take to work?"

"Like I said, it depends. Anything up to half an hour. We have to wait it out."

The doorbell for the ward rang and Amy watched the nurse go to open it. She was surprised to see Cerys striding across the room, in full uniform.

"Are you a class A moron?" she asked him, voice taut. "Hi Amy."

"We think we've found it," he said, pushing the open jar of peanut butter towards her.

"Of course, you've already eaten the bloody stuff, haven't you? Idiot. Come with me before you do something stupid."

He stood up, reluctantly, then gripped the edge of the table. "It's starting."

"Shit." Cerys yanked on his arm. "We need to get out of here."

"What's going on?" Amy said, suddenly afraid. "Is he allergic?"

"Last time he tried this, he had a bad trip. A very bad trip."

"Has this man brought drugs on my ward?" Miriam had come over at the commotion and looked like she would try to take Jason out there and then.

"He's under arrest," Cerys said, quickly. "Hopefully, he'll come quietly."

"Don't you need to read him his rights?" Miriam was sharp, sharper than Amy had given her credit for.

"He's in no state for that right now," Cerys said. "Maybe he'll sober up in the car."

"The lights have come on," Jason mumbled, his eyes glazed. "Where's Lewis?"

"In prison. Where you'll be going if you're not careful." Cerys was backing him out of the ward like a hostage.

Amy hated the way he stumbled, staggered - she wanted to hold him, tell him it was okay. But he wasn't really there.

"Dad's coming, isn't he?" he said.

Cerys bit her lip. "Not now, okay? We can talk about him later."

"I miss him."

"Me too."

"You're not a police officer. You're this man's brother!"

Amy cursed Miriam. "She's trying to help him," she protested. "What are you doing? You should be treating him!"

"I don't work with addicts," she said stiffly.

"You worked with Mordecai," Amy said, watching Cerys' progress. "The doctor never told you the truth, did he?"

"Don't stir, Amy," Miriam said. You need to work with us if you want to get out."

Get out. How would they get out? The nurses held all the key cards, the windows were all on safety restrictors, and the garden was surrounded by a massive fence. It would have to be the front door.

Amy looked up at the nearest camera, imploring. Had she given Corelia access to the security locks as well as the footage?

No time. There was no time.

Quick as a flash, Amy lunged for Miriam and pulled at her badge. The special lanyard around her neck snapped open, dropping the ID badge and swipe cards into her hand.

"You assaulted me!" she cried.

But Amy was gone, pelting for the door and bashing the badge against the reader. The door popped open and she pushed it.

"Cerys - come on!"

Cerys towed Jason, who came unresistingly with them, and closed the door behind her. Amy opened the second door, as the alarms started blaring. *Shit.*

"If they lock us down, we're screwed."

They got through the second door but the automatic doors at the entrance remained stubbornly shut. The nursing staff would be right on their heels, and they would target Amy. She was their priority, after all. Who cared what Cerys and Jason did, as long as they kept their crazy little prisoner?

Amy looked around for another exit - and seized on a little red box, with a clear panel in the centre. She smashed it with her hand, a second alarm adding its screech to the first. The door sprang open, unlocking due to the emergency override.

Amy started for them, but realised Cerys and Jason weren't with her. Jason had planted his feet and was talking to someone in the middle distance, laughing and crying at the same time. It scared her - but she didn't have time to be scared.

"Jason!" she called but he didn't seem to hear her.

"Help me!" Cerys shouted.

Amy grabbed hold of Jason's other arm and together they tried to drag him towards the door.

"We can't leave him!" he shouted. "Let go!"

"Jason, we have to go now!" Amy cried. "I need you!"

He looked at her then and nodded, once, waving at whatever he could see. They made it through the doors before the fire alarm cut out and they slammed shut again.

Bryn had the engine running in the car park, frowning when he saw Amy. "That was not part of the deal."

"We need to get to Emma Mason's house," Amy said, pushing Jason into the back of the car. "It's the peanut butter."

Bryn stared at her, then took one look at Jason. "I'll call for backup. Where is she?"

"Somewhere near Swansea."

"Start driving," Cerys said, climbing in the front seat. "I'll call it in."

"Maybe we should drop you off," Bryn said.

Amy shook her head violently. "If he's got to her again, you'll need me. She'll listen to me."

It took a moment for him to relent, but he hit the accelerator to take them out of there. Towards Emma, and whatever hell she had been plunged into. The hell that Amy should've seen coming.

Right now, she didn't have time for guilt. She had to do something to make amends, to bring Emma back from the brink. To stop her brother poisoning her mind and driving her towards the edge - and over it.

Chapter 48: Road Trip

The car was expanding and contracting at such a rate that Jason felt he was inside an accordion and would soon be compressed to death.

"Am I dying?" he asked his father.

Dad gently shook his head.

"You're not dying." Amy, blunt as ever.

He wanted to hold her hand but his palm and fingers were too big, like their Sunday morning brunch frying pan and five fat sausages, bursting with animal fat and raw pink flesh. She sounded worried, beneath the blunt, and he vaguely thought he might've caused that. Should he say sorry? He should, really. Sorry might not make it better but she might like him more.

"Shut up, Jason." That was Cerys, ahead of him, a million miles ahead. "You have to shut up. It'll wear off soon."

"It could take several hours," Amy warned, her voice like an alarm - blaring, too loud, why wouldn't she shut up?

"Jason! Fucking stop it."

"He doesn't know what he's doing." A man's voice, but not his father. Probably Bryn. His second father. "You can't tell him anything."

"He's going to be no use like this." Cerys sounded just like their mam. Exasperated with him. Exasperated. It was a good word, echoing around his head like the rush of a fast-flowing river.

"What if he vomited?" Amy wasn't a nurse, but she could be one, with her good ideas and her instinct to take care of him.

"Will you be my nurse?" he asked her, or he thought he did. It was difficult to keep track of who was speaking, when he was silent and when he was loud, why the sky was pink or was it black and how many legs did he have anyway?

"What have you got in the car?"

"Not in my car, Cerys."

"Then we'll need to stop - two minutes, once he's puking. What have you got?"

"Nothing!"

"There's energy drinks in here."

"Caffeine is a bad idea."

"It's fizzy. What about salt?"

"Salt I have. Those little restaurant packets - in the doors."

Salt was white and small and grainy. He loved it on chips, after a night out. He loved it on skin, the kiss of sweat after you'd fucked a girl. He wanted to taste it on Amy.

"Eww. Shut up, Jason. Please shut up."

"We…uh…need something, to mix it in."

"Water bottle?"

"Yeah, half full. It's warm."

"Give it here."

He already felt sick - *slosh-slosh-slosh* went the tea in his stomach, and now it had to come out. The car was flying apart like a star exploding into a black hole, but now it was stopping, and all the rest of the world was flying past instead. Would he explode or would he fly? Would his father be waiting for him?

"Out. Fucking get out."

He stepped out into the frigid smog of the motorway, coughing as he tried to breathe, his lungs and his heart and his skin all turning inside out with the force of it. His eyeballs would explode, leaving red smashes in the centre of his face.

Cerys made him drink, warm salty water, and then his stomach flipped and turned and tore itself apart. Out-out-up! He was streaming green and yellow and salt and all that fucking tea.

"Shh…shh…you're okay…"

Amy was there and Amy made it better and, fuck it, why couldn't he be in bed with Amy instead of crying on the side of the road? He had clearly made some fucked-up life choices in the recent past and this was God's way of punishing him.

"That's what you get for trying to play hero. Get back in the car."

Jason obediently did as he was told, his whole body shaking and wrung out. He closed his eyes and tried to sleep, wanting everything to go away, and for his father to stop whispering in his ear.

"Is it over?"

Bryn glanced at Jason in the rear-view mirror and then pulled back out onto the motorway. The traffic was easing off after the rush hour, the skies already dark with dusk and the threatening rain.

"The worst of it," Cerys said, darkly. "Idiot."

Bryn's car radio told them that units from Swansea were on their way and would meet them at the house. They had no time for a warrant, for a judge's blessing - this was a life-saving operation and Bryn intended to sell it as one after they had all emerged from this shit.

How had he ended up with a car filled with a rebellious probationary constable, a drugged-up ex-con and one hacker escaped from a mental hospital? Of course, Owain should be there, to inject some measure of sense and normality, but Bryn suspected he would never be there again.

Cerys' phone rang beside him. "Corelia - hi."

Another civilian caught up in this bloody mess. Why the hell was the child ringing now? Bryn had known this situation was slipping out of his hands from the beginning but after all his words about keeping everyone safe, he hadn't managed to protect even one of them during this case.

Amy learned forward, her hand clasping Jason's tightly, straining to hear what the girl was saying, and Cerys put the phone on speaker.

" - scanned the boarding card at the time the pre-pay was purchased. He was flying to the north of Mexico, which is smack-bang in the middle of peyote territory."

"That's good work," Amy said, obviously impressed. "Do we have a name?"

"Amy." The single word managed to convey a world of admiration. "Yeah - Maximilian Mason. Documentary filmmaker. His latest project, according to his website, is spending six months following the Tarahumara people. His social media is full of all this bitter shit about how he can't get distribution."

It fitted perfectly with what they already knew. "We only need motive," Bryn said.

"Who's that?" Corelia had all of Amy's suspicion.

"A friend," Amy said. "What do we know about his family?"

"Father's dead - helicopter crash about three years ago. His mother runs the family business now. Something about civil aviation. He has an older sister - "

"Emma," Amy said.

"That's right. Groomed for the business until she fell off the radar after her father's death. There aren't any pictures of her after that - the whole family seemed to go underground."

"We've found them. You've been amazing," Amy said, warmly. "Thank you."

"Any time. I mean it - any time."

Amy met Bryn's eyes in the mirror. "It's definitely him. He's trying to get rid of her, maybe the mother too."

"What do you know about him?"

"I don't know much. It was his idea to get Emma out of there. His mother isn't much better. He's a dead-eyed bastard."

"He's had her for over twenty-four hours," Cerys says, worrying at her thumbnail with her teeth. "We could be too late."

Bryn put his foot on the accelerator and started up the blues-and-twos. "Not on my watch."

Chapter 49: Knock Knock

They left Jason in the car to sleep off the last of his trip. Amy wanted to stay with him, to comfort him when he woke, to chase away the nightmares and the past, but she had to stay with Bryn and Cerys. She had to find Emma.

They should've waited for backup, but Cerys' words had fired Bryn into action. They had already left it so long, with Emma at the mercy of the murderer.

Without a warrant, however, they needed to play it safe. Bryn approached the front door of the beautiful modern house, backing onto the magnificent Caswell Bay, and politely knocked.

"We're less than a mile from where the van was found," Cerys said.

The light came on in the hall and a middle-aged woman in a dressing gown opened the door only an inch, peering out at them suspiciously. "What is the meaning of this?"

"Detective Bryn Hesketh, South Wales Police. Can I come in?"

"It's not a convenient time, detective. I was just going to bed with a headache."

"Mrs Mason - "

"It's Ms Phelps, actually. I never took my late husband's name. I take it this is about Emma?"

"Is she at home?"

"The doctor said she must not be disturbed. Come back in the morning."

She made to close the door but Bryn jammed his foot in the crack. "Ms Phelps, your daughter is in immediate danger. She has been poisoned by the same person who killed Ffion Ellis at the hospital. It is important she receives urgent medical care."

Ms Phelps gawped at him. "Then why haven't you brought an ambulance?"

"It's on its way," he lied.

Amy looked at her watch impatiently. An ambulance wasn't the worst idea.

"I know you." Damnit, she shouldn't stayed in the car. "You're that criminal girl from the hospital."

Cerys thought on her feet. "She's been working undercover."

Ms Phelps looked far from convinced. "You were with my Emma on that clifftop. Maximilian said you drove her to it."

"I was talking her down!"

"That's what the police record says, Ms Phelps." Bryn wasn't wasting any more time. "We must speak with Emma."

The woman groaned and let the door fall open. "Do what you will. There's no help for the wretched child anyway."

No help. Amy recognised the diagnosis, saw her own mother in that heavily made-up face, and balled her hands into fists.

"We have to find her now," she said, and headed down the corridor and into the living room beyond.

The last vestiges of daylight clung to the sea, orange and pink and deepest purple reflected into the room. The remnants of afternoon tea sat on a tray by the French doors, the crumbs of biscuits and empty cups telling it was well-enjoyed. The last dose well-administered.

A mound of blankets shifted on the sofa. Amy tore off the top layer, and a large black cat yelped and leapt out at her. It flew across the room and out of a side door she hadn't previously noticed.

Amy stepped out of the door into a little porch, full of gardening tools and weather-proof boots. The outer door was swinging back and forth, the wind off the sea stronger than she"d have imagined. The clouds were darkening to coal and jet, and the tranquil sea she had seen from the living room was actually alive and bucking like an untamed horse.

Amy stepped into the porch doorway, cheeks stinging from the force of the wind and the cold water saturating the air. The garden was plain but carefully-groomed, with a little gate at the bottom leading straight onto the beach beyond.

On the beach, there was a woman.

Amy tried to call her name, but the wind stole it from her. Without thought, she ran down the garden, her feet threatening to disappear from under her on the damp paving stones. She threw open the gate and the wind ripped it from its hinges, sending it tumbling across the beach.

Still, Emma walked, her feet sinking into the sand as she touched the water's edge.

Amy stopped, staring into that heaving mass of water, and remembered: she could not swim.

She had splashed in paddling pools and worn armbands once or twice in the shallow end, but she hated the water on her face and she had revolted, refusing to ever venture into the water again. Then she had spent ten years in her house and swimming had seemed like a distant fantasy.

There was no time. Bryn and Cerys were still inside the house, and Jason was in the car. Amy was alone with Emma, who took her first bold step into the sea.

"EMMA!"

But she would not hear, or could not, and she was marching determinedly into the water now, wading in under the waves crested above her waist.

Amy hesitated on the water's edge, but she could not stand and watch while Emma gave herself over to the sea. Emma, who was floating now, the water up to her chest…her neck…

Amy ran in after her.

Chapter 50: Man Overboard

Jason woke up on the edge of space, wrung out and wanting nothing more than to crawl into his own bed.

Except he was instead lying down in the back of a police car, the wind howling around it like a hurricane and piercing his aching head. How the fuck had he ended up here?

He checked his wrists - no cuffs. That was a first. And this wasn't a police car, was it? It was a car belonging to a police officer. Specifically Bryn. Though it wasn't parked outside the station or Amy's house or the hospital…

The hospital.

Jason bolted upright, his stomach lurching with the sudden movement. They had been at the hospital, he had eaten that bloody peanut butter, bad shit had gone down, and now he was here. Wherever here was.

The car kicked to life, thrumming beneath his body in that juddering, old washing machine way. Bryn really needed a new car. After this case was over, Jason was going car shopping with him. Something practical, yet fast. Maybe a bit of fancy trim.

The vehicle swerved violently out of the drive, almost hitting the gate post, and out onto the lane beyond. Jason was wide awake now. Bryn didn't drive like that - he might be in a hurry, but he was always careful.

He craned his neck, expecting to see his erratic sister behind the wheel - but it was a stranger. Distantly, he thought he could hear Cerys shouting. What the fuck was going on?

The man was twitchy, clearly wired, one hand on the wheel and the other running a fringed scarf over and over his fingers. It was mesmerising, the colours still too bright and too loud, but Jason forced himself to concentrate.

He clearly had no idea Jason was in the car, but he had stolen it, was making a run for it. Which probably made him guilty as sin.

Maximilian Mason. The name came back to him, through a haze -

where had he heard it? The more pressing question was: what the hell was Jason going to do about him from the back seat of the car without them hurtling off the road?

The car suddenly veered down a broad dirt track, past a blurred farmhouse, and onto little more than a coastal path. They were climbing now, up a hill towards the crest. Out of the left-side window, Jason could see the sea - and the ground falling away to nothing, inches from the wheels.

The sky opened and a torrent of rain hit them, pelting the car with the fury of the storm. Max swore and struggled to keep control of the car. It drifted dangerously close to the edge - and Jason seized his chance.

Surging over the driver's seat, he grabbed for Max's arm on the wheel. But he overreached, hitting the wheel itself, and only just managed to hold on.

"What the fuck?!"

Jason seized the wheel with both hands and yanked it down to the right. The car jerked over, but Max hit the accelerator in his panic. Jason tried for the handbrake, but too late. The back wheels kicked out, over open water, and the car teetered on the edge for one moment, two.

Then tipped over into the water below.

As the back wheels hit the sea, Jason pushed at the car door to open it - but nothing. Max must've locked it, or the mechanism had seized, because it wouldn't budge an inch. The car was sinking fast, as leaky as a sieve. If the whole car submerged, their chances of getting out alive would plummet towards zero.

Jason tore at the back passenger seat, scrabbling to find the mechanism that would release them. The seat suddenly shot forward, water following after and blinding Jason with salt. He fought against the rising swell, tugging at the boot lining to look for the tools underneath. Bryn must have a crowbar, a jack, something, anything to smash their way out.

Except he didn't need that, did he? He was in the boot now - he could release the lock from the inside. And then watch the car flood and falter. He would have to move fast.

Suddenly, he remembered the man in the front seat.

"Oi!" he yelled. "You coming or what?"

He looked at Jason, terrified, and he clearly saw the devil where a man should be. The shifting of his eyes, the way he pressed himself into the corner of the car, away from the spectre before him. Shit.

"Mate, you have to come with me."

Though he wasn't his mate, was he? He was a killer and a poisoner and a twisted fuck. Wouldn't it be better for everyone if he just drowned?

Jason didn't work that way, not anymore. Justice, the law - he believed in those things, had to believe in them and his second chance.

He leaned forward, intending to grab at Max and haul him out. The man flailed, clawing at the door, the monsters behind his eyes too vast to consider the alternative. The handle gave way beneath his hand, the door pushed open despite the pressure of the water, fear and desperation driving him.

In came the flood.

Jason took a deep breath and went under. The water was murky, filled with sand and shells, and he groped blindly for the man who was trying to get them both killed.

His fingers closed on water alone.

He surged up to the top of the car and gasped a breath with his lips against the inside roof. He dived down, fumbling his way towards the boot and reaching for the catch. His foot tangled in a seatbelt, dragging him back. He wrestled with it for what felt like hours, his lungs burning with the need for air.

Black spots played across his vision as he finally broke free and both hands hit the inside of the boot. His numb fingers shoved at the catch once, twice, three times - before the boot opened an inch. He shoved it, against the weight of water, and forced his body through and up.

Jason sucked in the briny air above the sea, feebly kicking his legs to keep afloat. The car was a dark receding shape beneath the increasingly choppy waves, which battered at his chest. He looked around for Max but the light was dim, the air thick with the mist rolling in from the Bristol Channel. Was he still trapped in the car? Had he escaped?

The wind carried echoes of voices across the water, though too far away to be him - or was it? Jason turned around, looking into shore, and saw two figures in the shallows. Who went for a swim at this time, in a storm? Why were they wading out further?

Even with salt-stung eyes and exhaustion in his limbs, Jason would recognise anywhere the slight figure battling the waves.

"What the fuck is wrong with you?" he muttered, to himself and to the exasperating woman hurling herself into the stormy sea.

Mustering the last of his energy, Jason swam towards them. Praying he wouldn't be too late.

Chapter 51: Amy Lane vs The Sea

The force of the water was already overwhelming and Emma was moving further and further away from her. Amy had to swim.

She took one stuttered leap forward, the water pushing her up before guiding her back down. The water was up to her chest now, and the chill was starting to eat into her skin. Her hoodie weighed her down, but there wasn't time to take it off, or her jeans, or shoes. No time.

She pushed on, until the sand fell away completely and left her suspended. She did not sink, though her clothes were leaden, and she tried to kick and flail and *move*. Though it was the water that carried her, dragging her out with the tide.

Emma was still standing, much taller than Amy, and she collided with her. She seized hold with both arms, pressing her mouth close to her friend's ear, not letting go even when Emma screamed.

"No! Leave me alone!"

"It's me - it's Amy! You're okay!"

"I can't...I can't..."

"You have to come back. It was Max. It was all Max."

Emma was trying to push her away, threatening to plunge them both under the water. Amy held on as if her life depended on it - her life, and Emma's, both sitting like fragile eggs within the grasp of Amy's hands.

"He'd be better off without me! They all would!"

"It's not true. It's a lie your demons tell you." The wind tried to whip away her words, but Amy would not let it. "I know, Emma. I've been there!"

"Why do they keep coming for me?" Her voice was filled with tears, though Amy couldn't see them through the spray, the churning of the water.

"It's poison. It will go, I promise. It was Max."

"Why do you keep saying that?"

"He poisoned you! He's been poisoning you all along!"

"No!"

Emma tried to shake Amy and they both fell, the water over their heads.

Amy inhaled, choking on it, the waves overwhelming. They pulled her away from the shore, away from the struggling shape of Emma, ripping her away from her friend and the shore and her life. She was tossed about like a pulped piece of paper, rippling on the surface until it thins, tears, sinks.

She sank, her clothes dragging her down, her limbs unable to fight against the force of the sea. She was going to die here - and she wanted more than anything to live. She wanted to run along the beach, she wanted to make a new home, she wanted to kiss Jason one more time. She wanted more than that, so much more - to really, truly live.

Her only enemy was the sea. She had no air, no hope, buffeted by the waves and lost from view. She couldn't save herself, let alone Emma. Where were her friends, her family? Where were the police, the coast guard, anyone - anyone at all?

She forced her eyes open, looking up through the murk of the water to the darkness above. Her feet touched the bottom, but it slipped away from her, her legs cramping and refusing to hold her upright. The surface might as well be a million miles away, though it was calm here, beneath the storm. Looking up at the chaos.

Amy closed her eyes and thought of nothing. Her chest hurt, the water hurt, everything felt distant and disconnected. Her heart was slow, like a stopping clock, winding down to its last seconds. She was dying, she was dead - she wasn't sure anymore. It was all over. Everything she had built for herself was being washed away with every press of the waves.

Something grabbed hold of her, constricting her chest, forcing the last bubbles from her lips. She had no energy to fight, carried away by Leviathan, limp as a broken doll in its grasp.

She broke the surface and breathed, cold air hitting the back of her burning throat and making her gag. The world was dark and terrible, as if the apocalypse had come, but she was alive and she was held and her story wasn't ending yet.

"Amy? Amy!"

The shouting was muffled by the water clogging her ears, but she knew that voice.

"I'm okay," she tried to tell him, but it came out as a harsh coughing sound.

"Fuck, you're alive!" Jason said, his grip only strengthening on her body.

"Emma?" she said, and the word came out more whole.

"I don't know," he said.

She couldn't see her friend and her heart ached for her. She wanted to look for her, insist Jason find her, but she was too selfish for that. She wanted him here, she wanted him to save her, to keep on saving her. She couldn't risk losing him in finding Emma, no matter how much her friend meant to her.

Jason awkwardly turned them around and started towards shore. Amy clung onto his arm, trying to kick her legs to help their progress. After a while, she drifted, staring up at the dark clouds fuming impotently above her, throwing down their burdens in a tantrum but unable to make her wetter and colder than she already was.

" - see her?"

"Only the clouds," she said.

"Shit, Amy - make sense." He sounded scared. She'd forgotten how much she'd hated hearing fear in Jason's voice.

"What can you see?"

"Something floating. Cerys has got her - I think it's Cerys. Police too."

Warmth and dread flooded Amy's limbs and she kicked a little harder, clumsily finding her feet as Jason dragged them onto the beach, the sand no longer falling away beneath her feet, streams of water flowing from her clothes as if she were a human waterfall.

Bryn tried to smother her in a blanket and lead her away up the beach, but she stood, took root, watched. Her friend was lying on the sand, motionless. Cerys and another police officer pressed at her, breathed into her, but Emma remained a corpse on the beach.

Amy had never seen a dead body before Ffion. She never wanted to again.

"Come inside."

"Not yet."

Jason would never stop trying to protect her, but she had to see this through to the end, to face the consequences of being too late, too slow, too selfish. She had to know it in her bones before she could take her rest.

Emma spluttered, life flowing back in all at once, and Cerys heaved her over to cough up the sea. Returning the water to its sandy home, though Amy feared neither of them would ever be truly dry again, entirely free from the sea's grip.

The paramedics hurtled down the beach, too late and yet their work just beginning. Amy sank backwards, Jason's solid form breaking her fall, and they fell together onto the sand. They watched the medics do their work, strap Emma to their stretcher, and carry her away up the beach.

"Where are they? What have you done with them?"

The confused voice rang out from the top of the beach. Stumbling out of her garden, Emma's mother looked out at the chaos sprawled over the beach, trying to make sense of what she saw laid out before her.

"Where's Emma? Where's my son?"

Amy tensed, scanning the beach hastily, as Emma's mother was intercepted by police and led to the ambulance. "Where is Max? What happened to him?"

"I lost him," Jason said, shortly - too short, and Amy could hear the reticence behind the words. "He might still be out there."

"He stole my car." Bryn appeared in her peripheral vision, hovering again, a crude square of gauze taped hurriedly to his forehead.

Amy gripped Jason's hand. "You were in the car."

"And now I'm not." His voice was even, and that scared her. Something bad had happened, but he didn't have the words yet - or at least wouldn't share them with her.

"I don't want to know where my car is, do I?"

"You might need a dredge."

Bryn's scowl was audible, but he wouldn't shout. Not here, not now - not with their lives so exposed, on this beach under the gathering starlight.

"Amy?" Bryn crouched down in the sand beside her, trying to gain her attention. "We need to go now."

"Go where?" Jason was immediately hostile, defensive.

Amy knew the score. "I need to go back."

Jason wrapped his arms around her, infusing her with heat and jealously guarding her. "She is not going back to that place. They have no fucking clue what they're doing!"

"Jason. I need to go back."

She twisted to look at him, his face blurry in the dim lights carrying down from the houses. He reached for her cheek, his fingers wrinkled from the water, the texture strange across her skin.

"Why?" he asked, almost petulant.

"I have to finish this. I need to be better."

"You don't...you don't have to change for me. You don't have to change for anyone. Do you get that?"

She smiled, something inside her breaking at the words - breaking open, released from its cage.

"I have to change for me."

Chapter 52: The sea will give up her dead

The dredge knocked against the buoy marking its mooring point, as the coastguard looked on and police divers suited up to secure the evidence. They lowered the chains into the murky seawater, fragments of the crew's shouts carrying to shore on fickle gusts of wind.

On the clifftop, Bryn was immobile against the freezing rain. He watched as the corpse of his car was slowly lifted from the grip of the Bristol Channel and laid out on the dredge's deck. Somewhere before him, his best coat was rotting alongside his battered, black umbrella and a mixtape his daughter had made him when she was thirteen.

"Did you want to say a few words?"

Cerys' eyes were mischievous beneath her soaking-wet fringe, her uniform almost black from the rain's efforts. She must have been standing there for some time, though Bryn had entirely failed to notice her.

"Don't you have college?"

"I'm starting again next term. 'Extenuating circumstances.'"

She shrugged one shoulder, as if she couldn't quite believe her luck. For the Carr family, becoming embroiled in a murder investigation was becoming just another day at the beach rather than something worthy of note.

"They pissed off about Jason?"

"He has that effect on people. Especially police."

The SOCOs were already poring over the wreck beneath a white tent bowed by rainfall, but Bryn had seen enough. He was never driving that car again, and they had already made sure Max's body was nowhere near it.

Where was it? True, the storm had been fierce and he could've been carried far out into the Channel, but it was a busy shipping route with plenty of shore for a body to wash up on. Bryn had a sinking feeling that they hadn't seen the last of Maximillian Mason.

"Are we standing here for any particular reason?"

Catriona was dressed for a Welsh monsoon in a yellow cagoule and waders, staring at them with their bare heads and sodden jumpers as if they had lost their minds.

"Bryn's saying his goodbyes."

He forcibly turned away from the sight of the dredge. "How's it going up at the house?"

Catriona grinned. "We found a number of cacti under industrial lights, and some dodgy-looking seeds at the back of a wardrobe. Max's laptop has the same footage on it as the camera - minus the flaming van, of course." Her smile faded. "We can make a good case *in absentia*."

He could see she felt it too, the lack of closure. With no man in custody and no body, justice felt absent. At least he could tell Ffion's children how their mother came to die, even if they could find little comfort in it. Eating the wrong chocolate at the wrong time. Collateral damage, in a plot over inheritance. Would such knowledge bring them solace?

"How's Ms Phelps holding up?"

"She's left for some wine spa in France. Possibly because she drank the cellar dry."

Emma was beginning to look like the most well-adjusted member of this family, and she was currently resident at Cliff House. Against everyone's better judgement, Frieda had refused to move Amy and therefore Emma had decided to return to the place. His pet hacker did have the most bizarre taste in friends.

Yet those friends had a burning loyalty towards her. He couldn't shake the image of Jason standing protectively over her on the beach, trying to keep a handle on his own shivering body to comfort her. After he'd almost drowned in Bryn's car, fighting with a murderer.

He hadn't taken Jason's statement after the incident, because they were in enough shit as it was. Bryn could've done without a question of 'aiding and abetting escape from detention' on his record, which was already black as night from Amy-related exploits.

"Take the laptop back to the station and see if you can make the final links to the stolen number plate and the forum posts. Without a…without a confession, we need this case to be airtight."

Catriona nodded and jerked her thumb towards the track. "You coming inside? We brought our own tea."

With one last lingering look at his car, Bryn followed Catriona back towards the farmhouse, Cerys at his right shoulder. They sat at the kitchen table, drinking tea and eating the chocolate digestives one of the SOCOs had brought. Now he was further inland, his old battered mobile had signal again and his emails started updating.

Indira had sent him an initial autopsy report for Ffion Ellis. He had no idea how she could do it, go back to that moment in her mind and coolly note down facts about the body she had examined - before she had been struck a devastating blow to the head. The second examination had been conducted by one of her trainees, but she had summarised the toxicology reports and made her conclusions, all from her hospital bed.

He had never been so proud of a person in his life. He wanted to tell her just how much his heart swelled when the doctors told her she would likely return to work. He wanted to take her out for a pint, or maybe dinner, something to show her how much he appreciated her. How badly he had taken her for granted.

He settled for a slowly-typed professional message that thanked her for her work and told her to get more rest. Other words could wait.

Looking around at the two women, he felt that same sense of pride at his team. Yet he felt one absence keenly, the easy jokes and reliable enthusiasm at his side. He missed the stellar detective sergeant, the bright shining future of Heddlu De Cymru. He missed his friend.

"Have you heard from Owain?"

The two women glanced at each other, unsure who exactly was being asked.

"You haven't heard?" Catriona said.

"What?" A hundred things leapt to mind, all of them worse than the last.

"He handed in his resignation. Word is that the National Crime Agency headhunted him."

"Frieda." The venom in Cerys' voice spoke of more than just that woman's crimes against her brother and Amy.

Bryn wasn't sure if this wasn't the worst outcome of them all. He remembered all too well how Frieda Haas had manipulated Owain, using him to get to Amy. The boy had been damaged by their exploits, unable to think straight, and she had swooped in to add another malign influence to his mind. Bryn hadn't seen it, hadn't protected him like he should.

Yet now he had chosen that path with the full knowledge that he was getting into bed with a viper. Bryn could only pray he knew what he was doing.

He shook his head sadly, returning to his phone, to the work. To anything that might mask the loss, that could make him forget how much he had let that boy down.

There was an email from Owain.

It simply said "I'm sorry."

Bryn ate his biscuit, then drained his mug of tea.

"Me too," he replied.

Chapter 52: Sunset, Sunrise

Dr Al-Dosari had decided she was making progress. With a tentative smile, he had praised her efforts towards recovery and made noises about how much she had benefited from Cliff House's care. Amy still thought he was a waste of space more interested in his own reputation than her mental health, but she couldn't deny she felt calmer. More ready to meet the world outside.

In exchange for taking all the doctor's prescribed pills and humouring her therapist, she could step outside the walls of the hospital. As soon as he'd heard the doctor's pronouncement, Jason had been keen to take her on an excursion. She had managed not to scream at him down at the phone, mumbling that she would think about it, before running from the nursing office as fast as ever she could.

Then she had stopped and thought about it. Reminded herself that she was trying to get better, to move forward. She was not a scared little girl anymore. She had so many things that threatened to confine her - she could not afford for her mind to cage her too.

She had called Jason back and agreed to a trip outside today. Away from the hospital, away from the safety she had found in its solid walls and predictable routine. She would have Jason, but would he be enough to counter the fear of stepping into the unknown, the terrible uncertainty of the world beyond Cliff House?

Despite the weather, she and Emma were spending more time out in the garden, watching the sea, talking quietly about how exactly Amy would take those steps without the world falling apart.

"You ran into the ocean after me. What could be worse than that?"

Amy felt Emma was underestimating the role of impending doom in her ability to cope with the outside world. Jason wanted to go into town, he said, where there would be crowds and people, all watching her, waiting for her to collapse and fail and die...

No. Stay in the moment. Remember to breathe.

Emma's hand on her shoulder grounded her, like Jason always had before her. It made the breathing easier. It made everything easier, knowing someone cared enough to stop her falling over the edge.

"Dr Al-Dosari thinks I can go home in a few weeks."

Amy looked at Emma's left hand, balled in her lap, fighting the urge to touch something and even up the sensation of Amy's back against her right palm. She was winning. Slowly, surely, she was winning. After Max's poisons had left her system, it was only her old demons she had left to fight. *Only.* As if that somehow made it easier.

"What do you think?"

"I think I might get my own place. Maybe in Cardiff. We could go out for tea."

She felt warm in Emma's gaze. "I'd like that."

"Amy? You have a visitor."

Taking another deep breath, Amy rose to her feet, letting Emma's hand fall from her shoulder. She could not delay the inevitable. She walked through the dining room, nodding to a couple of the new patients before entering the lounge.

Owain was standing before her.

"What are you doing here?"

"Can we talk in private?" He looked on edge, but his face was giving nothing away.

Amy wasn't sure to what extent she trusted him anymore, but they had been through fire together. She owed him the opportunity to speak, at least.

He opened the door to the Conference Room and she followed him inside.

"Good morning, Amy."

Take a breath. "Frieda."

She could see the agent was disappointed. Bringing Owain here, surprising her like this - she wanted Amy wrong-footed, off-kilter. Yet Amy could maintain the façade at least. It was one thing for which she was grateful to her father. Growing up with him had taught her how to wear a mask and his recent reappearance in her life had ensured she relearned the skill. For moments exactly like this.

She sat in the chair opposite Frieda, watching as Owain sat at the agent's right hand.

"Have you considered my offer?"

"I have."

Frieda gestured towards Owain. "I have kept my side of the bargain. The rest is in your hands."

Making her responsible for so many people's fates was Frieda's trump card and she knew it. They wouldn't dance around the issue anymore. If Amy wanted her friends to live free of the NCA's claws, if she wanted Jason to remain out of prison, she had to take Frieda's job. Yet she wouldn't just roll over like a good dog.

"I want to work from home."

Frieda's jaw clenched. She hadn't been expecting demands. "You'll use our computer and our server."

"I'll use my methods and my tools."

"You will give us access to your remote server."

"I will not."

"You won't communicate with Miss Martinez."

Corelia would be unhappy about that. "Fine."

"Anything else?"

"I need an assistant."

Frieda snorted. "Your puppy can have an allowance. What else?"

"Why is Owain here?"

Frieda didn't even glance at him, her ice-cold eyes fixed on Amy. "He will be your handler at the National Crime Agency. All your reports, all your intelligence - it goes through him. You succeed or fail together."

She was binding them to each other, to command their obedience to her. Whatever loyalty was left between them would be used to Frieda's advantage. Whatever Amy thought of Owain now, she wouldn't sell him down the river. She wished she could say the same of him.

She alone carried the weight of their future on her shoulders. Not just Owain's, but Jason's too. How would he feel about being the lackey of the National Crime Agency? What would that even look like? Would Frieda allow him to be more than her personal shopper and cleaner, allow him the freedom to pursue mysteries and leads as he had with Amy?

Would he take Frieda's coin in order to stay at her side?

"Do we have a deal, Amy?"

Chapter 54: Lamp in the Window

They still hadn't found a body.

He'd heard Bryn's car was good for nothing but the scrapyard, but Cerys hadn't let Jason see the salvage photographs. He knew they were bad from the way she hugged him before she went to bed that night.

He couldn't afford to dwell on that night in the water, how very differently it could've ended. If he hadn't found the latch, if he hadn't found Amy...he couldn't think about it without feeling sick, tasting the fear beneath the seawater in his mouth.

But if he had made it out of the car, out of the water, then the same could be true for Max Mason. With all the demon-fuelled adrenaline pumping through his veins, he could've outswum the storm. Jason could do without collecting any more enemies.

At least Amy had made a friend. Emma and Amy were coming to the end of their time together at Cliff House, both determined to get better and get out. They seemed to draw strength from one another, like two flames sharing a warm pool of oil. Jason wondered if he should be jealous.

She wasn't the only one making a good recovery. Corelia had been discharged from hospital and was thinking about school again, though Jason suspected she'd rather be thinking about making her name in hacking. Indira had been transferred to a specialised rehabilitation centre, though Bryn wouldn't say where. They were both aware that Max's body was missing, and that the man himself might want to finish what he started.

They couldn't live like that, though. Under threat from a ghost that might've departed, that might not give a damn about them even if he lived. They had to look to the future, even if it was still full of unknowns.

Jason was Amy's best friend, her assistant and companion, her... something else, maybe. That made him responsible for her happiness, at least in part. When Amy's sister Lizzie had reached out to him, he'd hesitated - was this really what Amy would want? Lizzie was adamant, though, and he couldn't do anything to stop her. With Amy getting better by the day, the doctor and nurses encouraging her to spend time off the ward, he couldn't keep this from her much longer.

"Why are we here?"

Jason paid the taxi driver before leading Amy away from the road and towards Roald Dahl Plass, the swanky statue-littered square in front of the impressive Wales Millennium Centre which stretched towards Cardiff Bay and the sea. "You don't like the Bay?"

Amy looked at him strangely. "I've never been."

Of course she hadn't. Until very recently, Amy hadn't been much outside her own house. Standing out here, with the sun hitting her hair just-so, and an almost-smile on her lips, it was easy to forget she was still in hospital, still so limited by her illness. The scars on her arms and cheek were red and pink now, fading though the memories weren't.

"Well…here it is!"

She laughed at him. "You're acting very strange today. You've been strange for a week or more."

"I have something to show you."

She followed him trustingly, staying close in the open space but relaxing a little more as they moved towards the houses and flats. Away from the people, and the crowds. Away from the things that scared her.

A confident man in a suit met them at the door to the block of flats. "Nice to see you again, Mr Carr."

Amy looked startled but said nothing as they rode the lift to the fifth floor, staring intently at the buttons. The man opened the front door to 5C, and then stepped away.

"After you," Jason said, gesturing for Amy to step inside.

She crossed the threshold warily, her steps increasing in confidence as she followed the corridor round to the right and into the living room. Jason kept close to her, watching her take in the warm wooden floors, the little kitchen space at the back, and the balcony view over Cardiff Bay.

She turned back to him, uncertain. "What is this?"

"Lizzie's in charge of your grandmother's money, though it belongs to the both of you. She's decided to sell the house and buy a new place."

"Lizzie lives in Australia," Amy said, though he could see the re-alisation in her eyes, though she was too afraid to believe it was true.

"We can live here," he said.

He and Lizzie had chosen the flat together, both agreeing that house-hunting would put too much stress on Amy. They had viewed a dozen flats, enduring the suspicion they were a couple over and over again, and finally decided this was the most promising. After a couple of hard weeks clearing out the old house and Jason putting his best cleaning skills to work, they had found a buyer and were ready to move on this Bay-view flat - if Amy liked it.

That was the big question, wasn't it? Jason scrutinised every inch of her face, looking for some sign that she approved.

"You want to live here, with me." She was stunned, he could tell, but he wasn't sure if it was in the best or worst way.

"Do you want to see the rest?" he asked tentatively.

"It needs security systems and cameras," she said. "I want a better lock on the door."

"We'll find a way to pay the bills," he told her.

"I took Frieda's job."

"You…what?"

"We won't starve. The Government pays its spooks well, even if they're behind a desk."

Jason was sure he was gawping at her, but he couldn't find the words to respond.

Amy hugged herself, rocking side to side and staring at her feet. "They pay their assistants well too."

"Frieda wanted me too?" His bewilderment restored his power of speech, though he was still reeling, trying to restore his balance.

"I want you." Her voice was quiet, as she dared to look at him again.

Jason wasn't sure how to take that. "She's trouble."

"She's letting me out of jail with a slap on the wrist. We're ready for her this time."

Amy wasn't the only one getting out of jail free. He knew Frieda would've threatened her with a shadow over Jason's future as well as her own. He wasn't happy owing Frieda Haas a favour or taking her money, but he wanted to move on with their lives more than he want-ed vengeance. At least, for now.

"She…she said I could work from home."

Home. "You'll be needing a home to work from then."

"Yes."

"Should I ask Lizzie to make the offer?"

Amy looked at him, her eyes intense, deepening brown and green and bronze as the light faded from the sky. "Are you sure about this? Are you sure you want to be here - with me?"

Despite Frieda and the mess they were in, Jason had never been more sure of anything in his life. Her doubt floored him, leaving him speechless. He leaned in unconsciously, his body longing to reassure her.

She closed her eyes, lips parting slightly. Trusting him.

"Amy," he said, and touched her shoulder.

Her eyes fluttered open, hurt and disappointment blossoming over her face.

"Listen to me," he said, heading her off at the pass. "I like you. I *really* like you. And I want you to be at your best before we leap into anything. Until we can talk it through. Make absolutely sure it's what we both want." He rubbed at his forehead. "Shit, I'm not making sense."

"I'm not going to change my mind," she said, obstinate, as always.

He smiled at her. "Neither am I. But I want to do this right."

She rolled her eyes at him, an exaggerated movement that threatened to cast them clean out of her face. "When did you develop this sense of chivalry?"

Since I met someone I could love. "What's that supposed to mean? I'm a gentleman, I am."

Amy laughed and socked him in the arm, and he grabbed hold of her, lifting her off the floor and swinging her round.

"Put me down, idiot!"

He did as he was told, grinning all over his face. "What do you want to do with the rest of your leave? We could walk along the front, grab an ice cream?"

She pulled a face. "In December?"

He'd almost forgotten they were so close to Christmas, that the year was almost over and they might get to start the new one in a better place, with something to look forward to that wasn't solving a murder. Not that he minded the odd murder.

He guessed there wouldn't be much of that anymore, running all about town to uncover clues for her and chase down suspects. More shopping and cleaning and watching old movies with a pizza box between them. He could live with that. He could live with pretty much anything if she was on the other side of that sofa.

"You know…" Amy looked at the kitchenette and then back out at the living room. "Lizzie isn't flying back until New Year. We could have Christmas dinner here, your family and mine."

Jason set aside his anxiety at cooking turkey for his mother and marvelled at Amy for a moment. She wanted to invite people in, to celebrate with them, to be part of his family and he part of hers.

They were journeying into a crazy new world, of working for the National Crime Agency and giving up everything they knew, but they were moving forward. They were coming home.

The man in the suit tutted quietly by the door and tapped at his watch. Jason shot him a glare.

"If you don't want ice cream, we could grab a drink somewhere?"

Amy beamed. "I'd love a cup of tea."